Dear Scarlett

by

Robin Kruger

Published by Robin Kruger Books

ISBN: 978-0-6399865-0-0 (epub)
ISBN: 978-0-6399865-1-7 (mobi)
ISBN: 978-0-6399865-6-2 (print)

Robin Kruger Books

Courting Justice
Dear Scarlett
Good Evening Merry Gentlemen
Shabeni
Suffer the Little Boys
Kruger Park – Heaven on Earth
How to Make (or Not Make) Money Trading Online

www.robinkrugerbooks.com

Prologue

It was drizzling the day Michael came to a stop on his bicycle halfway across a bridge in the university city of Cambridge. All traffic ground to a halt on Silver Street as an elderly lady battled to cross it in her wheelchair. About to go and help the lady, Michael casually glanced up at a window of a bus stopped alongside him.

Despite raindrops trickling down the window, he saw a young woman staring pensively into the distance up the River Cam towards the Mathematical Bridge. He was struck by the sadness of her expression. Suddenly she looked down at him and Michael saw the most beautiful pair of eyes he had ever seen, eyes that were to mesmerize him for years to come.

The traffic started moving again. Michael cycled alongside the bus, looking up as often as he could, trying to catch a glimpse of the young woman with the sad but beautiful eyes. He attempted a wave to attract her attention. As the bus squeezed him closer and closer to the kerb, he hopped up on to the pavement, deciding it would be safer. Desperate to know who those eyes belonged to, he weaved his way past pedestrians while trying to stay alongside the bus window. She still stared back at him, prompting Michael to gesture with one hand, urging her to alight from the bus.

Only at the last moment did he realize that he was fast approaching the Trumpington Street intersection. He frantically squeezed the brakes of his bicycle until his knuckles turned white, but the wet pavement caused it to skid slap bang into a lamp post. The impact hurtled Michael upwards and forwards, his head hitting the metal pole with a dull thud before he fell to the ground.

Shaking his head, a groggy Michael staggered to his feet, but with the front wheel of his bicycle buckled he could no longer cycle, so he doggedly set off after the bus on foot. Despite being well-built and athletic, he was no match for a moving bus but that did not deter him. He knew that at some stage it would have to come to a stop, and he would seek out the young woman. Unknown to him, this was no ordinary passenger bus and it did not stop at the usual bus stops. Still, he ran and ran. To his dismay, however, the bus eventually disappeared out of vision.

Only once he had lost sight of the bus, did Michael become aware that blood was trickling down his face from a split in his right eyebrow, courtesy of his collision with the lamp post. As he stood in the rain, blood and drizzle dripping off his chin, he stopped and yelled in desperation at the top of his voice, 'Nooo!'

1st January 1965

Dear Scarlett,

It is the morning of the first day of the new year, and I'm still humming the tune *Auld Lang Syne* that was played at a New Year's party last night. It is a nostalgic song for me. Each occasion as one year passes into the next, I'm reminded of times gone by. Happy times that bring so much joy to my heart, but also some sadness leaving them behind. Goodbyes! I hate them! So as we all say goodbye to the year 1964, I'm writing to you to keep alive the memory of what happened earlier in the summer.

First let me introduce myself. I am Michael, Michael Gibson, and I live in Cambridge. Lived here all my life. I have recently become an adult, at least officially, and am currently studying medicine at the University of Cambridge. Both my parents are medical doctors and I knew early on that I would follow in their footsteps. You see, medicine is a true calling for me. What I won't do, however, is follow my parents into academia. They are both professors in the medical school here at the university. But that is not for me. I do have one sibling, my sister Jean, who is five years younger than me, and my guess is that she, too, will follow the family obsession and study medicine. She's in her final year of high school, so I have a head start as I've just completed my fourth year at med school.

To escape the aftermath of last night's party, I am ensconced in my room at the residence of King's College. And as I sit at my desk writing this letter, I occasionally gaze out at the vast expanse of lawn that leads to the River Cam. Although it is mid-winter it is still a beautiful scene, one that I am privileged to see every day. And each day when I look out of my window, my heart sails up that river to a bridge not far away where I was lucky, or unlucky, to have seen the most beautiful young woman in the world, you!

Do you remember that day in August, a day when it drizzled, much like today? You were on a bus staring down the River Cam, a contemplative look on your face. Why were you lost in thought and why the look of sadness? I have wondered so many times about that.

And then you looked at me and I saw the most striking sapphire blue eyes, eyes that I can still see so vividly in my mind. Eyes that were set in a sculptured face of high cheek bones and a gorgeous complexion, all framed by long dark silky hair. There was an aura about you, a magnetism that drew me to you.

Of course, you probably remember how like a bumbling idiot I crashed my bicycle into a lamp post. That would have been hard to miss! Quite embarrassing, I might add! What you may not know is that I abandoned my bicycle and ran after your bus in the hope that I could meet you when you got off at a bus stop. But it didn't stop and I may never know why. I have wondered about that a million times, teasing and torturing my heart because I was and still am so desperate to meet the person behind those beautiful eyes.

What you also won't know is that my eyebrow cut open as I hit the lamp post causing it to bleed profusely. I am nothing if not persistent because although I lost sight of your bus, I was so desperate that you were slipping through my fingers that I ran on down that road, checking shops, looking down alleyways, even asking people if they had seen you. That caused quite a stir, I tell you! I know, as I could see it in the bewildered looks on their faces! Me with my bloodied face and clothes, asking if anyone had seen a beautiful young woman with mesmerizing eyes in the vicinity. What was I thinking, you may well ask?

I considered having my split eyebrow attended to in a hospital, but in the end decided that since I was a med student I should try to stitch the wound myself in my room. It was more difficult than I thought! Unfortunately, I did a bit of a botched job which doesn't auger well since I want to one day specialise in surgery!

Eventually, I had to come to terms that I had lost you. And that realization felt like my heart was ripped from my chest. But I am one who lives with eternal hope, so not a day goes by when I cycle to lectures or go grocery shopping or am just walking around the beautiful city of Cambridge that I don't look out for you. Of course, there may be the chance that you don't live locally, but I am ever hopeful that you do and that someday I will find you.

So why Scarlett? I had recently seen the film *Gone With The Wind* and you reminded me a little of Scarlett O'Hara.

Who are you Scarlett? And will I ever see you again?

All my love, Michael.

Scarlett

The young woman whom Michael called Scarlett, was not, in fact, native to Cambridge, but was instead a member of a South African swimming team. The team had recently competed in meets in the United Kingdom as a warm-up for the upcoming Olympic Games to be held in Tokyo. Just prior to boarding the bus that would take them on a tourist trip through Cambridge, the team was told that, due to the racial policies of South Africa, the members were to be banned from taking part in the Olympics. Scarlett was devastated by this turn of events and was deep in thought contemplating her immediate future when the bus came to a stop on the bridge across the River Cam.

The following day, on an aeroplane going back to South Africa, Scarlett again found herself looking out of a window, this time across the continent of Africa as she returned to her home country. For hours, she gazed out into the distance and thought about all the years of training and her single-minded ambition to become an Olympian. Now it seemed it was all for nothing. She swallowed hard, fighting back the tears until she felt drained of emotion and simply stared into the distance feeling numb.

Paul Rhodes, a fellow teammate, glanced at Scarlett, concerned. He knew how much work she had put into her training and how much the Olympic dream meant to her. He nudged her gently and asked, 'What are you going to do now, Missy?'

Paul Rhodes was shy, especially around Scarlett. Five years previously, when he first joined the Dolphin Swimming Club in Cape Town for training, he would address Scarlett as Miss Harrison, a title usually reserved for a teacher. As time went by and Paul lost some of his shyness, Miss Harrison was shortened to Missy. Soon everybody at the club would call her Missy.

Scarlett turned towards Paul, forlornly. 'I honestly don't know,' she said. After a strained moment of silence, she continued, 'It's the only thing I've ever wanted — to become an Olympian.'

'I'm truly sorry, Missy,' commiserated Paul. 'In your case you would've been a real medal contender. Not only in Tokyo but in future Olympics too. I know that I don't have the times to even get to a final, let alone medal. So for me, realistically, it's always been about the honour of becoming an Olympian, but after Tokyo my intention was always to go to university. I'm so sorry.'

'I love swimming so much,' sighed Scarlett. 'I don't know what else to do. Perhaps I could become a swimming coach,' she suggested tentatively.

'You've got to be joking! Missy, you're the dux at Rustenberg Girls' High, the brightest person I know. You have so much potential. I don't want to sound demeaning but you can't simply become a swimming coach. Besides, to what end? What would you be coaching swimmers for? Because one thing is for sure, South Africa will never be allowed back into the Olympics.'

Shaking her head, still in a daze, Scarlett answered, 'Then I simply don't know.'

Thoughtfully, Paul looked at her. 'Starting in the new year, I am going to medical school at the University of Cape Town,' he said gently. 'Why don't you think about joining me. You could always swim for the university team.'

The suggestion of swimming for a university team made Scarlett feel bitter. After all that hard work just to swim for a university, her chance to become an Olympian gone, and probably gone forever. She looked out the window again and never said another word for the rest of the 14-hour journey to Cape Town.

1ˢᵗ January 1966

Dear Scarlett,

Yes, it's the first day of the new year and again I find myself humming *Auld Lang Syne* while I write to you from my room at King's College.

I can't explain it, but I am besotted with you. Perhaps I don't look out for you quite as much as I once did, but that hasn't diminished the number of times that I think about you. I still wonder every day about the person behind those beautiful eyes, but since I don't know you my imagination runs wild. I do, however, live in hope that I may one day meet you.

So, another year has passed since I last wrote to you. I have now completed my fifth year at med school and will soon be looking to become an intern at a hospital. I can't wait. While it is true that we students have been dealing with live patients during the last two years, it has always been under the guidance of a teaching doctor, and I am itching to be let free, so to speak, to make my own calculated decisions, though, of course, I will have to bear the consequences of any ill-fated ones!

You may think that *Auld Lang Syne* is the only song I know. Well, that is definitely not the case. As much as I have a calling for medicine, my passion is music. And like *Auld Lang Syne*, music has a special way of taking me back in time, not so much of reliving memories but making me feel nostalgic about times gone by.

I simply love listening to music and am teaching myself to play the guitar. Because you would definitely not like to hear me sing, to add melody to my songs I play finger style on an acoustic guitar. Actually, a Gibson acoustic guitar! Playing causes huge callouses on the fingers of my left hand, which is just as well because I will need all the sensitivity in my right hand that I can muster to one day wield a scalpel.

So I guess that if I weren't trying to become a doctor I would like to join a band. And what a time to want to be in a music band! To me there has been a big change in music over the last few years. Groups like the Beatles and the Rolling Stones and artists like Bob Dylan have added a new and interesting dimension to the music scene. In the prophetic words of the latter, 'The Times They Are A Changin'.'

Were those tears in your eyes when I saw you last year or just droplets of rain against the window? And did you wave to me or were you just wiping the window clear of mist? And did you smile at me or did I imagine that? Will I ever know?

In the meantime, I'll close my eyes and dream that you are here, see the face I long to touch, to kiss, and believe that one day it will be for real.

All my love, Michael.

Scarlett

With a few months to think about it, despite having to prepare for her final school exams, Scarlett dug deep to figure out what she wanted to do with her life. She could not believe that all her youth she had swum towards one goal, to become an Olympian, the last five years waking up at 4 o'clock in the morning to train for two hours and then another two hours in the afternoon. For what? Only for her dream to be snuffed out at the last moment. Her mind travelled a myriad of pathways seeking a way to put her Olympic goal back on track, but each time she came back to the same conclusion. She had the misfortune of being born in the wrong country!

Many nights she cried herself to sleep, but although the bitterness never left her, the stark reality slowly dawned on her that her chance of swimming competitively was over. Now she wrestled with a new problem. What could she do with her life now that her dream was over? Paul's suggestion that she attend medical school at the University of Cape Town, commonly known as UCT, became more and more appealing. Finally, she made her decision. Her excellent school marks and her swimming potential enabled her to receive a scholarship and in February 1965 she enrolled at UCT and took up residence as a freshette at Fuller House.

§

On the second Saturday of the semester the boys from a neighbouring residence, Smuts Hall, constructed a makeshift catwalk for the traditional cattle parade, all part of compulsory initiation. That evening the freshettes, wearing mini-skirts, paraded in front of the freshers to the accompaniment of loud music which barely disguised much lewd commentary.

Each freshette took her turn on the catwalk, the ultimate compliment being a catcall reserved for the handful of girls with stunning legs. Once the parade was over the auctioning began, boys putting in bids for a date with a specific girl.

Scarlett thought the whole process demeaning, especially for those whose legs were not to die for. But she comforted herself that the money was to go towards a good cause through a fundraising event known as RAG, an acronym for 'reach out and give', a non-profit cause that gave back to society.

With her athletic figure and stunning eyes, Scarlett was the last 'cow' to be auctioned and at a very high price. The lucky bidder was André.

Beaming from ear to ear, André informed Scarlett, 'I'll pick you up next Saturday evening, around 6 o'clock.'

'No you won't,' Scarlett replied forcefully. 'As a med student I have work commitments.'

'But—'

'It's okay. You won't lose out. We can date on float building night.'

§

A couple of months later, André picked up Scarlett from Fuller House on float building night.

The floats were assembled with a light timber frame covered with chicken mesh and then adorned with papier mâché. Inevitably most students ended the night in a drunken stupor, but miraculously the floats were eventually completed by the morning for the parade down the city centre. Not only that, but most looked fantastic, probably courtesy of the fine art students.

Scarlett and André walked to the car park where the floats were being constructed and no sooner had they arrived when a beer was thrust into each of their hands. The float that Scarlett and André helped to build was a large Zulu hut. And much happened in the Zulu hut that night. A large vat containing a mixture of every possible alcoholic beverage in existence was consumed in vast quantities as the hut slowly took shape. The more alcohol the students consumed, the more they lost their inhibitions, and for many their virginity too.

Scarlett woke the next morning with a splitting headache, amongst a slew of bodies in various stages of undress, including herself. The sad realization dawned on her that more than just float building and boozing had taken place through the night. She skipped the float parade and instead, when her headache wore off, devoted her time to studying for a test on Monday morning.

§

A few weeks later, Scarlett's period was late. This was not uncommon for her. She had always put her irregular periods down to her heavy athletic training. But after a few more days a gnawing knot of worry tightened in her stomach.

A fortnight later, after returning from breakfast in the dining hall, she barely made it to the bathroom before vomiting. She sank onto the floor next to the toilet and put her head in her hands. 'Oh, no!' she whispered, despairingly. Her suspicions could no longer be ignored.

To get confirmation, Scarlett visited the nurse at the campus clinic.

'I think I may be pregnant.'

'If I got one rand for every time I've heard that, I could retire a millionaire,' the unsympathetic nurse said. 'And given the date, I suspect it happened on float building night. Were you drunk?'

'Sadly, yes.'

'You silly fool! Alcohol should be banned at universities. It causes more harm than good. And I know it because I see the results. One night of binge drinking can have serious consequences. Your whole life could be ruined! Not ideal circumstances to bring a baby into this world.'

Scarlett did not need a lecture but listened anyway, her head bowed. The nurse was not saying anything she had not already told herself.

'Come back in two weeks for the results,' the nurse said brusquely.

Scarlett's result came back positive but she knew from continued morning sickness that she was pregnant.

Returning to her dormitory room, Scarlett sat on her bed with her head in her hands. That damn cattle parade! Just one night! And why with André, of all people? He was a stranger to her. She had not seen him since the night of float building. Did he need to know about her pregnancy? She supposed she was obligated to tell him. She sighed. Yes, it was the right thing to do. Late one afternoon, steeling herself, she found out which room he occupied in Smuts Hall and knocked on his door.

After a few moments, André, dressed only in a pair of shorts, opened the door. 'Well, if it's not my little vixen,' he sniggered, a smirk on his face. 'I've been thinking of contacting you for a repeat session.'

'I'm pregnant!' Scarlett burst out.

André's smirk disappeared fast. 'What's that got to do with me?'

'Are you serious?' asked a bewildered Scarlett. 'You're the father!'

'How do you know that?'

'Because there has been no one else.'

'I find that hard to believe. Anyway, I'm having nothing to do with your child. Nothing. If I were you, I'd get an abortion.'

'But that's highly illegal,' stated Scarlett, incredulous. Knowing she did not want to give up her baby, she put her arms protectively over her stomach. 'Besides, I'm training to be a medical doctor and my goal is to save lives, not kill them off.'Type equation here.

'Fine by me, but I want nothing to do with the child.'

Scarlett swallowed hard, and after a few moments slowly nodded her head. 'Okay,' she said, 'but on one condition, that you have no future custodial rights to the baby. Not even the right to see the baby. If I'm to do it alone, then the baby is mine alone.'

'You couldn't have said it any better.'

§

André was the easy part. The scary part, Scarlett knew, was telling her family. Her parents were old-fashioned. The thought that their bright and talented daughter had gotten pregnant during a night of binge drinking would be very difficult for them to accept. She knew that they would be shocked and disappointed in her. Once more, taking her courage into her hands, she headed off to her family home. And there was even more riding on the line. The clinic nurse had reported to the matron at Fuller House that Scarlett was pregnant, and she was given until the end of that day to vacate the residence.

She made sure to tell her mother first, perhaps get some understanding before having to face her father. 'Mama, I'm pregnant.'

'Don't say another word,' a horrified Mrs Harrison said. 'Not until your father gets back home from work.'

'But Mama! I'm sorry! Please just listen' cried Scarlett.

'Not another word.' And with that, she left Scarlett sitting at the kitchen table, and disappeared into her bedroom.

§

Supper was a quiet affair. Scarlett hardly ate a thing. She waited for her parents and her brother Danny, two years younger than her, to be seated in the lounge before she plucked up the courage to make her announcement.

Standing in the middle of the lounge, Scarlett said in a soft voice, 'Papa, I know you are not going to like what I have to say, and I'm not proud of myself, but ...,' her voice trailing off, '... I'm pregnant.'

Scarlett's father said nothing at first. Simply glared at his daughter. Then he slowly rose from his armchair, walked over to Scarlett and slapped her across the face, shouting, 'You whore!'

A slight trickle of blood ran down from Scarlett's bottom lip as she bowed her head, looking away from her father's menacing gaze. She heard her mother gasp but Mrs Harrison made no move to protect Scarlett from her father.

'Just make sure you marry the father of your child before it is born, before it even shows you are with child.'

Scarlett raised her eyes to meet those of her father and said, 'Papa, I can't. The father wants nothing to do with my baby. Besides, I don't love him.'

Mr Harrison looked at Scarlett with piercing eyes and said, 'No daughter of mine is bringing shame on my family by bringing a bastard into this world. You have a choice, marry the father or leave my house.'

'Papa, I can't marry him,' replied Scarlett with tears welling in her eyes. 'I was drunk and, except for one night, I don't know him. It's not what I want for the rest of my life.'

'Well you should have thought about that before you foolishly got drunk.' Scarlett's father shook his head in disgust. 'We have given you a privileged life. A good home, the best schooling, paid for all your swimming training and tours, and this is how you repay us.' Sharply, he delivered his ultimatum. 'You either marry him or you will no longer be my daughter.'

'I can't, Papa,' Scarlett sobbed.

'So you've made up your mind. I'm going to bed. Pack up your belongings and get out of my house!' demanded Mr Harrison as he turned his back on his daughter and left the lounge.

There was a sudden silence. Scarlett held out her hands pleadingly to her mother, hoping for support.

'I'm sorry, Sweetie,' Mrs Harrison said tearfully. 'But you heard what your father said. I cannot go against him.'

Scarlett's mother turned reluctantly and followed her husband to their bedroom.

'And you, Danny?' Scarlett asked brokenly. 'Are you also going to condemn me?'

Danny, who had not spoken a word, comforted Scarlett with a hug and said that he would go and speak to them. After what seemed like an eternity, Danny returned with a rather grim look on his face and shook his head.

'Even Mama?' asked Scarlett.

Danny, with a mop of dark brown hair and the same colour eyes, nodded his head. 'You should know that she will always do what Papa decides. She gave me this to give you to help you get going.' Danny handed over a few notes of cash. 'Sorry, Sis. But please know I am here for you. Always.'

A tearful Scarlett looked at her brother and nodded her head in appreciation.

'What are you going to do tonight?' asked Danny.

'I don't know,' replied a forlorn and broken Scarlett. 'Perhaps sleep at the YWCA wherever that is. There should be one somewhere in Cape Town.'

Danny said that he would look it up in the telephone book while she packed her belongings. When it was time to go, Danny said that he would walk with her to the YWCA.

§

Sitting alone in a bleak room, Scarlett wondered in utter disbelief how quickly her life had gone from the possibility of winning a medal at the Olympic Games to being cast out of her family home and holed up in a single room at the YWCA. She then lay on the bed and cried, a deep ache in her belly. And what of her future? She had received a scholarship to attend UCT based on both her academic record and swimming prowess. But that would come to an end. She would need to find a job. And who would look after the baby while she was at work?

§

Scarlett found an evening waitressing job to pay for her accommodation at the YWCA.

Three weeks after being kicked out of the house where she grew up, Scarlett, still suffering from morning sickness, had to rush out in the middle of an early lecture, to throw up in the toilet. On her return, she caught Paul's eye and quickly looked away. But not before she noticed the concern in his expression.

After the lecture, Scarlett discovered Paul waiting for her in the corridor. He placed a hand on her shoulder and took her aside.

'Missy, I know something's wrong. And don't try to be strong and deny it. I want to help you. Tell me what's going on.'

Scarlett remained quiet but didn't object. A moment later she said quietly, 'Here's not the place.'

'Then let's go outside.'

'But what about our biology class?'

'This is more important.'

Holding her hand, Paul walked Scarlett to a grassy open space between two lecture theatres and sat next to her on a bench. 'Out with it,' he said, not unkindly.

Stumbling as she replied, Scarlett said, 'I'm pregnant.'

She told Paul all that had happened, the full story, leaving nothing out. She began with the cattle parade and finished with the waitressing job she had found to pay for her accommodation at the YWCA.

'I've been attending lectures, mostly to keep sane,' said Scarlett, listlessly, 'but soon I will have to stop.'

Paul cut her short. 'Nonsense! You can't let one mistake wreck the rest of your life.'

'But I can't continue. I'm here on a scholarship partially based on swimming and obviously I can no longer keep that commitment.'

'Mmm,' Paul frowned thoughtfully. 'Missy, I have an idea. My parents have a small flat above their double garage. You could stay there and continue your studies.'

'Thanks, Paul. You're a good friend but I think your parents might object to an unmarried pregnant girl staying in their flat. Besides, I couldn't afford the rent and who would look after the baby?'

'Leave my parents to me. We live in a mansion. The flat is standing empty and no one will know that you're even there. As for the baby, one of our maids can work as a nanny when you are at university.'

'Paul, I know you mean well but I can't accept charity. I'd feel terrible.'

'Then how about an agreement that in return for board and lodging you help me with my studies. I really want to become a doctor but already my marks are not up to scratch. Yours are way better than mine, Missy — even with all the personal problems you've been going through.'

'That all sounds good,' said Scarlett, 'but you haven't even asked your parents.'

'They'll agree,' Paul replied confidently. 'My family is wealthy and I sense an element of guilt has always made them want to help those in need. They already do a lot of philanthropic work. This can be an extra one added to their list.'

'What about the cost of my studies? There's no way the university will continue to fund my tuition.'

'Your help is my guarantee that I will graduate. Trust me, Missy, my parents will be willing to pay your fees.'

§

Scarlett moved into the flat above the garage of Paul's parent's house. It was modest, an open-plan lounge and kitchenette, a bedroom and a bathroom, but it was all she needed.

Her brother Danny was a frequent visitor, bringing updates about how her mother was faring. Scarlett never asked after her father. She loved him but he had hurt her deeply.

'Mama is torn up inside, Sis. She never smiles anymore.'

'Is there any chance that we can arrange to visit when Papa is away?'

Danny replied, 'She wouldn't take the chance. She is too loyal to Papa.'

§

On Christmas day 1965, Scarlett woke up in her flat and went to the toilet. As she stood up her waters broke, flooding the bathroom floor. Keeping calm, she called Paul who arrived to drive her to Groote Schuur hospital. On the way, they stopped at Scarlett's childhood home. She wanted her mother to know she had gone into labour.

Paul knocked on the door which, after a few moments, Danny opened.

'Missy has gone into labour. She wants her mom to know.'

When Danny came back he told them that his mother could not come to the hospital but that he, Danny, would love to join them. Instead of Scarlett's husband pacing up and down the corridor of the maternity wing, it was Paul and Danny.

After eight hours of labour, Scarlett gave birth to a baby girl. She called her Robin.

1ˢᵗ January 1967

Dear Scarlett,

Finally! I got to work as a medical doctor. Well, ... as an intern at Addenbrooke's Hospital. And sadly, it was rather disappointing. It turns out that 'intern' is just another word for skivvy! Think closing up wounds when all the 'good stuff' has been done!

But all that changed in one case that hit very close to home. In fact, it was in my home! After a long shift at the hospital, I arrived back at the house where I grew up. Last year I left my residence at King's College and moved back home, with my parents and sister, Jean. My Mom and Dad met me at the door and told me that Jean had come down with the flu. They wisely counselled me to stay away from her as it would be unethical to pass on the flu to my patients at the hospital.

When I went to bed that night, I lay awake a long time worrying about Jean. She is a real sweetie who was then in her second year at med school at the University of Cambridge. Being the lackey at the hospital, I get to see many patients, and could not recall any recent cases of flu amongst them. I fretted all through the night, unable to sleep. Early the following morning I made my way to Jean's bedroom. She was definitely not well! When I turned on the light, she groaned, turning her head away, pulling the bedcovers up to cover her eyes. This could have been a normal momentary response but her sensitivity to light did not abate. On further evaluation she also had a severe headache and high fever, both symptoms of flu. But it was first her stiff neck that had me worried and made me suspect something more serious. Unbuttoning her nightgown to inspect her torso confirmed what I was looking for.

I shouted out for my parents to come to Jean's room. They entered just as I had retrieved an empty glass from Jean's bedside table and pressed it against a rash on her torso. When the red spots did not fade under the pressure of the glass, I told my parents that Jean did not have flu, but in all likelihood, bacterial meningitis. Jean was not in a state to understand, but my parents were horrified that they had missed the signs

To be fair, my father specialised in ophthalmology and my mother in podiatry.

They had become professors at the University of Cambridge and had long since been out of medical practice. So perhaps it was easy to misdiagnose Jean's basic symptoms as a case of flu.

The Gibson family rushed off to Addenbrooke's Hospital where Jean was put into intensive care. A lumbar puncture did reveal bacterial meningitis. Sadly, Jean's condition deteriorated rapidly, and she went into a coma that lasted three weeks. Even if she pulled through, there was the chance that she could have permanent neurological damage.

But my sister is a strong person and was eventually declared well enough to go home. But even then she was in a compromised state for several months, her parents and brother watching over her like hawks for any signs of permanent damage. Jean had to give up her studies for the year but I can happily tell you that she is now back to her normal self and her experience has prompted her to one day specialise in neurology.

Phew! That was a scary few months! I love my sister dearly and would not wish for anyone to go through what she did. But the opportunity of dealing with a serious case such as Jean's, confirmed to me that my calling for a career in medicine was the correct one. If only I could speed up this internship business and get to deal with the serious cases, as long as they don't involve my sister!

I write this letter while singing the words to *Lara's Theme* from the film *Doctor Zhivago,* and I am heartened by the lyrics, 'Someday we'll meet again, my love. Someday whenever the spring breaks through.' It's winter now, so I am willing the days away until spring, my dear. Strangely, I am again writing this annual letter while looking at the River Cam, except this time I am looking out from my bedroom of the house that I grew up in. And looking at that river, of course, brings back memories of that special day when I saw you. Just so that you know, I still live in hope!

All my love, Michael.

Scarlett

Although she had lost her scholarship, Scarlett never gave up swimming. The water was a special place for her. A place where she could go into another world and dream she could do anything or be anyone she wanted as she swam lap after lap.

When Robin was six months old, Scarlett took her daughter to the swimming pool for the first time. After Scarlett had completed her laps, she unbuckled Robin from her pram, placed her on the edge of the pool and while still holding her daughter with one hand, Scarlett jumped back in. She lifted Robin off the edge and drew her to her chest, bouncing her up and down as she walked across the width of the pool.

Scarlett was about to end their joint swimming venture when she took the courage to take Robin under the water. Over her life she had seen many babies scream at this, but Robin kept her eyes open and when they surfaced she had a huge grin on her face, a grin that made mother purr inside.

§

Scarlett invited Danny over for supper every Friday evening, where Paul always joined them. Given that Paul's parents paid Scarlett's food bill, she was always frugal in her shopping and cooking, despite protestations by Paul. Tonight it was cheap yet tasty spaghetti bolognese. Paul always brought over a good bottle of wine to wash down the rather simple food.

It was at these weekly meals that Scarlett bombarded Danny with questions about her parents. Was there a softening in their feelings towards her? No! How were they keeping? How was their health? Danny would always say that their mother wore a veil of sadness that had not existed before the revelation of Scarlett's pregnancy had caused the rift in her family, but her loyalty to her husband was paramount.

'The day after tomorrow is Christmas Day,' Scarlett said to Danny. 'I don't suppose it's worth speaking to Papa, but please will you remind Mama that it's also Robin's first birthday'

'I will, Sis, but don't expect her to come over or acknowledge it in any way.'

Scarlett looked at Danny sadly. Family was important to her. All her growing up life she imagined that she would always be close to her family, that birthdays and Christmases would be special family occasions. She still could not believe that her parents had cast her aside and cut all ties with her. That they would never share in their grandchild's life, especially on milestones such as birthdays and Christmas.

'But I'll be here to celebrate,' added Danny, 'though I'll only be able to make it in the late afternoon or evening as I'll have to be with Mama and Papa for Christmas lunch.'

Scarlett nodded her head in appreciation and said, 'Thank you, dear brother. I'm so grateful Robin and I still have you!'

When Danny was about to leave, Scarlett gave her brother two Christmas gifts, one each for her father and mother. She did the same for their birthdays. And she would continue to do so despite being estranged from them.

'You're wasting your money, Sis. They haven't opened their presents from this past year and I don't think they ever will.'

'That's okay,' answered Scarlett resignedly, 'but it's important for me that I still make an overture to them. After that, it's up to them.'

§

After attending church that Sunday morning, Scarlett joined Paul and his parents for Christmas lunch.

Later that afternoon Danny arrived at Scarlett's flat. There was a very small Christmas tree and Scarlett had made snowflakes out of paper sprinkled with glitter which she stuck on the lounge wall.

'Happy Christmas, Sis,' greeted Danny, giving Scarlett a big hug. 'And where is the birthday girl?'

Danny spotted Robin sitting in her pram, squatted down and handed his niece a gift. Robin tore at the gift wrapping paper, the sound of which earlier in the day had given her more pleasure than the gifts she had received from Scarlett, Paul, and Mr and Mrs Rhodes.

Danny's gift to Robin was a teddy bear. This time the gift appealed to Robin more than just the opening of it. Her eyes lit up.

'It's a teddy bear, Robin,' explained Danny. 'A teddy bear cub.'

'Cub!' repeated Robin to add to her growing vocabulary. And from that moment the teddy bear's name became Cub, and for reasons unknown to Scarlett it was as if it were Robin's best friend that would accompany her for many years to come.

1st January 1968

Dear Scarlett,

I'm bubbling with excitement! But more about that in a moment.

So, I have completed my internship and am now a bona fide qualified doctor. Working at Addenbrooke's Hospital this past year became more rewarding as the leash around my neck was gradually loosened. Loved every moment of it and am so utterly sure that my drive to become a doctor at such a young age has been worth it.

Worth it, too, has been learning to play the guitar in an era of music that seems to be getting better all the time. That sounds somewhat disparaging to music of the past and that's not my intention, it's more a case of the variety that has entered the world of music. Sweet pop music with wide appeal may be heard on the radio but such an array of alternative groups keep popping up with music from the music gods, if one knows where to look for it. Such a choice for me to play on my guitar.

But there has been something else that has caught my attention. At the grand old age of 24, I have watched with keen interest a railing against establishment that is being played out mainly in America and this often reflects in the music I listen to. I am against war and discrimination of any kind. So to borrow from Scott McKenzie's song, which I so enjoy playing, I would have loved to have been in San Francisco to see up close what the 'summer of love' was all about, though I am not sure I would have worn a flower in my hair! I am a conflicted soul in this counterculture movement because I identify a lot with the ideals, but I've also been brought up with old-fashioned values. Does that make me a fence sitter? Perhaps. Time will tell.

So why am I bubbling with excitement? I'm sure wherever you are that you would have heard that the first human to human heart transplant took place just four weeks ago. This has left me stunned, as it has the whole medical community. I'm sure! There was a rumour in the air that a heart transplant was imminent, but the race to be the first to do one was taking place in the USA. How shocking, then, that it happened in Cape Town in South Africa at a hospital called Groote Schuur. I have to confess that I hadn't even heard of that hospital. I'm not sure if that's just me being an ignoramus or because here in the UK we're always looking to America for great things to happen.

This heart transplant has had a profound effect on me, though I'm not sure why. Perhaps because medical science, particularly surgery, has come such a long way in recent years. Can you believe that just over two decades ago if you got shrapnel to the heart during the war they would give you a morphine shot and simply allow you to die. Nowadays, open-heart surgery is becoming more and more commonplace and four weeks ago a heart transplant! My head swirls when I think of this development, especially since my dream is to become a surgeon. Excuse the pun, but we really are in an era of cutting edge stuff!

So the last four weeks I've been doing a lot of soul-searching. I've now completed my internship and was due to specialise in surgery here at the University of Cambridge. But I've lived all my life in Cambridge and feel that I'm due for a change, and what better place to specialise than at the teaching hospital where the first heart transplant took place, Groote Schuur in Cape Town.

Scarlett, I still keep looking out for you when I walk or cycle around Cambridge. I've even wondered if you're a nurse or someone studying to be a doctor and have kept my eyes open for you here at Addenbrooke's Hospital. A small chance, yes, but sadly it would appear that is not the case. Although I have not yet heard back from the University of Cape Town, I have applied to continue my studies there. That, of course, will involve spending a lot of time at the now famous Groote Schuur hospital which operates in conjunction with the university. Who knows, I might even get to meet the most famous doctor on the planet, Dr Christiaan Barnard! But it will also mean that I'll be very far from you and that's the one thing that makes me sad about my decision, that I may never get to see you again.

All my love, Michael.

Scarlett

After lectures and before studying in the evening, Scarlett would pick Robin up and head off to Newlands Swimming Pool where she would swim 40 laps of 50 metre lengths, to keep in trim but mostly because she loved the feel of the water. A place of solace. Each time she finished training, Scarlett would undress Robin and, holding her daughter to her chest, get back into the water. Robin's face always lit up with a smile. The two would spend as much time together in the water as Scarlett could afford away from her studies.

When Robin was a year and a half old, Scarlett no longer restrained her in her pram. Instead, the little tot would pace up and down the paving on the side of the pool waiting for her turn to get into the water. Scarlett would do 10 laps of each stroke. Always freestyle first, then butterfly, followed by breaststroke and lastly her beloved backstroke. One particular day, on the third breaststroke lap, Scarlett raised her head to take a breath and immediately saw that Robin had fallen into the pool on the far side. Panic set in and her heart pounded in her chest.

Scarlett was a third of the way along the length of the pool. She faced an agonising decision. What was the fastest way to get to her daughter? Swim to the side, get out and run to the far end of the pool or trust in her ability to swim directly to Robin? She made her decision in a split second. Scarlett had never swum in an Olympic final, but now she swam for what was most dear to her heart, something more precious than a gold medal.

A million thoughts raced through her head. Her precious daughter could not drown in a swimming pool. If that happened in Scarlett's peaceful place it would be beyond cruel. As she neared Robin, she lifted her head above the water level and what she discovered shocked her. Robin had not fallen into the pool but had got in deliberately and was floating on her back, doing little kicks with her legs just as Mom did. Scarlett slowly walked up to her daughter and witnessed a smile on Robin's face, and shock turned into relief which turned into joy. Her daughter was a water baby!

§

Later that year when Paul knocked on the door of Scarlett's flat to join her to study, his heart was beating loudly in his chest from what he had just heard on the radio.

'Have you heard the news?' Paul asked excitedly, as soon as Scarlett opened the door.

'That depends, but not the news you've heard given the smile on your face.'

'There's a chance that South Africa may be allowed to participate in the Olympics in Mexico City!'

Scarlett gave Paul a piercing stare and said sharply, 'Paul, I am up for a joke as good as anyone, but that would be below the belt.'

'I'm serious. Just heard it on the radio. Some cockeyed arrangement where South Africa has agreed to send an integrated team but there will be two trials, one for whites and one for blacks, and an eight person committee, half black and half white, will compare performances and choose a squad.'

By now Scarlett's heart beat had also started racing, but she was highly sceptical. 'Surely the rest of the world would not accept that arrangement.'

'You'd think not, but the IOC is going to send a committee to South Africa later in the year to see if any progress in race relations has been made and, if it has, then South Africa will be invited to compete at Mexico City next year.'

'Well, that's not going to happen!' Scarlett stated in a matter of fact tone.

'Missy, there have been a few changes. Even with our few visits to Groote Schuur hospital we can see some improvements. But the fact that South Africa has agreed to send a mixed team will surely be seen in a good light. Maybe those against South Africa will see sport as the catalyst for change.'

'I have to be honest, Paul, I'm not so sure.'

'Well, let me ask you this, if we are invited back would you want to go for it?'

'Are you seriously asking me that question?'

'Well, what I'm saying is that if, and yes it is a big if, but if they do invite South Africa to compete then you need to be ready.'

Scarlett slowly nodded her head, trying to digest this turn of events. Then she asked Paul, 'What about you?'

'I'm afraid not, Missy. My goal was just to get to the Olympics, become an Olympian. I always knew that I had no chance to medal. Besides, I'm nearly halfway to becoming a doctor—'

'So am I.'

'But Missy, you're bright enough to train and still keep up with your studies. Even if you took next year off, you could return to your studies and breeze through your exams. I'm a slogger. A slogger at swimming and a slogger at studying. If I stopped now my hope of qualifying as a doctor will go up in smoke. And unlike you, I've not kept up my swimming, so I'm not even sure I would make the team. But it's different for you. All I'm saying is that you should keep your options open.'

And Scarlett did. She woke up at 4 o'clock every morning and trained her heart out. Her late afternoon swimming with Robin took on a new dimension, training to improve rather than to keep in shape.

And she loved it. And she hated it. A chance to become an Olympian but still in the hands of politicians.

1st January 1969

Dear Scarlett,

I have big news! I was accepted to specialise in surgery at the University of Cape Town and spend a considerable time at the teaching hospital, Groote Schuur, now famous as the venue of the first human to human heart transplant.

The excitement of that heart transplant had not diminished by the time I arrived in South Africa in mid-January last year. In fact, the hospital was abuzz because a second transplant had just taken place, and as I write this letter the recipient is still alive, which is quite an achievement. Everywhere I went, people spoke reverently about Dr Chris Barnard and his team.

As you know, until last year, I had lived all my life in Cambridge. It's quite something to now experience a new city in a different country. And what a difference and where to begin to describe!

Let me start with the easy part. I have always thought Cambridge to be a beautiful city, which it is. But Cape Town is breathtaking! The city is nestled between the sea and an iconic mountain. If you approach Cape Town by sea, the first thing you see is the majestic Table Mountain, and I'm sure I don't need to explain its name. Sometimes the view of the mountain is crystal clear with a deep blue sky behind it, and on other occasions it is blanketed by a white cloud as if it were a table covered by a table cloth. Absolutely stunning! Table Mountain is flanked by several other mountains — Lion's Head and Signal Hill to the right and Devil's Peak on the left, and together they form an amphitheatre that is a dramatic backdrop for the city below, a city that looks out towards Table Bay. My university is on the slopes of Devil's Peak and not far to its left is Groote Schuur hospital where I spend much of my time. Behind Table Mountain are several leafy green southern suburbs and I live in one called Rondebosch that is not too far from UCT.

The odd occasion when I've had spare time, I've driven along the waterfront, meandering through Sea Point, then past the golden beaches of Clifton and Camps Bay before climbing up Chapman's Peak, where one overlooks the glittering Atlantic Ocean that is coloured in a profusion of shades of blue. Once I continued down the peninsula to Cape Point which has so many beautiful lookout spots, then motored up the east coast passing through quaint fishing villages. The sea along the way looks stunning, but there is one big problem, the water is cold! Too cold for swimming! And there are sharks!

Another time I drove north from the city and visited some of the wine estates for which Cape Town is famous. These estates are 'chocolate box' beautiful and offer wine tasting, along with delicious food in their gourmet restaurants. I'm becoming something of a wine connoisseur and bought a couple of select vintages to take back with me. You know the saying — when in Cape Town, do as the Capetonians do!

I can't comment on the rest of South Africa because I work very long hours and haven't had the opportunity to visit other parts of the country. I'm hoping that in the near future, I'll be able to visit a game reserve. I'm longing to see South Africa's famous wild life!

That's the easy part, now for the hard. The people! As I write this, my head is swirling thinking about how best to describe South Africa and its people. Out of the blocks, let me say that I'm an easy going guy who wishes that everyone could live peacefully and happily together!

Okay, let's start. It's impossible to tell you about the people without telling you about the politics of the country. But even that is not easy. I have been here a year now, and I'm still struggling to come to terms with the history of this country and how it got to where it is now. What the world knows is that there is a minority group of white people and there is a majority group of black people. Only whites are allowed to vote and the present government rules with an iron fist implementing a policy of racial segregation where white people are advantaged. And that is true. But it's so much more complicated than that.

So, how do I begin to explain? Let me try. For starters, around nine different black tribes comprise the majority group of black people. I'm led to believe that these tribes are as different as say Germans and French people. And we all know where Germany and France stood just 25 years ago! But despite different cultures and languages, they do have a common purpose and that is to gain equality with the white minority.

To compound matters, the white population is made up of two prominent groups, the English and the Afrikaans, the latter originally coming from Holland and France. And at the beginning of this century they were bitter enemies fighting each other in the Boer War. I sense that there is still a feeling of enmity between some of them. Also, amongst the whites are Jewish people, Italians, Germans, Greeks and many more.

And now it gets even more complicated. My understanding is that a person of colour in say, America, is considered to be black. Not here. Over the centuries, offspring of illicit inter-racial affairs coalesced to form a distinctly separate group of people called coloureds. And then there are a sizeable number of Indians from Asia, though they mainly live in the province of Natal.

Also, to add to the mix, there are a people known as the Khoisan who, I believe, were the true indigenous people of the land that is now mapped out as a country called South Africa. Sadly, much like the native Americans or the Aborigines of Australia or the Maoris of New Zealand, it would appear that they have been decimated, in South Africa's case by both the whites and blacks.

Bizarrely, by law there is a pecking order of racial groups in South Africa. Whites come first, then the coloureds and then the blacks. Where the Indians fit in I am not sure, but I surmise they would exist somewhere between a white and a black, even though the ones I have seen appear blacker than the blacks! As for the Khoisan people, to be honest I haven't a clue.

How is South Africa different from other countries that have been colonized? It's simple. In South Africa the white population is in the minority whereas in America or Australia or New Zealand the white population became the majority. And why does this matter? Well, there exists in South Africa this vast continuum ranging from people who are still hunter-gatherers to highly qualified doctors performing groundbreaking surgery. The whites originating from the United Kingdom and Europe are as a whole more educated and civilized in a western world sense and fear that if everyone had an equal vote they would be voted out and lose their very good standard of living. Despite countries like America, Australia and New Zealand only giving their darker shade of inhabitants the right to vote in recent times, there was never quite the same fear amongst the whites that they would be outvoted and lose their privileged status.

South African history is a very complicated and convoluted story and I'm not sure anyone can with any degree of accuracy explain how the country got to this point. The bottom line, though, is that the present government continues with its apartheid policy of legislated segregation. As far as I can see, at some point in the future something has got to give for things to change. Either a civil war or a miraculous change of attitude by all the people of this country! The latter is not inconceivable. They do have an election every few years, and although only whites have the vote there is a sizable number who vote against the ruling party. Time will tell.

So, what's it like living here in South Africa? Interesting! With such a hotchpotch of people of different shades of colour, different cultures and so many languages, everyday life presents difficulties and challenges. Just the language divide quite often means I haven't a clue what someone is saying to me. On the other hand it allows for an indulgence in a variety of cultures and foods. I'll say it again, interesting!

I said earlier that I am an easy going guy who wishes for everyone to be peaceful and happy, so how do I deal with this very complicated situation? As individuals, I find most people in all the different groups to be extremely friendly and hospitable, more so, perhaps, than any other place I have been to. So I try to do my bit each day to bring people together. And I'm pleased to say that, by and large, the people where I work have a similar attitude.

And that's my take on South Africa. It surely is one of the most beautiful countries in the world with beautiful people who have unfortunately made things complicated for themselves.

Is there anything that I don't like about South Africa? Yes! It seems as if everything starts an hour earlier than anywhere else in the world, and I have always been a night owl!

There's a song that was released by a South African artist during this past year called *Lazy Life*, so I'm not sure if you would have heard it in the UK. It conjures up images of lying on a blanket, picnicking in the park under blue skies, sunshine on one's shoulders, birds singing, butterflies floating from flower to flower, and kids running free with much laughter and gaiety, capturing all the joys of a lazy life and leaving one's problems behind. Oh, how I wish it were you on that blanket with me so I could play the song for you on my guitar.

Instead, I am now living at the bottom of the African continent and I feel so far away from you. I would dearly love to meet you and bring you out to South Africa to experience this wonderful but somewhat crazy country.

All my love, Michael.

Scarlett

In the new year, both Paul and Scarlett registered as fourth year medical students which meant that they would be working with live patients for the first time at the teaching hospital, Groote Schuur.

The day they arrived at the hospital, it was buzzing. During the summer holidays at the end of the previous year, the first human to human heart transplant had occurred. And by the time the students had returned to university a second transplant had happened. Naturally a lot of talk centred around this new turn of events and their hospital had gained worldwide attention. Would they get to meet Dr Chris Barnard? Could they take a peek at the new heart transplant patient? Was it morally right to take a heart out of a fellow human and place it in a different body? The excitement was palpable.

That excitement soon came crashing down when the workload started to pile up. A typical day for Scarlett would be a 4 o'clock start for two hours training in the pool just in case South Africa were readmitted to the Olympic Games. Then lectures in the morning, followed by patient visits in the afternoon at Groote Schuur, requiring intense concentration in order to correctly answer the difficult questions posed by the teaching doctors. In the late afternoon, Scarlett would always fetch Robin from home, where she was looked after by a nanny belonging to the Rhodes family, and take her to the swimming pool. Mother would do a further two hours of training while her daughter would escape into her own world in the kiddies pool. At the end of Scarlett's training session they would swim together in what they called the big pool. Scarlett tried to keep it fun, but Robin displayed an unfathomable desire to want to learn to swim properly. That for her was fun.

In the evenings, Scarlett would cook and eat with Robin. Then Paul would come over and the two students would study late into the night. An exception was Saturday evenings when Scarlett and Robin would join Paul and his parents for supper. On a Sunday, Paul, Scarlett and Robin had a standing lunch date at one of the many restaurants somewhere in the Cape winelands, followed by a stroll in the beautiful estate gardens before returning home.

§

In February, Paul once again knocked on the door of Scarlett's flat to deliver good Olympic Games news.

'Missy, I've just heard on the radio that the committee that was sent to South Africa last year decided that the South African National Olympic Committee had made sufficient progress and based on that the IOC members had a postal vote. They've decided to invite South Africa to participate at Mexico City. We're in!'

'But?'

'What but?'

'Paul, there always seems to be a catch.'

'No, the invite is definite. It is, however, on the understanding that any remaining discrimination will be ended by the 1972 Olympic Games.'

'So there is a but.'

'Yes, but, to use that word again, the invite still stands for Mexico City. Whether South Africa eradicates discrimination by the Munich Games will be a decision for another day.'

What Paul said made sense, so Scarlett contacted her old coach Graham O'Brien and together they set about priming the swimmer for the Olympic Games later that year.

'Graham, I can't pay you now, but in a year's time I will get a small salary as an intern and will reimburse you then, if that's okay with you.'

'Missy, you don't have to pay me anything. Working with the greatest talent I've ever had is payment enough.'

Scarlett was so engrossed in her swimming training, studying and being a good mother, that she paid little attention to what was transpiring politically around the world. Various bodies indicated that they would boycott the Olympic Games if South Africa participated and eventually the Mexican organising committee, concerned that its Olympic Games would become a fiasco, asked the IOC to reconsider.

At the end of April, Graham arrived at the swimming pool, where Scarlett was already training, to deliver the bad news.

'Missy, you need to get out of the water to listen to this,' said her coach.

A nervous Scarlett climbed out of the pool.

'You'll need to sit down,' he said, grimly. After Scarlett sat on a bench, Graham read from the newspaper, 'In response to Mexico's request to the IOC to reconsider its decision to readmit South Africa to the Olympic Games, the IOC executive board met on the 21st April 1968 to seek a diplomatic formula under which to exclude South Africa, finally agreeing that due to the international climate, the executive committee was of the opinion it would be most unwise for South Africa to participate.'

Scarlett's face crumpled, and she sobbed her heart out. Sitting next to her, Graham put an arm around his star student to comfort her.

When Scarlett finally managed to regain some composure, Graham said, 'Missy, I would give my house away to enable you to compete, but I'm afraid that the forces against you are just too great.'

Scarlett looked at Graham with tear-filled eyes. 'Thanks, coach,' she said. 'You're a good man.'

§

In September that year while sitting in a restaurant on the Spier wine estate in Stellenbosch, Paul asked Scarlett, 'How did you enjoy working on a cadaver this past week?'

'Do you have to ask that when we're eating?' Scarlett enquired, feigning annoyance. On her plate was roast lamb with cranberry jelly, roast potatoes, pumpkin and peas. If she had bothered to glance at the table behind her she would have seen Michael Gibson enjoying the same meal. She cut a piece of the roast lamb, held it up with her fork and said, 'If the cadaver were as tasty as this dead meat it would have been more fun but—'

'Mommy, why is the meat dead?' asked Robin, a few months away from her third birthday, her dark hair now long and held in place with an Alice band.

'Now look what you've started,' said Scarlett, and then turned the tables saying, 'Paul will explain.'

'What!' exclaimed Paul, lost for words.

'That'll teach you to open your trap about cadavers when we're eating.'

'Mommy, what's a trap?'

'That's one way of getting out of answering a child's awkward questions,' Scarlett said to Paul with a triumphant smile. 'Change the subject.' Then she explained to her daughter, 'Sweetie, it's what Paul has for a mouth when he asks stupid things.'

'I want a trap.'

'Then ask a stupid question. But be careful,' teased Scarlett, 'because you might just fall into your own trap.'

'Why do I call you Mommy but I don't call Paul Daddy?'

Scarlett nearly choked on her roast lamb. This question had come sooner than expected. Scarlett quickly cut another piece of meat and offered it to Robin to buy time and Paul helped her out by asking, 'Now that lectures and practicals are getting to the nitty gritty of medicine, are you still happy with your choice of career?'

'It's the least of all the other evils, so I suppose yes. But I feel it's my right to swim in Mexico City next month. I could live a million years and I would still never understand why I can't compete. I've heard all the arguments. I don't have a racist bone in my body, yet I'm being banned from becoming an Olympian. Why can't they have a bloody neutral team in which all the so-called lepers can compete?'

'Bloody!' exclaimed Robin.

'No Sweetie, don't say that word.'

'Bloody!' exclaimed Robin again, with a wide smile.

'Robin, what happens if I cut my hand with a knife? What will come out?'

'Blood.'

'And my hand will become all bloody.'

With Robin's fascination with the word diminished, Scarlett bit her lips, almost drawing blood, and she became teary-eyed. 'All I have ever wanted to do is swim against the best.'

'Mommy, can we go and swim?'

'Yes, Sweetie,' answered Scarlett. She knew that she would find solace in the water with her precious daughter.

Paul looked at Scarlett and a great empathy overcame him. He had never been as ambitious as Scarlett. Even if he were as talented as she, he may still not have had the drive. He could only imagine the heartache that Scarlett must feel to have been so close to twice participating in the Olympic Games, only for those chances to be scuppered at the last moment.

1st January 1970

Dear Scarlett,

This past year can only be described as a crazy one. In addition to trying to complete my doctorate in surgery in as short a time as possible — I'm itching to get slicing and dicing — I'm having to put in 18 hour days which means I literally live at the hospital from Monday to Friday. In the middle of the year, a series of things happened that gave me both a rush and a downer at the same time. It started on a high just before 5 o'clock in the morning on the 21st July as I headed off to Groote Schuur. News came through on the radio that Neil Armstrong had set foot on the moon. I felt an adrenalin rush as I heard his famous words, 'one small step for man, one giant leap for mankind', and thought of the astonishing human conquests of recent times, climbing Mount Everest, the first human heart transplant and now man landing on the moon.

We don't have television in South Africa. In my opinion, the government is afraid it could be used as a tool against its racial policies. Nevertheless, the newspapers and radio carried the moon landing story for days. It was a big deal! I was especially excited because not long afterwards, I was due to fly out to America in early August to deliver a paper at a conference at both Stanford University in Palo Alto near San Francisco and later at Harvard University in Cambridge. Not my Cambridge, obviously, but the one in Massachusetts. The paper is related to the work I'm doing for my doctorate in surgery. This would be my first visit to America and I could imagine the excitement of the moon landing still permeating the air when I got there.

An odd side thought. When you live in Cape Town, one feels that the big things happen in Johannesburg which is the biggest city in South Africa. My sense is that if you live in Johannesburg that things in London are a step up from South Africa. And having lived most of my life in the UK, there was always that feeling that things were bigger and better in the United States of America. I wonder who the Americans look up to?

When I arrived in America in early August, there certainly was a buzz in the air about the moon landing. Before delivering my paper at Stanford University, I visited San Francisco nearby and tried to imagine what it must have been like during the 'summer of love' only two years earlier, then spent a day roaming the campus of the University of California in Berkeley, home of the free speech movement. All the time I was trying in my mind to marry the two opposites of established America and a revolution that preached 'make love, not war'. There was a part of me that wanted to join the revolution and promote peace, but there was also a part of me that valued established norms, perhaps due to my upbringing.

I then presented my paper at Stanford University. It was there that most people in the medical fraternity expected the first heart transplant to take place, so when the guests heard I was from Groote Schuur in Cape Town, the atmosphere became somewhat prickly. I was bombarded with questions about the hospital and was repeatedly asked about Dr Chris Barnard.

I was a bit annoyed because I felt that my paper was worth discussing on its own merits. So I had to take a deep breath and explain that Groote Schuur, while not in the same league as the renowned hospitals in the USA, was actually a fine institution with medical teams imbued with an incredible pioneering spirit. Regarding the famous heart surgeon, I explained that I had never met Dr Chris Barnard, having only seen him once during a guest lecture.

And then I was questioned about the racial policies of South Africa in quite an unfriendly tone! I abhor discrimination of any kind, so I felt that the attack was undeserved, especially since in my own everyday life I try to advance changes against inequality. But I kept my cool and explained that while I could not speak about the rest of the country, Groote Schuur was making great strides in treating people of all races as equals. Not there yet by any means, but moving in the right direction, and I found it somewhat hypocritical having to defend myself to an audience whose country had only recently passed laws to end discrimination, and from what I had observed in my short stay still had a long way to go before it would play out in society. Nevertheless, I felt I won them over when I steered the audience towards my own research which was well-received and precipitated a lively debate.

And then the buzz of the moon landing was shattered with the news that the actress Sharon Tate along with a few others were murdered by some madman that I had not heard of. It spooked the world of Hollywood and became major news, especially since early evidence suggested that it was associated with the counterculture movement. I, too, was stunned and saddened.

I had a small break before I was due to present my paper at Harvard and as luck would have it, my time off coincided with a music festival to be held at Woodstock, not too far from where I was heading. It was billed as '3 Days of Peace & Music'. That appealed to me as I found the atmosphere in San Francisco to be somewhat toxic. I needed some peace and music!

Well, what can I say? It had recently rained, and since the festival was held in a field on a farm, there was mud everywhere! To add to the woes, the organizers expected 50,000 people to turn up but that swelled to 400,000 which made life unbearable in many respects. Sanitation was inadequate, food was in short supply and the queues tested everyone's patience. And in that queue of people, can you believe it, yours truly helped deliver a baby!

Again, I had mixed feelings about the counterculture revolution. It was peaceful. The vibe was festive. In the words of others, 'It was groovy!' However, there were some worrying aspects. Though I'd helped deliver one baby, maternity wards were going to be rushed off their feet in nine months! I'm not a prude, so I understood that. But there was an element of degradation that concerned me, mostly of the festival goers having no purpose in life and looking for the high that the use of psychedelic drugs could give them. For someone training to save lives, I briefly wondered how many concert goers and performers would still be around in a few years, and came away with the feeling that while the cause of these people was noble, I was not convinced of the method for change.

But the music was great! The concert ran over time and only a few of us got to see Jimi Hendrix perform magic on his guitar, including, can you believe it, a rendition of *The Star Spangled Banner*. I left knowing that I still needed to keep my day job!

After a tour around the picturesque Boston area, the presentation of my paper went well at Harvard University, and then it was on a plane back to South Africa.

On the journey, my mind was in a turmoil regarding what had transpired since the moon landing. I struggled to make sense of it all. What I did know was that I had a purpose and was itching to get back and complete my doctorate in surgery and start practising. And I wanted to focus on trauma surgery which would mean even further studies. Why trauma? I'll be honest, the adrenalin rush!

Something else happened on that journey back to South Africa. I had lived most of my life in Cambridge in the UK, visited both the east and west coasts of America, but I felt a sense of calling back to South Africa, a special place which for the first time I considered my home.

As soon as I got back home, a new song was released by the Bee Gees which I have been practising on my guitar when I can steal a spare moment. Scarlett, I don't know what was going through your mind when you saw me five years ago, but if I had a wish it would be that you are now singing the words of the new song that I have learned, 'Don't forget to remember me, my love.'

All my love, Michael.

Scarlett

One evening in March, Scarlett was studying at the small dining table in her flat, waiting for Paul to join her while three year old Robin sat on the floor paging through a picture book. There was a knock on the door.

'Come in,' shouted Scarlett.

As the door opened, Scarlett remarked, 'You're a little early for your extra lessons.'

When there was no reply, she looked up to see André standing in the doorway. The blood drained from her face, and she rushed to the door, trying to block his view of Robin and prevent him from entering further.

'What are you doing here?' she demanded in a low voice.

'No need to be so uppity,' replied André. 'I'm just here to see my daughter.'

'No you're not!' spat Scarlett, turning to see her child watching them, eyes wide! 'Robin, go into the bedroom and close the door,' she said in a no-nonsense voice. Obediently, the little girl scurried towards the bedroom.

'So my daughter's name is Robin,' André said.

On edge, Scarlett kept silent.

André continued, 'I have a right to see her, you know. She is my daughter.'

'No, you gave up that right — years ago. You made it very clear that you wanted nothing to do with our child. My child.'

'She's my blood.'

'André, please! Don't make a scene. Just leave!'

André grabbed both Scarlett's wrists, marched her across the room and flung her on the couch.

'You're drunk!' cried Scarlett.

'That didn't stop us last time.'

Unbuckling his belt he uttered, 'If you're so callous that you won't let me see my daughter then perhaps we'll just have to make another one.'

By nature Scarlett would have fought like a caged leopard, but she was desperate to spare Robin from what was about to come. She lay back and said, 'Do what you must, but do it quietly.'

Suddenly, a cold, deadly voice spoke behind André. 'I don't know who you are, but let go of Missy now or you'll regret it until your dying day.'

'Paul!' Scarlett cried out.

André slowly turned. 'Who are you?' he asked with a sneer.

Scarlett put her finger to her lips and nodded towards the bedroom door, indicating to Paul that Robin could probably hear every word. Quick to sense the situation, Paul remained calm. Even though he had not kept up his swimming training like Scarlett had, he was naturally strong and wiry. Taking André by the scruff of the neck, he hauled him out of the garage flat, warning Scarlett to lock the door behind him

As soon as the door was locked, Scarlett hurried to her bedroom and found Robin sitting on the edge of the bed. The look in Robin's eyes deeply worried her. Scarlett lay on her bed, her head and shoulders propped up against the wall, and drew Robin onto her own body, laying her daughter's head on her chest.

After a moment of silence, Robin asked her mother the question she feared she would. 'Is that man my daddy?'

'No, Sweetie. He's a monster.' Then gently stroking her daughter's long dark hair, Scarlett surprised herself by saying in a tender voice, 'I'd like you to think of Paul as your daddy.'

It wasn't long before Robin fell asleep with her head on Scarlett's breast. It was only then that fear took over Scarlett's mind and body. She trembled. And she questioned over and over again. Why did this have to happen? Why after so many years?

Mother and daughter lay there for three hours before Scarlett heard a knock on the door. She got up from the bed, entered the living room cautiously. 'Is that you, Paul?' she called.

'Yes, open up, Missy.'

Relieved, Scarlett unlocked the door and was about to thank him when he stopped her. Grasping her hands firmly in his, he asked in a stern voice, 'Who is that man?'

Scarlett took a deep breath before answering, 'He's Robin's father.'

'Did he rape you?'

'No — no. But he was going to. You got here just in time.'

'I mean before, when—'

Scarlett cut in saying, 'We were both drunk. I honestly can't remember much, but I feel I'm just as responsible.' After a brief pause, Scarlett continued, 'We were only together for a night. On the one hand, I regret terribly that it caused me to be disowned by my parents. On the other, it gave me Robin, and she's the centre of my life. Would I have liked the circumstances to be different? Yes! Would I like for her to have a different father? Yes! Especially after what happened this evening.'

Paul nodded his head and said decisively, 'Missy, don't ever ask me why, but that man will never harm you ever again!'

Perhaps it was the relief of hearing that news, perhaps something deeper, but Scarlett released her hands, reached around to embrace Paul, then kissed him, lightly at first and then with passion. Several moments of tender kissing passed, before Paul pulled back and said, 'Missy, we need to talk.'

They made coffee and sat next to each other on the couch. Paul, with a fervour Scarlett had never seen before, looked into her eyes and told her what was in his heart, what had always been in his heart. 'Missy, from the day I first laid eyes on you, when we swam for the junior Dolphin Swimming Club, I had a crush on you. But, and I am not ashamed to say this, I've always been shy with girls and women, and even more so with you. You've always come across as being so strong that I've been a little scared of you. Not as much since you moved in here but definitely when we were younger. And, of course, that's why I called you Miss Harrison. But from the beginning I've yearned to say that I like you or later on I love you, but I just didn't have the confidence. Well, now I am saying it. I love you!'

Scarlett started to speak but Paul put his fingers to his lips to silence her. 'I don't know how you feel about me. I'd wish for you to return my feelings, but if not then that's okay. From my side it's important for me to tell you that I love you. Always have. And if you don't feel the same way, then it's still fine for us to continue as we have been doing. You don't need to feel that things have changed because in a sense nothing has.'

Scarlett leant over and kissed Paul, then whispered, 'I want you to be Robin's father.'

Confused, Paul said, 'I'm not sure I follow.'

'It's true that when we were young, I noticed you were a bit awestruck in my presence. If truth be told, I've always really liked you, but something in me would not allow me to lose focus on my dream of becoming an Olympic swimmer. And I am sorry for that. But since moving in here, I've developed feelings for you. At times, I've been really confused and I don't know if it's because you've been such a rock in my life, my saviour, or if it's love that I feel. It's hard for me to understand. I know that I long for your company each evening when we study together. This may sound strange, but we've known each other for so long that I feel that I've skipped the infatuation stage and instead have a deeper love for you — like a long time married couple.'

Paul was stunned, but had the clarity of mind to ask Scarlett, 'What do you mean by wanting me to be Robin's father?'

'Earlier when you were away, Robin asked me if André was her father and I told her to think of you as her daddy. It just slipped out. But over the next couple of hours I thought about us a lot. In many ways we've been like family and you've been the closest that Robin has for a father.

And I started thinking what it would be like if we really did become a family.' Scarlett, looking a little confused, continued, 'What if we took this in small steps towards that direction.'

'Are you saying we're engaged?' asked Paul. 'That we just skip a courtship?'

'In a way we've had a courtship, just a strange one because my Olympic ambition did not allow a normal one.'

'I don't know what to think. I love you Missy and would love to be married to you, it's just that I am not sure you feel the same way about me.'

'Would it help if I told you a little secret that may give insight to how I feel about you. When I registered Robin for her birth certificate I put your name as her father. Her name is officially Robin Rhodes, daughter of Paul Rhodes.'

Paul seemed stunned.

Scarlett continued. 'Normally to make us a complete family you would have to adopt Robin. That part is done.'

Paul got off the couch, knelt down, and took Scarlett by the hand. 'Missy, my darling, will you marry me?'

'Yes!' replied Scarlett before they kissed.

After a moment, Scarlett withdrew and said, 'Paul, this has all been unusual, so I think we ought to go slowly, especially for Robin's sake.'

Paul teased, 'It's been a slow journey so far. I think I can wait a little longer! But to seal it I want you to join me tomorrow to select an engagement ring. I know diamonds are supposed to be 'a girl's best friend' and I'm a bit out of my depth here, but I think a sapphire would match your beautiful eyes.'

The following day Scarlett selected a sapphire engagement ring, the precious gemstone surrounded by 14 solitaire diamonds and together set in 18-karat white gold. Paul took Scarlett in the cable car to the top of Table Mountain where he bent down on one knee and proposed. Their engagement was official!

1st January 1971

Dear Scarlett,

As you know, the first human to human heart transplant carried out by Dr Chris Barnard and his team at Groote Schuur hospital in Cape Town was instrumental in me relocating to South Africa. Something about that historic occasion moved me, so much so that there was no other place that I wanted to train to become a surgeon.

This past year my cohort had a few lectures by Dr Barnard, but I had no personal contact until late last year when he called out to me just as I was about to go to sleep at the hospital. Of course, you may be wondering why I would be sleeping at Groote Schuur. And the simple answer is to save time because in addition to completing my doctorate in general surgery, I have now started studying my diploma in trauma. Because the meeting with Dr Chris Barnard meant so much to me, I want to relay to you exactly the way it played out.

'Young man,' a voice called out to me as I was entering the storeroom that I used for sleeping.

I turned around and there was the world's most famous heart surgeon just a few paces away. Tall, dressed in surgical greens and with his signature white surgical cap covering most of his short black hair. I tried to say something, but I was star struck, made a fool of myself and blushed.

Dr Barnard said, 'I've noticed that you spend many hours late into the night here at the hospital.'

I nodded my head.

'Sleeping here, are you?'

'Yes.'

'Working 18 hour days?'

'Yes.'

'That's a good sign. It's the only way to rise to the top.'

I honestly didn't know what to say and stood there like I was stuck in the mud with my mouth glued shut.

'Would you like to see it?' he asked.

'What?'

'The place where the first heart transplant took place.'

I was overwhelmed and excited all at once and quickly replied, 'Yes!'

While we walked over to the heart transplant building, we chatted. Mostly he was asking questions about me.

'Your accent?'

'I'm from Cambridge in England. I did my medical degree there.'

'A fine university, Cambridge. Why did you leave to come here?'

'When you did your first heart transplant it made such an impression on me that I knew Groote Schuur was the place for me to continue my studies.'

'Cardiothoracic surgery?'

'Actually, no, general surgery.'

'That's a pity. We need fine surgeons like you in our cardiology department.'

I didn't know whether to take that as a compliment or if he was disappointed in me, so I switched topics and said, 'Tell me about the recipient, Louis Washkansky.'

'Washy. That's what we used to call him. A good-hearted fellow but with a bad heart, obviously.'

'Why him and not someone else?' I asked.

'We simply weren't ready to do a heart transplant before that. We didn't have the knowledge. But it came to a point where we felt we were not going to improve any further without taking that giant leap.'

'Are you aware that you've just used the same expression that Neil Armstrong used when he stepped on the moon last year?'

'No. I wasn't aware,' the heart doctor replied.

'Was there a race to do the first heart transplant like there was between America and the Soviet Union to land a man on the moon?' I asked.

'Most definitely!' replied Dr Barnard.

'When I was at Cambridge the speculation was that it would most likely occur at Stanford.'

'Shumway. Norman Shumway,' said Dr Barnard, nodding his head. 'Did you read his quote in the Journal of the American Medical Association about the way being clear for a trial of a human heart transplantation?'

'Yes. And we all felt that it was imminent and that he would do it.'

'Yes,' said the heart surgeon, 'that's what most people were thinking. But there were others too. Like Richard Lower and Adrian Kantrowitz in America and even Vladimir Demikhov from Russia. We all dared to do the impossible.'

'Then why here in Africa? Quite frankly, it shocked both me and the rest of the world, I'm sure.'

'That's an interesting question,' noted Dr Barnard. 'I sense that all of us were ready and it was just a fortuitous set of circumstances that allowed us to be the first. In some ways we were not in the league of our colleagues in America. Our budget was a fraction of theirs. I'm not sure if you know but I studied at the University of Minnesota, which at the time was the leading institution for research in cardiac surgery. After obtaining my PHD in cardiothoracic surgery, the head of department, Owen Wangensteen, wanted me to stay on and work under him, but South Africa was in my blood and I wanted to come back home. He kindly arranged for the American National Health Institute to give me a De Wall-Lillehei heart-lung machine as a parting gift to take back to South Africa. When it arrived by ship, we assembled it only to discover that we did not even have an autoclave at Groote Schuur to sterilize it. We had to take it to the Red Cross War Memorial Children's Hospital and have it sterilized there. That's just one example of many where we had limited resources. And then there was the South Africa situation.'

'Meaning?'

'With apartheid, South Africa was becoming increasingly isolated. All science is based on building on what has gone before. But here there was a stem of the flow of information. We were only receiving medical journals months after they were being published in America and other countries. Such were the challenges here in South Africa.'

'So what made the difference?' I asked.

'We had one huge ace up our sleeves. In the US the heart transplant surgeons were subjected to draconian legislation that accepted only the absence of a heartbeat as the definition of death, whereas we benefited by a looser definition. It was not one hundred percent clear so before the heart transplant I consulted a professor in forensic pathology, Lionel Smith, and asked for clarity. He said that South Africa had purposely left open the definition of clinical death. This meant that it was up to the doctor to decide if a patient was clinically dead, and brain death declarations were legal.'

'So how did that help you?'

'My gut feel is that the Americans may have been ready earlier but were cautious, afraid that they might be charged with murder if the donor was brain-dead but the heart was still beating. But once we had completed our transplant it opened the way for them. Kantrowitz did his first transplant only three days after us and Shumway a month later.'

'So a technicality in the law helped you to win the race?'

'Only partly,' replied Dr Barnard. 'There were a lot of factors that needed to come together to make the perfect storm, so to speak. A candidate for transplantation being the most obvious one and it had to be someone where all other treatment had been exhausted and the patient was going to die. Washy was only handed over to us for a transplant in the second week of November. And then, of course, there is the availability of a donor heart and one that matches the recipient. That was a big issue, the timing.'

'And you had to wait until early December for a donor?'

'Actually, not many people know that we had a donor heart two weeks earlier, but we couldn't use it,' declared Dr Barnard.

'Why not?'

'The donor was a coloured man.'

'Were you under instructions by government authorities not to go ahead?' I asked.

'No. It was a decision taken between me and the head of cardiology.'

'But why?' I asked, somewhat bewildered. 'From what I've heard, you're against the racial policies of South Africa. Instrumental in a lot of changes here at Groote Schuur.'

'I am steadfast against the apartheid policies of our government,' said Dr Barnard, 'but our hands were tied. If we had used the heart of a coloured donor or even did the first transplant on a coloured or black person, we feared that the world would accuse us of experimenting on non-white people, and we didn't want to bring Groote Schuur into disrepute.'

'So, given that you never knew when an American surgeon might attempt a transplant, you risked the chance to be first.'

'I'm glad you brought that up, young man,' said the heart surgeon, 'because there are still those who feel we gambled with someone's life just to be first. The truth is that we gambled with someone's life by not transplanting the heart of a coloured man into Washy just to satisfy world opinion that we were not experimenting with non-white hearts.'

'Non-white hearts!' I laughed. 'That sounds ludicrous. They all look the same and bleed the same colour red.'

'Exactly!' exclaimed Dr Barnard. Looking ahead he said, 'We're approaching the building where the transplant took place. Basically there are two theatres, Theatre A for the recipient, Washy, and Theatre B for the donor, with two rooms separating them, the scrub room and the instrument room.'

'Tell me about the donor, Denise,' I requested.

'Denise Darvall. Then let's first go to Theatre B where we removed her heart. I'm told that she was 25 years old, worked at a bank and was the breadwinner of the family. Apparently she was fond of ballet, classical music and romantic novels.'

'There've been conflicting reports about that auspicious weekend,' I noted. 'Start at the beginning. I want to hear it in your own words. After all, that weekend changed my life.'

'It didn't start too well,' said the heart surgeon. 'After we turned down the idea of a transplant two weeks earlier, Washy went into depression. On Saturday morning two cardiologists popped in to see him before leaving for the weekend, saying that they would see him on Monday. When I visited him early in the afternoon he was very down, believing that the cardiologists had gone fishing and were leaving him to die. We had promised that we would give him a new heart but I got the impression that he felt he would not make it through the weekend alive. And I think he was probably correct.'

'You genuinely thought he was that close to death?'

'Yes!' replied the heart surgeon emphatically. 'Remember that we would only consider a transplant for someone when there was no other treatment available and death was imminent, be it days or weeks.' Dr Barnard looked pensive and said, 'There was a strange coincidence of events that occurred that day, almost as if it were orchestrated from above.'

'What do you mean?' I asked, somewhat puzzled.

'Washy's wife, Anne, was with him early in the afternoon trying to lift his spirits. She then left to go home about mid-afternoon and shortly afterwards I decided to go home too. As I walked out into the car park, I distinctly recall that it was a glorious summer's day in Cape Town. And I've calculated that when I got into my car was the exact moment that the accident happened.'

'Denise's car?' I asked for confirmation.

'Yes. She, together with her parents and one brother had decided to visit friends in Milnerton. Denise was driving the car, with great excitement, I'm told, because she had just received a raise at the bank and had recently bought herself her own car. The family took a detour to buy a caramel cake at Wrensch Town Bakery in Main Street, a kind gesture, but a fatal mistake as it turned out. Edward, the father and Keith, the son, stayed in the car while Denise and her mother, Myrtle, crossed the road to visit the bakery. On returning to their car, a lorry obscured their vision, and they failed to see another car speeding to beat the red light. Sadly they were hit by the car. Myrtle died on impact but Denise was thrown into the air and, on landing, hit her head on the hubcap of the car's wheel causing a compound fracture of her skull. They were only five minutes away from Groote Schuur so an ambulance was soon at the scene. But can you believe that Washy's wife, Anne, drove past the accident on her way home, slowed down and saw both women lying on the road. Little did she know then that the next morning the heart of one of those women would be beating in her husband's chest!'

'Wow, if you had written a script like that people wouldn't have believed it. Too far-fetched!'

'Amazing, isn't it,' replied Dr Barnard, before continuing. 'I went home, felt exhausted, took a nap and was woken at 8 o'clock in the evening by a cardiologist to say that we had a potential donor. I sped over to Groote Schuur, filled with hope and anticipation. When I got there two registrars said that the neurosurgeons had already confirmed there was nothing more they could do and had handed Denise over as a donor. But I wanted to hear it in person and called the head neurosurgeon and the head of cardiology to confirm that Denise was brain-dead but also that there was no cardiological damage to her heart. And based on their answers I gave the green light to call in our entire heart transplant team.'

'How many of them were there?' I asked.

'A team of 30. Fellow cardiothoracic surgeons, anaesthetists, a blood tissue specialist and several nurses.'

'But how did you get hold of them so quickly?'

'Good question because they were scattered all over the peninsula. One doctor was camping and some nurses were at a fancy dress party, so it wasn't easy. But they had been on standby for three weeks and were instructed to notify the sister on duty of their whereabouts at all times. They came in at various stages and there was this sense that something big was going to happen. I guess like soldiers who are on standby before being called to war.'

'Did you know at that stage that Denise's heart was a match for Washy?'

'No,' replied Dr Barnard. 'But the blood tissue specialist had already started, and said that he needed two hours. Meanwhile, Denise was put on a ventilator. It was all coming together.'

'And how were you feeling?'

'You know, young man, there was a surreal moment when my brother Marius and I were alone in the scrub room and I said to him that here we were, two Afrikaners from a poor family who came from a small town in a semi-desert in the sparsely populated Karoo, ostracised by the white community because my father preached in a church to a congregation of coloured people. We lived in a country at the foot of Africa that didn't even have television, yet here we were, about to attempt the most daring operation in medical history.'

'No panic? No self-doubt?'

'I would be lying if I denied that. Marius suggested that he open Denise's chest, but that it was important for me to excise the heart to get a feel of it for when I inserted it into Washy's chest. He then left me and for a brief moment panic set in. I was alone. I closed my eyes and steeled myself and went into a zone of total concentration.'

'I've heard about your famous concentration. Also, that you expect utter professionalism from everyone else.'

'It's nothing personal. I demand it of myself,' the heart surgeon said.

'So, with two theatres, where did you place yourself.'

Dr Barnard laughed and said, 'Everywhere! To begin with I was like a husband pacing up and down a corridor in a hospital with his wife in a difficult labour. Each person had his or her own role to play, but to begin with I visited each theatre several times trying to coordinate the progress on both donor and recipient.'

'I assume the blood tissue test came back as a match and that was the first big test you overcame.'

'Yes. The next big hurdle was dealing with Denise's heart and making sure it did not deteriorate. At some point Marius switched off the ventilator at which time I gave the go-ahead in Theatre A for Washy to be put on bypass and then went to do a final scrub. In the scrub room I could hear the saw cutting through Denise's chest. I returned to Theatre B, cut out Denise's heart and placed it in a metal dish containing an ice-cold saline solution.'

'And then the famous 31 steps!'

'Oh, so you've heard that the distance between the two beds was 31 steps,' remarked Dr Barnard.

'Yes!' replied Michael. 'Weren't you nervous that you might trip?'

'Are you actually asking me that?'

I felt a fool, as he'd already told me that after his brief moment of self-doubt that he'd gone into a zone of total concentration for the rest of the operation.

We walked over to Theatre A and Dr Barnard continued, 'I faced Washy and suddenly there was this moment of reckoning, because although his heart was sick, it was still beating. Once I removed his heart, there was no turning back.'

Even then, after nearly three years, I felt the importance of that momentous occasion.

Dr Barnard continued, saying, 'I cut out Washy's heart and my first impression was how could he have still been living with such a diseased organ. I placed it in a dish and when I looked back at the huge cavity in his chest it struck me that we were looking at something that nobody had ever seen before, a person without a heart being kept alive by a machine!'

Again, the enormity of this first transplant struck me! How lucky I was to be getting a first-hand account from the very surgeon who carried it out.

'I took Denise's heart which was pink, firm and cold as to be expected, but very small. A woman's heart is twenty percent smaller than a man's and here I was about to insert this dainty heart into a cavity that moments before had housed a diseased heart that had doubled in size! It seemed as if Denise's heart would float around in Washy's chest, but we'd reached the point of no return, so I stitched it in and incredibly her heart became one with Washy's body.'

'And then the moment of truth,' I declared. 'Would a heart you had allowed to die, start up again?'

'Yes, the question to which we all wanted to know the answer,' replied Dr Barnard.

'I can imagine your own hearts beating at an all-time high.'

'Funny you should say that because the doctors and nurses from Theatre B came over and sat in the gallery of Theatre A to watch the remainder of the transplant. Marius claims he could see a vein in my neck throbbing, and he roughly counted it to be beating at 130 per minute.'

'If only you could have transferred some of those beats to Washy's new heart,' I said light-heartedly.

'If only! Instead, I asked for the paddles of the defibrillator and placed them on either side of Washy's new heart. Finally, the moment we had all been waiting for. I nodded for a current to be sent through the paddles. At first, it appeared that nothing was going to happen. The wait seemed interminable. Then suddenly, the heart contracted.'

'And is that when you famously pronounced, 'It's going to work!''

'Yes, but it wasn't quite over. We still had to ween Washy off the bypass machine which, as you would know, was successful because on that early Sunday morning, just before 6 o'clock on the 3rd December 1967, Denise Darvall's heart began to beat by itself in Louis Washkansky.'

Dr Barnard's eyes suddenly seemed to moist over as if he were reliving the moment so close to his heart. 'What was the reaction of everyone?' I prompted him.

'Some cheered, I could see some had tears in their eyes above their masks, tears of joy and wonder, and some laughed, perhaps nervously.'

'And you?'

'I was exhausted and asked for a cup of tea!'

We both stood quiet for a moment. After a while I broke the silence, saying, 'And then the media insanity!'

'That's an understatement! We were besieged. One thing they begged for was a photograph of the operation. Offered us a million dollars! But can you believe that it didn't enter our minds to take one.'

'Why not?'

'We were so focussed on the job at hand. Yes, we wanted to beat Shumway. Who doesn't want to be first? But our prime goal was to save Washy. We weren't thinking about fame. We didn't expect the reaction we got.'

'For me, the climbing of Mount Everest, man landing on the moon and the world's first heart transplant stand out as *the* human conquests of the century,' I declared. 'You must have given it some thought since then, so why do you think there was such a media circus after the transplant?'

'Firstly because it was the heart,' replied Dr Barnard. 'Surgeons had been doing kidney transplants for some time. We did one here at Groote Schuur a little more than a month before the heart transplant, but there was little attention given to that. But the heart was seen as some mystical organ, the seat of love, and for some, the home of the soul.'

'Which caused certain people to criticize the transplant. Whose soul would be in Washy's body?'

'That's correct,' said Dr Barnard. 'And that's somewhat understandable, I suppose. But if you're a doctor you know that the heart is merely a pump.'

'You said 'firstly'. Was there another reason?'

'The fact that the operation was performed in Cape Town. It would have been big news in America, but I think that it shocked the world that the first heart transplant was done in the dark continent of Africa, a continent that many around the world think is one country. But the fact is, we were ready. While we lacked the amenities of some hospitals in the States and around the world, Groote Schuur is a good hospital, and we had assembled a team which, though inexperienced, made up for that inexperience with passion. And that has been proven with the success we've had in subsequent heart transplants. Our patients are far out living those in other countries.'

Aware that Dr Barnard's charisma had charmed the world, I suggested a third reason. 'Possibly it was also due to a certain person who Washy described as 'the man with the golden hands'.'

Dr Barnard laughed and said, 'You mean the man with the swollen hands.' He held up his hands and said ruefully, 'These are a surgeon's greatest weapon, but sadly mine are riddled with rheumatoid arthritis. If Washy knew that, he may not have wanted me to operate on him!'

Dr Barnard looked almost vulnerable then, as if he knew that his disease would one day end his career.

After a moment's silence, he said, 'There were a lot of heroes that day. Think of Denise. For a heart transplant to happen, one person has to die for another to live. And what of her father? He'd already lost his wife, and then he was asked if we could harvest Denise's organs, and he barely gave it a moment's thought. He said that Denise was a giver and it would have been what she wanted.'

'Why do you say organs as if there were more than one?'

'Edward Darvall donated his daughter's kidneys as well. They were transplanted into a coloured boy that same night.'

'And you intentionally mention that the boy was coloured as if to say that transplanting kidneys in a non-white was okay but not the heart.'

'You're quite sharp, young man,' commented Dr Barnard. 'The answer is yes, because the first heart transplant in South Africa had to be a white donor with a white recipient. World opinion dictated that. Thereafter, it did not matter, as is proven by the fact that the second heart transplant performed at Groote Schuur just over a month later, was a coloured heart into a white man.'

'You're known here at Groote Schuur as someone who has pushed back at South Africa's racial policies. I'm aware that you insist that if a black sister is more capable than a white one then the black sister must be in charge of the ward. From what I've heard, it can be quite dangerous to antagonize the South African government. What advice do you have for a foreigner who is not used to this legislated segregation?'

'That depends,' replied Dr Barnard, 'because unlike you, I now have a platform. I believe that people are entitled to fight discrimination in their own way. We should not be dictated to that there is only one way to go about this fight. I've been criticized for being pro-South Africa. But I was born here! I'm a patriot! Where is the sin in that? But I'm also anti-apartheid and will fight segregation in the way I feel I'm best able to. For someone like you, my advice would be to go about breaking down barriers as best you can, in your own small way, in your everyday life. Become a small beacon of light. You might change one person's attitude and that person becomes another beacon of light. And so it can spread with a multiplier effect. This country is not going to change overnight and you won't change everybody. But one day, perhaps a long time from now, it will happen. Do your bit and you'll be a small but vital part of the solution that will allow South Africa to one day show itself in all its glory.'

I nodded my head to show acceptance of his advice. There was, however, one more question that I had for him. 'Back to the transplant. Has there been a moment since when you considered the magnitude of what you had achieved? A 'why me' moment?'

'I am not sure I questioned the magnitude or why I was first. But when I drove home that day there were tears of thankfulness in my eyes. I prayed to God, thanked him for giving me the chance to do the heart transplant and to do it to the best of my ability. My humble father had always been so proud of his children, so I asked God to tell my father what Marius and I had done to save a life.'

By now we had left the building where the first heart transplant had taken place and were heading back towards the storage room where Dr Barnard had called out to me earlier that night.

I was about to thank him for the special guided tour when he asked me, 'If Shumway had won the race would you have gone to Stanford?'

'No,' I said shaking my head without having to think. 'I would have stayed in Cambridge. It was the unimaginable fact that the first heart transplant had occurred at a hospital called Groote Schuur in a place called Cape Town in Africa that made me want to come here. I reasoned that if you could pull off such a feat here, then this was the place for me. And so far I don't regret it one iota.'

'Well, Cambridge's loss is our gain,' said Dr Barnard with his toothy grin. 'If ever you change your mind about general surgery, please know that there is a place in our cardiology department.'

I thanked Dr Barnard and was about to enter my 'bedroom' when he stopped me again. 'Young man, are you married?'

Somewhat confused at such a question, I answered, 'No. Why do you ask?'

'Because people like you who are married to their jobs don't stay married to their wives for very long.'

And with that the doctor turned and left. Puzzled, I opened the storeroom door, slumped onto my makeshift bed and fell asleep.

And there you have it. A step by step account of my meeting with the very man who was instrumental in me coming to study and work in South Africa.

I'm so happy that the hard work I put into my studies is reaping rewards as I slowly shift over to practising surgery. And I love Cape Town. But although I have many acquaintances here, I've not yet developed any close friendships. Perhaps I study and work too hard! I do miss my family. And, of course, I miss what I could be having with you. Last night was the first time I can remember not attending a New Year's party. I spent the time alone in my apartment, lonely. So I brought out my trusty ol' friend and at some point played *Bridge Over Troubled Water*, a song I'm sure you must have heard by Simon & Garfunkel. And while strumming, I imagined you singing to me, 'When times get rough and friends just can't be found, like a bridge over troubled water I will lay me down.'

I need you Scarlett. I need a friend.

All my love, Michael.

Scarlett

'Paul,' Scarlett remarked, 'I don't have a sister and I treat all my friends as equals, so I'm not comfortable picking just one to be my bridesmaid. I don't want to hurt anyone's feelings.'

'Missy, that's fine by me. As an only child I've no brother and though I've never thought about it before, I'd also feel awkward choosing between my friends to act as my best man. Besides, darling, I decided a long time ago that a wedding day belongs to the bride. I'll abide by any decision you make.'

'Does that include you wearing a pink tutu when you say your vows to me?' teased Scarlett.

Paul ignored his fiancé and asked, 'Are you going to have a special place for Robin?'

'Yes, I would like her to be my flower girl.'

§

Paul and Scarlett's wedding took place at the Rondebosch Congregational Church. The groom stood alone in front of all the seated guests as the organist played the wedding march. He turned around to see Robin smiling shyly at him, dressed like a fairy in a rose pink satin dress and tulle confection, pink ballet slippers on her feet and a coronet of pink flowers on her shiny, dark hair, scattering rose petals in front of her as she walked up the aisle. Scarlett and Danny followed close behind, sister holding onto her brother's arm, with the bride wearing a simple but elegant white satin dress covered with lace, extending into a short train. Like her daughter, Scarlett also wore a coronet of fresh flowers in her dark hair, and she carried a bouquet of white roses. Scarlett smiled at her fiancé as she joined him in the front of the church, then turned to face the minister.

'Dearly beloved,' he began, 'we have come together in the presence of God to witness and bless the joining together of this man and this woman in Holy Matrimony.'

Much of the rest of the ceremony was a blur for Scarlett until the minister addressed the guests, 'If any of you can show just cause why they may not be lawfully wed, speak now, or else forever hold your peace.'

Scarlett's heart beat in her chest like a caged bird. Despite Paul's promise that André would never again be a problem, a small part of her feared that his ugly spectre may appear at that moment. But no unwanted voice disturbed the silence. And Scarlett thanked Paul under her breath.

With the bridal couple facing each other the minister addressed the bride. 'Paul, will you have this man to be your husband, to live together with him in the covenant of marriage? Will you love him, comfort him, honour and keep him, in sickness and in health, and, forsaking all others, be faithful unto him as long as you both shall live?'

Amongst much murmuring from the guests, Scarlett burst out laughing and said, 'No!'

A shocked and rattled minister asked, 'Why not?'

'Because you called me Paul!'

'Oh, dear!' the minister said apologetically. 'Well, will you take Paul as your husband?

With a big smile on her face, Scarlett said, 'I will.'

The minister repeated the same question to Paul, then asked, 'Who gives this woman to be married to this man?'

Scarlett's mother, hiding behind a pillar at the back of the church witnessed her son Danny stand up and say, 'I do.' As much as they both loved Danny, Scarlett and her mother were deeply sad that it was not the father who gave the bride away.

Still facing each other, it was time for the giving and receiving of the wedding bands. Then the minister declared, 'Bless, O Lord, these rings as a symbol of the vows by which this man and this woman have bound themselves to each other, through Jesus Christ our Lord. Amen.' He smiled at the couple and said, 'I now pronounce you husband and wife.' And to Paul, the obligatory, 'You may kiss the bride.'

After kissing Scarlett, the newly married couple walked down the aisle, followed by the guests. After posing for photos, the bridal party and their wedding guests met in a local hall for the reception. At the bridal table there were two missing people. There was a deep sorrow in Scarlett that her parents were not there to celebrate this wonderful occasion.

§

Scarlett and Paul honeymooned in the Seychelles. Joining them was their daughter Robin.

The setting was idyllic, white sun-kissed beaches and blue seas. Not unnaturally they spent some of their days swimming in the warm Indian Ocean.

Sitting under a thatched umbrella on the white beach sand sipping an exotic drink, Scarlett remarked to Paul, 'It's the first time I can recall not wearing a Speedo swimming costume. I feel half naked in this.'

'You are more than half naked,' corrected Paul, eyeing Scarlett in her skimpy pink bikini. 'And very sexy, too, I might add.'

'Oh, Paul, you're insatiable. You need to go and cool off. Come, let's join Robin in the water.'

After frolicking in the sea for some time, Scarlett suddenly noticed that Robin was nowhere to be seen.

'Paul!' Scarlett called out in alarm. 'Paul, where's Robin?'

Both panicked.

'She can't be far,' Paul said, trying to calm his wife, though he knew the situation was serious. 'I mean, she was here with us only a moment ago.'

After a few minutes of near hysteria, Scarlett spotted Robin way in the distance out to sea. Both she and Paul set out to swim to her as fast as they could. But before they reached her, Scarlett said to her new husband, 'Wait, Paul. Look at her. She's enjoying herself, swimming like a dolphin.'

The couple slowed and nonchalantly swam to their daughter, not wanting to show Robin how fearful they had been.

'Look Mom! Look Dad!' exclaimed their four year old daughter. 'I found a silver fish and swam all the way out here with it.'

Scarlett was both relieved and ecstatic. Relieved that her baby was safe, ecstatic that she was literally in her element, water.

1st January 1972

Dear Scarlett,

I hate saying goodbye. Whether it's at the end of a holiday with a group of friends, or saying goodbye to the year gone past. Hence *Auld Lang Syne* is such an emotional song! I have sometimes wondered if my reason for writing to you each year is to keep alive my memory of you so that I don't have to say goodbye.

I love my job but, as I said, I hate goodbyes. Unfortunately the two are inextricably intertwined.

For as long as I can remember, I have wanted to be a doctor. The older I got, the more I realized that I didn't want to be a physician, dispensing pills to patients with flu. I knew I would specialise and the more I thought about it, the more my mind turned to surgery. Definitely not an ear, nose and throat specialist or a paediatrician! That might sound a bit harsh, but I wanted something more, something new every day, something where I lived life on the edge. Also, I didn't want to specialise in just one type of surgery and say, do four back ops every day for the rest of my life.

There is no question that being a general surgeon in trauma would give me the variety I was looking for. It may sound glamorous, but it is not. Hippocrates once said, 'He who wishes to be a surgeon must go to war.' And what I had not counted on was how often in that war I would confront death, the ultimate goodbye.

The relatives of patients think I am God. That somehow I can make it all come right. And while it is true that a child who has been smashed up in a car accident or a man who has been shot does depend a lot on my skill, unfortunately I cannot save everybody and a certain number of patients under my care do die. So the pressures are enormous. While my arms are up to their elbows in stomach innards, or I'm carefully reconstructing a skull oozing bits of brain matter, I'm acutely aware that the patient's loved ones are in the waiting room with their anguished minds and hopes depending on me.

When I am successful it is almost as if they believe that I was God sent to earth to save their loved ones and I feel their joy. But for those I lose, suddenly I am a mere mortal. Fortunately, they don't blame me. Never had that. But their sense of loss is so palpable and that takes its toll on me.

Trauma surgery is much like a seesaw. On the one end are those who have a high probability of survival due to my intervention. On the other end of the seesaw are those who are simply a lost cause. Then there are those somewhere in between where it is my job to tilt the seesaw in the direction of life. Those are the most challenging ones because they can go either way.

I can't say for myself, but the impression I get from others is that I am a skilled surgeon, and getting better at my craft. As time goes by, I feel more and more pressure to tilt the seesaw of near impossible cases in favour of life. Of course, I get great satisfaction when that happens. The worst case is when I lose someone who was on the living side of the seesaw. Unfortunately, there are just so many variables that come into play that the outcome is never a sure thing.

Strangely, the worst I felt was a case that occurred just two weeks ago, and oddly, it was a patient that I knew was never going to make it. But there was a reason for me feeling so heartbroken. I had just finished my shift late at night and as I exited the doors to the hospital I witnessed a stabbing below on the pavement. I quickly called for a stretcher and went to assist the victim. Her name was Shannon. A beautiful 16-year old blonde haired girl in a white dress lying on the pavement with blood pouring like a fountain from her abdomen. It was a stark image, like a bright red blood stain on virgin snow. Things did not look good. I first blocked the flow of blood with my own hands, then placed both her hands over the gaping wound to stem the flow of blood and asked her to press down as hard as she could. I then ripped off part of her dress and stuffed it into the stab wound. As we waited for the stretcher to arrive she looked at me with desperate eyes and said several times, 'Please don't let me die.' Of course, I tried to comfort her by saying that she was in good care at the best hospital. But I knew.

The staff were wonderful and quickly wheeled her into theatre. I had no time to scrub, simply put on surgical gloves and waited for an anaesthetist. All the time Shannon's eyes looked at me pleadingly while I applied cotton swabs to her wound. Suddenly a look of fear swept across her face. She looked directly into my eyes and asked in a soft voice, 'Am I going to die?'

I hate, hate, hate being put into that position where someone is pleading to live, hoping that I am God, when I know they have gone beyond the point of no return. Scarlett, it is not easy for me to lie, but I console myself that a reassuring answer is a final word of comfort I can give to a patient before they depart. Her life slowly ebbed away with her eyes still open and looking at me. When she passed away the pleading look in her eyes changed to a vacant stare, so I closed them. I should have used a cotton swab because I smeared blood all over her pretty face. In case her parents got to see her soon, I carefully wiped away the blood and felt devastated that someone so young, with so much life to live, had to die so long before her time. What a tragic waste! And that is why I was so upset.

I left the theatre and sat hunched over on a couch in the corridor. As a witness to a murder, I knew that the police would want to question me, but mostly I needed to be there for her parents when they would come rushing to the hospital hoping to find their daughter still alive.

When Shannon had not arrived home by midnight, her parents phoned the police. They were informed of a stabbing of a young girl matching the description of their daughter and directed to Groote Schuur. I can imagine that they would have asked the police if she was still alive and I knew that they would respond that they did not know, even if they did, that it was best to get to the hospital as quickly as possible.

Sitting in the corridor, I thought about the fragility of life. How this teenage girl could have lived another 70 years, but for one action by a jealous boyfriend. And how would her life have turned out? Might she have been one of the lucky ones where she would meet her knight in shining armour and live happily ever after? Or would the harsh knocks that some experience wear her down so that she would endure life rather than live it to the full?

Oh, how my mind flitted all over the place trying to make sense of it all!

Half an hour later, Shannon's parents came walking down the corridor. It's always in the eyes. The fear. Fear that could turn to utter relief or utter despair and sadness. That short distance is a long walk. It is the worst part of my job. When they neared me I stood up, my surgeon's scrubs still soaked in Shannon's blood, and I slowly shook my head. Sometimes there is screaming, sometimes sheer disbelief, this time resignation with lots of tears, their reaction always guiding me how to respond. There were a few questions. Did it take long? No. I also explained that there was no chance of survival. On this occasion I was relieved when they didn't ask me the worst question, did she suffer?

And with that, Shannon's parents walked back down that lonely corridor while I sat down again and pondered what it was all about. How could someone live 100 years, perhaps taking all sorts of risks, yet here, a vibrant 16-year old was cut down in a moment with no way back. No way back! It's my job to bring them back, but sometimes there is just no way back. And what must Shannon's parents be feeling? They were in bed, ready to go to sleep and wake up the next day to live the rest of their lives watching their daughter grow into a beautiful woman, get married, have their grandchildren and live happily ever after. Instead, their lives shattered in a brief moment. The death of life can be so cruel. So final. The final goodbye. I hate goodbyes!

I only go to funerals of patients I have lost if asked by family or friends. I went to Shannon's. It was sore, but dignified. As on previous occasions, it brought to mind how difficult it must be to bury a child. The sight of the coffin of a teenager being lowered into a grave is an assault on the natural order of things.

Afterwards, I sat in my car for a long time and wept uncontrollably.

I am sorry, my dear Scarlett, to offload like this, but it is still raw. Still a part of my job that I have not got used to, and maybe never will.

And talking of goodbyes, it breaks my heart that I may never see you again, and that will mean it's goodbye to you too.

But the year wasn't all bad because most of the time I did manage to tilt the see-saw in the direction of life, even when the odds were heavily stacked against me, which makes me believe I am getting better at my craft.

And despite working long hours at Groote Schuur, I like to think that my guitar playing is improving too. When I end this letter I am going to play a song on my guitar by The Archies, a song called *A Summer Prayer For Peace*. It became a huge hit in South Africa, but I believe the song was not widely released because it was considered an anti-Vietnam War song, so you may not have heard it. Somewhere in the lyrics are the words, 'Three billion people together forever. Three billion people sing a summer prayer for peace.' Here's hoping that 1972 is a year of peace and no more stabbings.

And especially a year of peace for you, my dear!

All my love, Michael.

Scarlett

Six months before graduating, Paul bought a doctor's practice and a week after qualifying, Scarlett arrived for her first day at work. She had dealt with several hundred patients during her internship but the butterflies in her tummy were a touch flighty.

Scarlett picked up a file from the top of the pile at the secretary's desk, read the name on the file and called, 'Miss Lagerström?'

A very attractive young woman rose from her chair in the waiting room.

'Hello', Scarlett greeted her. 'I'm Dr Rhodes.' Pointing down a small passageway, she said, 'Shall we go into my consulting room?'

Together they entered Scarlett's new den. She seated herself behind her desk, and indicated that her new patient should take the comfortable chair facing her.

'How may I be of help to you, Miss Lagerström?'

'You can call me Anna.'

Scarlett was dying to suggest that her patients also call her by her first name, but they were taught at med school to keep things formal, at least until a patient became a regular visitor.

'Well then, Anna, what can I do for you?'

'I've been getting bouts of a combination of numbness and also pain or tingling in my thumb and fingers, and it sometimes goes up my arm.'

'Just one hand or both?'

'Both.'

'Anna, what do you do for a living?'

'I'm a pianist, playing both professionally for an orchestra and I also give private tuition.'

'Any hobbies?'

'In my spare time I like to play tennis.'

'And that would be just one hand. Are you right or left-handed?'

'Actually, well, I am right-handed, but I'm one of very few people who use a double-handed backhand. So I guess you could say that I use both hands when I play tennis.'

Scarlett walked around to the front of her desk and did a physical examination of Anna Lagerström's hands.

'Is there any particular time of day when it gets worse?' Scarlett asked.

'Yes. Mostly at night when I am sleeping.'

'Anna, I'm convinced what you have is carpal tunnel syndrome.'

'Okay. Is that a bad thing?'

'No, mostly an annoying thing,' Scarlett said. 'Unfortunately, it's probably coming from your piano playing, possibly made even worse by your tennis.'

'Well, that doesn't sound good. Piano and tennis are my life.' Anna asked, 'Can anything be done?'

'Let me explain briefly what the problem is. You have a median nerve that runs down the arm, through a tunnel at the wrist called the carpal tunnel and into the hand. Through repetitive use, such as your piano playing, the tissue surrounding the nerve can swell and that puts pressure on the nerve which results in the pain, numbness, tingling, and weakness in the hand.'

'And?'

'The first thing is to stop doing what is causing the swelling of the synovium tissue but—'

'I can't do that! It is my livelihood and playing piano and tennis are the two greatest pleasures of my life.'

'Yes, I was going to say that in your case it would be very difficult to stop the repetitive action, therefore some intervention needs to take place. The cautious approach is for me to give you a cortisone injection, but my understanding is that with your repetitive action, it simply delays the inevitable, in which case surgery will be required.'

'What do you suggest?' asked Anna.

'We're nearing the end of the year. Do you have much in your diary by way of playing the piano?'

'Very much so. Several nativity concerts and—'

'Then I would suggest that I give you a cortisone injection in each wrist. That will give you temporary relief to get you by. With any luck your symptoms may just go away, though I have my doubts. If in the new year the symptoms return then I suggest that you have surgery. It is a fairly simple procedure, though the surgeon will probably do the operation on each hand a week or two apart.'

'Who would you recommend as a surgeon?'

'Well, Anna, earlier I said that it is my understanding that with continued repetitive action surgery would inevitably be required. You may have noticed that I didn't say 'in my experience'. The reason is that I am brand-new on the job. In fact, you are my first ever patient.'

'Really? You seemed to diagnose carpal tunnel syndrome very quickly and confidently.'

'Thank you. During my internship at Groote Schuur, even though I've never met him, the word was that Dr Gibson is the go to surgeon. So I would recommend him if that's okay with you.'

'Absolutely fine.'

'Then I'll write a referral letter to him. Even though I'm very confident in my diagnosis, he'll be able to confirm it.'

After writing the referral letter, Scarlett gave Anna Lagerström two cortisone injections. While administering them, she asked, 'Why did you make an appointment to see me, especially given that I am a newly qualified doctor?'

'I have been coming to this practice for a few years. Not often, as generally I am very healthy. But word got around that a female doctor was joining the practice and I thought that it would be a nice gesture to support you especially since there don't seem to be many women doctors in South Africa.'

'Well, thank you. I appreciate that,' said Scarlett. 'You have a slight foreign accent?'

'I am originally from Sweden. Perhaps that played a role in me wanting to see a woman doctor.'

'The male doctors are no good in Sweden? I find that hard to believe.'

'No, they are very good. It's just that it is a more equal society there. Definitely more women doctors than here and I thought I would do my bit to help.'

'All done,' said Scarlett. 'Please let me know how you get on.'

1st January 1973

Dear Scarlett,

This is an extremely difficult letter to write. I met a girl. Or should I say a woman, a lady. Actually, she met me!

Okay, that all sounds confusing, so let me explain. Towards the end of January last year, a lady by the name of Anna came to see me at Groote Schuur. She had been referred to me by a Dr Rhodes and when I mentioned that this doctor had been sending me a lot of patients lately and that I ought to meet him one day, Anna said that Dr Rhodes is a she. I told her that might explain why most of the referrals were women. Dr Rhodes had diagnosed carpal tunnel syndrome in both Anna's wrists and if I concurred with the diagnosis she recommended that I operate on them.

The lady's wrist problems were indeed carpal tunnel syndrome. It would appear that the cause was excessive piano playing as she is both a concert pianist and piano teacher, and the problem may even be aggravated by her playing tennis.

Cortisone injections had only given her temporary relief and since the patient's livelihood depended on the repetitive use of her hands, rest was not an option, so she needed an operation on both wrists. When I told her that her wrists needed surgical intervention, Anna made it very clear that her hands were her life, to which I replied that mine were too, so I completely understood. In a case like this I only operate on one wrist at a time to allow the patient some use of a hand for everyday functioning.

I did the first operation and when visiting the patient for a post-op checkup, it struck me what a lovely person she was. She spoke with a slight accent and when I asked her about it, she said she was originally from Sweden. A couple of weeks later, I operated on her other wrist and thankfully both operations were successful. And that would have been that if it were left up to me, and how dumb I would have been!

On the 29th February, I got a phone call from Anna. I was somewhat surprised, but we had a pleasant conversation, and then even more surprised when she asked me if I knew the date. Obviously I replied in the affirmative. She responded by saying that according to leap year tradition, as a woman she could ask a man out for a date but, since I was already married, sadly, she was unable to ask me out! Okay, now I was really confused. What do you mean married, I asked? She laughed and claimed that I was married to my work! Thinking quickly on my feet I enquired if I got a temporary divorce from my work would she reconsider inviting me on a date. She strung me along for a while, teasing of course, but then formally asked, to which I replied with a resounding yes.

Our first date? Anna wanted me to come around to her apartment so that she could cook a meal for me. The following Saturday evening I drove to her home in Newlands, which is a neighbouring suburb to where I live in Rondebosch. In the interim, I spent a lot of time mulling over Anna's comment about me being married to my work. And it only struck me then how right she was. At school, I pushed myself to get into medical school as soon as possible, finishing my A levels at the age of 16. I became a doctor at a young age, then worked 18 hour days to become a surgeon in record time. And now that I'm qualified, I spend my mornings working in general surgery before joining the trauma department in the afternoon. Officially, I am only employed for the day, but trauma is never-ending so inevitably I work most evenings until late, often getting home after midnight.

When I knocked on Anna's front door, my heart was pounding like a schoolboy going out on his first date. And in a sense, it was my first date. Yes, I had invited partners to various dance evenings at university, not wanting to attend on my own, but the truth is I had never formally set out to date a person of the fairer sex because, after all, I was married to my work! Of course, I hadn't set out to date Anna either because she invited me. And how glad I am that she did.

Did I mention that I had met a lady? What can I say about her? A most beautiful person, inside and out, is the short answer. But she deserves more than just a short answer. Her name is Anna Lagerström. She was born in Västervik in Sweden, which is on the east coast about a four hour drive south of the capital, Stockholm. She is an only child and lived there until she was 15 years old when her parents emigrated to South Africa. Her father is a missionary and her mother a nurse, and they live in a small town called White River which is in the Eastern Transvaal, quite close to Kruger Park, which you may have heard of.

Due to her love for music the family decided that Anna should complete her schooling at Rustenberg Girl's High School where she boarded at Erinville Hostel. Post matric, she did her basic and master's degree in music at the University of Cape Town and is nearing the completion of her doctorate.

Did I say she was beautiful? Well, she is gorgeous! Yes, she has that stereotypical Swedish long blonde hair and blue eyes, but there is so much more. When she opened that door it felt as if a ray of sunlight from a fresh dawn poured out of her apartment. At 26 years old she is three years younger than me, but she has remarkable poise and confidence. I was dressed in my casual best, but she was barefoot! And comfortable with that. Is that a Swedish thing?

Before arriving, I wondered why Anna wanted a first date to be a meal prepared at her apartment. I had heard rumours about a revolting dish that is part of Sweden's culture called Surströmming. Apparently soured herring that stinks to high heaven! Thankfully we had a fondue meal of cheese, bread, mini meatballs, vegetable skewers and potato wedges, followed by a dessert of brownies dipped in chocolate. And lots of red wine.

And we talked and talked and talked. The more we talked about me it became all too obvious that I was married to my work, so I would gently steer the conversation back to find out more about Anna. She was obviously a music prodigy when growing up, attending some special music school in Sweden before the family left, and now performs in all sorts of concerts in the major theatres and halls of Cape Town. What is refreshing is that she loves all types of music.

Anna has a piano, a baby grand, in her apartment and when I asked her to play it she willing obliged and, although I didn't know many of the songs, they sounded as if performed by the angels. I felt rather reluctant to tell Anna that I played the guitar, especially when she asked about all sorts of genres to which I sheepishly replied that I only ever played modern rock and pop songs. Then she disappeared to her bedroom and returned with a damn guitar! What could I do? I was so nervous! My fingers were shaking or at least it felt like they were! Not a good thing when you're trying to impress someone who is a brilliant musician and to play a guitar well requires precise finger placement on the strings in a fret, a finger precision that comes so easily to me when wielding a scalpel. Was it nerves because I felt she was so much better a piano player than I was a guitar player? Or was it that she was already stealing my heart?

I felt like a dumb idiot not knowing what to play, so Anna suggested that I play the song that I was currently learning — Led Zeppelin's *Stairway To Heaven* which was released a few months before. Halfway through she accompanied me on the piano. I asked her if she was also learning that song, and she said no. She really is that good a pianist!

Anna said she was impressed with my guitar playing. Of course, I seriously wondered if she was just being polite, but as I got to know her over the year I realised that she would only have given an honest appraisal, so I now take that as a compliment.

So what happened over the next year? I visited Anna more and more frequently for supper on Saturday evenings. It made no sense for me to entertain her because, except for a hasty bowl of oats porridge for breakfast, I never cook for myself, always eat at the hospital canteen.

Our time together expanded on the weekends as Anna persuaded me to learn tennis and join her every Saturday afternoon at Claremont Tennis Club. Being so focussed on my studies and then my career in medicine, apart from regular jogging to keep fit, I had never played any sport. But I have come to thoroughly enjoy tennis. I even go for coaching once a week and play league tennis against other clubs but now is not the time to tell you which team I play for!

Sometimes Anna and I play tennis on a Sunday. My goal is to beat her before I die! Other Sundays are spent hiking up Table Mountain, or motoring to the beautiful wine estates near Cape Town. Mostly we'll have a picnic and then sample wines and buy several vintages to have with our regular Saturday meals.

I guess by now you'll realise that I am in love with Anna, which makes this letter so hard to write. But more about that later.

In early September I proposed to Anna. I wanted it to be special but also unique, so I booked a weekend away at the Springbok Hotel — separate bedrooms, I might add — which is in a town called Springbok in the heart of Namaqualand. The springbok, the national animal of South Africa, is an antelope which was once upon a time prolific in this area. It is also the national colours of a South African sports team. So, if you represent South Africa in rugby or cricket or tennis or swimming, you will be awarded Springbok colours in the form of a green and gold blazer, although that is happening less and less as the country is becoming increasingly isolated due to its racial policies. As far as I'm aware, I don't think South Africa is even allowed to participate in the Olympics anymore, which may have been just as well this past year. If memory serves me correctly, the Olympic Games in Munich were on the go while we were on our 'engagement weekend' and newspapers were reporting a tragic terrorist attack.

Namaqualand needs to be explained because Mother Nature gave her all to this region. For most of the year the landscape is one of arid, dusty plains that span vast distances to dramatic mountains in the distance. But in the months of August, September and October, after the winter rains, the desert is suddenly transformed into a magical carpet of flowers as far as the eye can see. They say that a picture is worth a thousand words, but I'm afraid that I could not do justice to the beauty of this natural wonder of the world, so you'll just have to take my word for it that it is heaven on earth.

Anna and I packed a picnic lunch and drove various roads that reaped different fields of flowers of single colours while others were a kaleidoscope of brilliant hues from a master painter's palette. As we came across a field of yellow daisies, she suggested that we stop. When I asked if she meant for our picnic she said yes, but also for 'you know what'. How she knew I was going to propose to her in a field of yellow daisies still baffles me to this day. But yellow is her colour and what better setting than to lay out a blanket on a carpet of yellow daisies and propose to the love of my life.

And that is why this has been a difficult letter to write. My heart fluttered when I saw you on that bus eight years ago. I dearly wished to find out who was behind those beautiful eyes, never did, but fell for a person that I have never met. Is that weird? Can one really fall in love with a person who is a figment of one's imagination? Can one love someone in person and also love some imaginary person at the same time? I don't have the answers to those questions. Ever since Anna and I got engaged, I have dreaded this day arriving, the first day of the year. The reason is that I have not told Anna about you. Well, not about you so much, since I don't know you, but that I write an annual letter to you. There is a part of me that would feel embarrassed telling her I write to an imaginary person. But mostly it would be that I have kept this a secret from everyone, including Anna. And I'm not sure why in her case because there is no other part about me that I have shielded from her. So why this? I'm sure she would understand, but I think it would be reasonable for her to expect me to stop, so maybe it's just that I don't want to let go of you. And lately that has been driving me insane because who would I be letting go of? Someone I don't even know! These last few months I have wrestled hard with my conscience about writing to you, but in the end I've convinced myself that instead of writing a love letter, I will treat it as more of a diary of my thoughts and what has happened over the past year.

I so wish I could meet you so that you can meet my precious Anna.

All my love, Michael.

Scarlett

After their marriage, Paul and Scarlett bought a house in Rondebosch. One evening after supper and Robin was in bed, they retired to the lounge. It was the 5th September 1972. Paul picked up the newspaper he had bought on the way home from work, sat down on the couch and remarked to his wife, 'You've seemed rather subdued these last few days, darling. Is everything alright?'

'Well, you know where we ought to be, at least where I ought to be.'

'At the Munich Olympics. I know. And swimming is making quite a splash with this American fellow Mark Spitz.' Immediately turning to the sports section at the back of the newspaper, Paul announced to Scarlett, 'Well, he's done it. Seven events, seven golds and seven world records! Astonishing! And I can see why you're glum. When I see the times for your favourite 100-metre backstroke, there's every chance you could have been in the mix. And since adding the 200-metre backstroke to the swimming programme at Mexico City, I think you may have had an even greater chance at a medal, possibly gold because—'

'Paul!' Scarlett interrupted sharply from an armchair opposite her husband, having just noticed the newspaper's front page headline.

She quickly joined Paul and turned the newspaper to show him the front page. 'Oh, no!' she exclaimed. 'There's been a terrorist massacre at the Games. Let's put on the radio to hear if there are any updates.'

Paul and Scarlett heard further details about a Palestinian terrorist group called Black September taking 11 Israeli Olympic team members hostage and then killing them along with a German police officer.

'Maybe it's just as well you're not there, darling.'

'Never, Paul! That's like saying don't ever fly in an aeroplane because it might crash. Besides, with the way Robin swept all her races last summer I'm hoping that I'll still get to the Olympic Games — even if it's through her.'

'Did you hear what you just said?'

'What do you mean?'

'Missy, I don't want to sound nasty or upset your plans, but it seems to me that you're trying to live vicariously through your daughter. That you hope to live your Olympic dream through her.'

Sheepishly, Scarlett replied, 'Is it that obvious?'

'Yes!' replied Paul emphatically. 'It's important to let Robin be a kid who just happens to have a special swimming talent. If you're desperate for her to become an Olympian, she'll feel it. She'll feel the pressure and will most likely fail. Let her grow up and become a well-adjusted young woman and if she swims in an Olympic Games one day then view that as a bonus. Trust me darling. Be more like your parents were. They never tried to motivate you, because that needs to come from within, but they were there every step of the way to help you succeed.'

Scarlett nodded her head, not quite sure how to take this advice from her husband.

'And if you really want Robin to succeed,' Paul continued, 'your best chance is to take a step back. And to do that I would highly recommend that you stop coaching her.'

'What?' cried Scarlett.

'I mean it, Missy. A parent coaching a child is not a good thing. Up to a certain age, perhaps. But at some stage you have to let go or you'll smother her. Robin is strong willed, just like you, and you risk building a wall between the two of you, especially when she becomes a teenager.'

'But—'

'No buts, Missy. Let me rephrase it like this. Your father supported your swimming. But he is also strong willed, unbending. How long do you think you would have lasted if he were your coach?'

'So what are you saying?' Scarlett asked. 'That after nearly seven years with Robin, I just hand her over to someone else to coach.'

'In a nutshell, yes!'

'And I play no role?'

'Of course not. You can go to her practices. You can swim with her, even train with her. But hold back on the coaching and—'

'But what if I detect that she's doing something technically wrong?'

'Then you discuss it with her coach without Robin present,' Paul advised. 'And especially hold back in pushing her. I'm not saying you do that now but you're so competitive that there's a good chance you may do so later when she is competing for local and hopefully national titles.'

It was hard advice for Scarlett to digest, to let go of her precious daughter.

'Trust me, Missy, the best chance for Robin to succeed is for you to take a supportive role. Be there for her every step of the way, but take a back seat when it comes to how she ought to swim. And if she were to lose a race, never show any disappointment if she tried her best.'

'Okay,' Scarlett relented. 'It isn't going to be easy, and I'm not sure that Robin is going to be happy.'

'She'll come around to the idea.'

'And who do you think should coach her?'

'That's obvious. Your old coach, Graham O'Brien. You and Robin are carbon copies of each other. He did wonders for you and I promise that he'll do the same for Robin.'

§

One night later that week, after Scarlett had done much soul-searching, she broached the subject with her daughter while tucking her into bed with Cub, her teddy bear, next to her.

'Daddy and I have done a lot of thinking, and we believe that it's best if you have a new coach instead of me,' Scarlett said, purposely casual, but expecting the worst.

'Why?' Robin demanded. 'Why can't we just carry on as we have been. After all, I've won every race I've entered.'

'Sweetie,' responded Scarlett in a soothing voice, 'it's worked well until now but everyone says that parents should not coach their children. That it leads to problems down the road.'

'Well, we're not them. Why can't we be different?'

'I was a good swimmer, Sweetie, but that doesn't mean I would make a good coach.'

'But we've been together all this time and I like you teaching me.'

'Okay, then let me ask you this. What do you want out of swimming?'

'Mom!' Robin answered in a tone that suggested Scarlett was asking the obvious. 'You know that I want to be the best swimmer in the world. To become an Olympian, to compete against the best and try my hardest to win.'

'Then let me say this. I can carry on coaching you, but I've no experience and you run a high risk that if I'm not a good coach then you won't reach your dream. Daddy and I thought that my old coach would be best for you. I promise that you couldn't wish for a better person to help you reach your goal. So, you can take a chance on me or go with someone who knows how to produce champions.'

Robin looked at the poster of her heroine, Karen Muir, that was stuck on the wall next to her bed. She sighed deeply and said, 'I hear you, Mom, and I accept that if having a new coach is what it will take for me to be like Karen, then that is what I'll do. But please promise me that you'll always be there for me.'

'Sweetie, I wouldn't have it any other way.'

1st January 1974

Dear Scarlett,

I'm married!

It was a very untraditional wedding. Anna said that she wanted to get married in the exact same spot where I proposed and, if you remember, that was in a field covered in a carpet of flowers in Namaqualand just outside the quaint town of Springbok. When I told her that it was at least six to seven hours drive away and it would be difficult for many of our friends to attend, she told me that she didn't want any guests other than her mother and father, and my parents, if they wished to attend. She suggested that we have a big party for all our friends in Cape Town after our honeymoon. I asked her if she was aware that, being autumn, there would be no flowers in Namaqualand as they only magically appear out of the desert landscape around springtime. She replied that she was well aware. I don't know if it's a Swedish thing to be different, but I was very happy with whatever Anna wanted.

And so it was back to the town of Springbok. Sadly, my parents were unable to attend due to my father presenting an important paper at a medical conference, so we agreed that we would repeat the celebration when next we were in the UK. In mid-April, Stefan and Ingrid Lagerström, my future in-laws, and Anna and I motored north to Namaqualand. We spent the first night at the Springbok Hotel, just as we had when we got engaged. Then the next day we drove out to the same spot in the same field where I proposed. There wasn't a flower in sight but there was no need for one. In the middle of a semi-desert landscape, Anna, dressed in a buttercup yellow dress and a circlet of yellow flowers in her hair that resembled a halo, looked like the prettiest flower that had ever bloomed in Namaqualand.

Stefan performed a beautiful ceremony, Anna and I signed the register, witnessed by Ingrid, and on the 14th April 1973, we became husband and wife. And immediately afterwards we spread a blanket on the dry sandy ground and enjoyed a delicious picnic lunch for a reception. As I said, maybe it's a Swedish thing, nothing like I ever imagined my wedding to be, but I would not swap it for anything else. It was so special, so intimate and Anna was a beam of sunlight.

I kept our honeymoon a secret all the way through until the end. Of course, I advised Anna what to pack, which made it all the more intriguing because it ranged from hiking gear to a ballroom dress and everything in between.

We spent the night of our wedding in the honeymoon suite at the Springbok Hotel, and the following day raced back to Cape Town and caught a taxi to the harbour. I got such a thrill watching Anna's facial expression as she tried to guess what was in store for her. Well, the first instalment was boarding the RMS Windsor Castle for a cruise to Durban, which is the main city in the province of Natal. How can I best describe the ocean liner? Perhaps the grand hotel of the high seas! Anna's face was a picture when she realised the huge ship was our destination!

As we boarded the luxury liner, a personal porter came to attend to our needs. And I say personal porter because I pulled out all the stops for this cruise, booking us into one of only 10 deluxe cabins — our own hotel suite on the ship, luxuriously furnished with armchairs, coffee tables, a writing desk, bookcases and cocktail cabinets. And, of course, it had its own private bathroom. With her father a missionary and mother a nurse, Anna's formative years were forged in frugal ways, so at first the opulence was a bit overwhelming. It was for me too, but we soon settled down for a cruise that created a lifetime of fond memories.

Once we were settled, the ship sounded its horn and we set sail. Our cabin faced land which offered us occasional glimpses of the country as we sailed up the east coast of South Africa. The next five days we spent our time holding hands as we explored the cruise ship or lazed around the swimming pool, having a dip every so often, read books while sitting on yellow and coral coloured deck chairs on the veranda overlooking the pool, and sipped exotic cocktails as the sun set over the coastline. Lazy days in the sun!

In the evenings we dressed in our finest, descended the flying staircase to the dining saloon and treated ourselves to scrumptious meals. Afterwards, we would retire to the lounge which, during the day, with its large curved windows served as a wonderful lookout to the world around us. In the evenings, with the curtains drawn, the attention drew inwards to an oval dance floor where we would dance the night away.

Despite having dated for over a year, we were inseparable, like two lovers discovering each other for the first time. Well, except when Anna visited the health spa every day — she is Swedish, after all! And there was another occasion too, when I was called to action. While sitting on the veranda, I heard a scream from a young boy who was in the swimming pool, so I quickly jumped in, hauled him out and laid him on a towel. After a quick assessment, it turned out that he had a nasty cut on his knee, a result of slipping and falling on the steps leading into the pool. It looked worse than it actually was but several crew members fussed about, placed him on a stretcher and marched him off to the infirmary, closely followed by his anxious parents. I decided to follow, too, just to make sure everything worked out fine, and just as well because the ship's doctor was somewhat under the weather, apparently from food poisoning! So, yours truly took over and stitched up the wound. I tell you this because it scored Anna and me a special invite to dine with the captain of the ship in a most elegant, intimate private dining room.

The skipper, a Mr Harold Charnley who introduced himself as Chuckles, had a great love for classical music, so he and Anna got on very well, especially when he played a selection from his vast record collection, causing him and my new wife to 'ooh and aah' during the evening. I am slowly acquiring the taste for classical music but that evening it was more the taste of food that made me 'ooh and aah'. I especially kept a menu to relate to you the delectable treats I savoured. Actually, it seemed as if you could order anything you wanted, which made me wonder how big the ship's pantry was! It also made choosing difficult, so I kept to the suggested menu of chilled paw paw, grilled Dover sole with lemon butter, roast leg of lamb boulangére, Viennese fruit flan with cream and, of course, a selection of cheeses and coffee.

On our last night before disembarking in Durban, while eating in the dining saloon, Anna perused the evening's entertainment offerings and commented that the theatre was going to screen her favourite film of all time, *The Sound Of Music*. When she asked me what my favourite song was from the film, I sheepishly had to reply that I had never seen it. The incredulous look on her face immediately determined what we were going to do that night! And I have to agree with Anna, it was fabulous. Afterwards, we walked out on deck and spent the remainder of our last night on the RMS Windsor Castle embraced in the warm air as we sailed up the coast of Natal towards Durban.

In Durban, we booked into the five-star Edward Hotel for two nights, a hotel that epitomized a time of Victorian elegance and is known as the Grand Dame of Durban hotels. When in Rome do as the Romans do, so, it was catching a rickshaw along the beachfront known as the Golden Mile! Dressed in colourful regalia, horns sprouting from his headgear and body attired with beads and wild animal furs, a Zulu man had us bobbing along the promenade as if we were in a Ben Hur film. We jumped on trampolines that were set in the beach sand, ate candy floss and popcorn while walking through mini town, a one in twenty-four scaled down version of a city that replicated many of Durban's famous buildings and landmarks, and swam in the warm Indian Ocean, trying to body surf decent-sized waves. Then we lay on the beach sand amongst other holiday makers, most of whom had portable radios sounding out the latest hit songs from a station called LM radio. We had noticed that there were so many Indians one could be mistaken for thinking that we were on the Asian subcontinent. For lunch, we decided to sample what an Indian man called bunny chow. What is that, you may wonder? So did we! It turned out to be half a loaf of white bread, hollowed out and filled with some sort of curried meat. What type of meat, I asked? Better that you not know, was his reply! Is it hot and spicy? If it's not hot, he replied, it's not a Durban bunny chow! So, sticking to our motto of when in Rome, we had bunny chow for lunch and discovered it to be delicious, a 'to die for' food, not only to taste but also for the after effects the following morning! That evening we had cocktail drinks in the ladies bar before tucking into the Edward Hotel's famous smorgasbord where we ate enough food to keep us going for the rest of our honeymoon.

Every day was still a surprise for Anna, but when we woke up the next morning I did warn her that the luxury part of our honeymoon was over.

Later that morning we hired a VW Beetle and slowly motored up the north coast of Natal. At some point we crossed the Tugela River and entered the territory of Zululand. Rolling hills of sugar cane dominated the scenery and when the stems of cane with their flower tops waved in the breeze it gave me the impression of hordes of Zulu warriors with their assegais, performing a war dance. Eventually we came to a little town called Mtunzini, perched on a hill that overlooked the sea. Below the town the Mlalazi River formed a lagoon before running parallel to the coastline for about four kilometres before entering the sea. A rustic log cabin in some dense bush at the lagoon was meant to be our accommodation for the next two nights.

We had eaten so much the last week that we went to bed early. But we couldn't sleep. Mosquitoes! Thousands of them!

The next morning we rose early, did a little boating, explored a grove of Raphia palms, and then at the recommendation of the owner of a small shop that mostly sold bait for fishing, we decided to walk to the river mouth along the edge of the river. It was a glorious autumn day that people from Natal will tell you is the best weather in the world. As the sun kept on rising, it glittered on the river where various species of fish like mullet and springer would jump high out of the water and land with a splash. It was a beautiful walk. The river on our left and a sand dune covered with bush on our right. Walking hand in hand, crabs would scurry out of our way and shoals of tiny little fish on the water's edge would swim away as, every so often, we cooled our feet in the water. After a couple of hours, we came across the river mouth.

It was an idyllic spot as river met sea. On the opposite side of the river mouth were some pine trees, so we waded across and found some relief from the midday sun. But every so often we would frolic in the water, with not another person in sight. Something we didn't notice was that the tide was coming in and soon the river swelled to a size that cut us off from the track back to our cabin, so, given that it was a warm evening we decided to spend the night sleeping under the stars. As we lay on our towels on the soft beach sand that stretched away from the river's edge, cuddled together, I couldn't help but wonder what a far cry it was from being drenched in blood at the end of a work day at Groote Schuur. It was truly blissful.

The following day when the tide went out we crossed the river and walked back to the lagoon via the beach. Only later in the year when reading up about that magical place did I discover that the river mouth where we swam for much of the day is one of the most shark-infested waters in the world! Oh, and there have been known to be a few crocodiles in the area too!

Next, we drove to what is known as the Drakensberg, a range of mountains that forms the western boundary of Natal. We camped in a tent at a Natal Parks Board campsite. In front of us were breathtaking mountains, the most famous being Cathkin Peak, Champagne Castle and Monks Cowl. These are serious mountains, so we dared not try to climb them, but we did a decent walk meandering through bush, rivers and waterfalls up to a rocky outcrop called the Sphinx and then on to a small mountain called Verkyker, both of us singing *Climb Every Mountain* from *The Sound Of Music* film we had watched on the RMS Windsor Castle. This grass-covered mountain is so symmetrical in rising to a peak, I told Anna it looked like a women's breast! And can you believe that when we got to the top there was a rock cairn, human made, which, I pointed out to Anna, looked just like the breast's nipple!

Again, the autumn weather in Natal was stunning. A crisp, clear, sunny day. Verkyker in Afrikaans, one of the many languages spoken in South Africa, means binoculars and it is obvious why it was so named. From that vantage point looking back, we could see way into the distance, a vast land of rivers and lakes and rolling grassy knolls that is Natal.

We sat there for a long time taking in the splendour before us and somehow got talking about our heritage. I'm English through and through, and although Anna is Swedish her one grandmother was also from England. We went back as far as we could and can you believe we discovered that we both had great-great-grandfathers who had fought for the British in the Anglo-Zulu War? And, what's more, both fought in the battle of Isandlwana.

Our stay in the mountains was meant to be the last leg of our honeymoon, but then Anna suggested that we visit the battleground of Isandlwana since it was not that far past the horizon as we looked back at Natal.

The following day we drove through Bergville, Ladysmith and then found a bed and breakfast at Dundee. Our host, Piet, offered to take us on a guided tour. We rose early in the morning and set off for the battleground and I will describe the tour as it happened.

'There she is,' said Piet in an Afrikaans accent, pointing to the sphinx-like mountain known as Isandlwana. 'It's a haunting looking mountain. And she has been watching over the scene of the battle for nearly 100 years. She remembers.'

As we walked closer to the mountain, the landscape below was dotted with aloes and cairns of white rocks which Piet told us marked the spot of buried British soldiers. Every so often we found a spent cartridge, a poignant moment as we pondered whether it was possibly fired from the Martini-Henri rifle of either one of our great-great-grandfathers. It was a sombre moment for us too as we knew that both our ancestral relatives had died on that hot day of the 22nd January 1879.

'The British camped here at the foot of the mountain,' Piet told us. 'But they made a big mistake by not forming a laager. They were too spread out making them vulnerable.' Pointing in the distance, Piet continued, 'The Zulu impis appeared over that plateau ridge at dawn. That's how they always fought, trying to catch you off guard.'

'How many Zulu warriors?' I asked.

'They say about 20,000. They attacked using their traditional tactic of encircling the enemy like the horns of a buffalo. And they would have been high on muti.' The questioning looks we gave prompted Piet to ask, 'You're from England?'

'Yes,' I replied, not wanting to confuse him with Anna's ancestry.

'Muti is medicine, but this muti would have been a concoction of dagga, er, marijuana, and other herbs from the witchdoctors. The Zulus always did this. It made them lose any fear, and they attacked ferociously, like madmen. But the British, man, they were like sitting ducks,' said Piet shaking his head. 'Like I said, they should have formed a laager like the Boers did in the Battle of Blood River. Then you have cover. And the Martini-Henri rifles gave off too much smoke so the red coats couldn't see what they were shooting at. The Zulus came in waves and soon it was hand-to-hand combat, rifle and bayonet against assegai and shield. In the end all but a handful of the British met their death.'

'All stabbed with assegais?' I asked.

'Yes. A gruesome death. No war is clean, but an assegai wound can mean a slow and agonizing death,' said Piet dispassionately, words that caused Anna and me to shudder at the thought. 'I see you don't like that, so I'll tell you some good news. The Zulus had a tradition of disembowelling the dead and dying.'

'And that's good news?' I asked, somewhat puzzled.

'Yes. It meant a quicker death.'

'But what did it matter to the Zulus?'

'In the hot African sun the corpses would putrefy quickly and the gases given off caused the stomach to bloat. The Zulus believed this was the soul trying to escape to the afterlife. So the warrior would cut open the stomach of his victim to allow the spirit to escape. If he didn't, he believed he would be haunted by the ghost of his victim, who would then inflict terrible horrors upon him, including causing his own stomach to swell, and eventually the warrior would go mad.'

'I suppose that is good news. That they died a quicker death,' I commented without much conviction.

'That's what I said,' commented Piet in a manner that suggested that I was somewhat slow to catch on.

'What I recall from school, that battle was Britain's worst defeat against an indigenous foe,' I told Anna, not proud of it. 'And as if to emphasize the moment of defeat, apparently a solar eclipse darkened the theatre of battle only for the sun to reappear to reveal the carnage.'

'But they learned from their mistake,' said Piet.

'What mistake?'

'Not forming a laager. You must always form a laager.'

'How did they learn if they were all dead?'

'A few escaped and told those at Rorke's Drift that the Zulus were coming for them too. Come, we'll go there now. Are you up for a good walk?'

'Yes,' we both replied, fascinated by this history lesson.

We walked for a couple of hours to a place called Fugitive's Drift where a handful of fugitive British soldiers had crossed the Buffalo River to inform those at Rorke's Drift, once a store but transformed into a makeshift hospital, that the Zulus were coming for them.

'We cross here,' Piet informed us.

'Here?' I asked, looking at the flowing river in front of us.

'Yes, just like the British did. Except the river was swollen then from summer rains. Now it is much lower.'

So swim we did! And I will give it to old Piet that he gave us a good tour. He made our experience feel very real, as if we had gone back in time to that fateful day.

As we came across Rorke's Drift, our tour guide said, 'Here they formed a laager. Not with wagons but sand bags. And even though the British treated my people very badly in the Boer War, I'll give them their due. They fought like real soldiers here. One hundred and fifty British soldiers, many wounded and sick, held off four thousand Zulu warriors. They had a laager, my friend.'

'Eleven Victoria crosses awarded for bravery that day,' I said, feeling proud.

'Yes,' said Piet. 'With a laager you can defend against a much bigger army than your own. They were brave.'

As we left our bed and breakfast later that day and drove back to Durban, our visit to the most famous battlegrounds of the Anglo-Zulu War, while sobering on the one hand, also gave Anna and me a bond to our past.

Our honeymoon was truly special. Until then, I'd not ventured out of the fairest Cape in my time in South Africa. Though different, Natal had its own special charm. My only regret was not having the time to visit a game reserve. I've been here for nearly six years now and can you believe that I have not seen a lion or an elephant or a giraffe or a zebra? And to think, we were so close to Umfolozi Game Reserve when we were up at Mtunzini. Perhaps another time. After all, I had a job to do in Cape Town. Anna did too.

Back home in Anna's apartment, one night while lying in bed, my wife started singing I'd Like to Teach the World to Sing. I asked if that was a dig at my pathetic attempts to sing and after a little chuckle she said not to take it personally, but she hoped that our children would inherit her singing voice. Well, I was fine with that!

The mention of children got us discussing our future. At our respective ages, 30 and 27, we decided that we should have children sooner rather than later. I'm over the moon to tell you that as I write this letter, Anna is nearly five months pregnant. We are so thrilled!

All my love, Michael.

Scarlett

'Paul, I've been thinking,' Scarlett interrupted her husband one evening while he was reading the newspaper.

'Uh, oh!'

Scarlett ignored Paul and said, 'With Graham coaching Robin I don't want to be at the pool every minute of her training, second guessing him and making him feel uncomfortable.'

'Well, I take my alarm back. I think that's a wise decision.'

'But that leaves me more time and ...,' Scarlett hesitated before continuing, 'as much as I like working in our practice, I feel that is not what I want to do all day.'

'And?' queried Paul with his voice rising, waiting for the bombshell.

'Well, ... spending so much time with Robin, raising her, coaching her, I've often been surrounded by children, and I love it. I feel I have a calling to work with children.'

'In what field?'

'Medical, definitely! I still want to be a doctor.'

'And how do you propose to work only with children?'

'A vacancy has become available at the Red Cross War Memorial Children's Hospital and—'

'Surely you have to be qualified in paediatrics.'

'I've already enquired and the superintendent said that as long as I study a diploma in paediatrics while I'm working, he'll accept an application from me.'

'And did you apply?'

'No, darling, I wouldn't make that decision without first running it by you. Besides, I feel bad that I would be letting you down by leaving the practice.'

'Missy, if paediatrics is where your heart is, then that's what you must do. Of course, I love working with you but you must follow your dream.'

'Aw, thank you, darling,' Scarlett said, giving Paul a peck on the cheek. 'One other thing, when you replace me in the practice, will you consider a woman doctor?'

'I most certainly will. The practice has been thriving and I can't help feeling that a large part of that is because ours is one of the few that has a woman doctor.'

§

Scarlett's application was successful and she was awarded the job at the Red Cross War Memorial Children's Hospital, a living memorial to South African soldiers who fought in World War II and donated two days of their pay towards the development of the hospital. She still woke up at 4 o'clock every morning to take Robin to training, except now she devoted her time there to studying books on paediatrics, but not without keeping an eye on her beloved daughter.

1st January 1975

Dear Scarlett,

This is not an easy letter to write. The year did not begin well, but at least it ended on a positive note.

Early in January, I came home from Groote Schuur one day and Anna told me that her baby had stopped moving. When I asked when she had first noticed, she replied about a week ago. Oh, Anna! Why she hadn't told me before, I don't know. Perhaps she wanted to spare me any anxiety, because it is certainly in her nature not to burden others.

I phoned a gynaecologist friend who works at Groote Schuur, and he told us that in all likelihood, Anna would experience a stillbirth. And she did. The following day Anna went into labour, I took her to Groote Schuur, and she gave birth to a lifeless baby.

How can I explain Anna to you? She must have been so sad at this terrible turn of events, but she remained calm and at peace during a time of mourning. Certainly more at peace than me! We were so looking forward to having our first child, instead we buried our little boy at Pinelands Cemetery.

Anna's personal doctor, a Dr Rhodes, recommended that we wait awhile before we try to have another baby. He said that Anna needed time to heal both physically and emotionally. But things don't always go to plan and not long afterwards Anna fell pregnant again. Although she had remained serene through her stillbirth ordeal, despite what Dr Rhodes had said, being pregnant again helped her mentally because there was definitely an extra spark in her eyes.

Sadly, the whole episode repeated itself in early June. And, I say this with tears in my eyes, again just six weeks ago. I was heartbroken and deeply worried that Anna might blame herself, even if subconsciously because she never outwardly expressed those emotions.

With three baby boys buried, we had a long heart-to-heart about having children and what could have been a difficult discussion was made a lot easier when Anna said that maybe it was just not meant to be. She brought up the subject of adoption but said that she would only be happy to go that route if I was okay with it. I desperately wanted to raise a family with Anna and was only too pleased that she was willing to adopt a child.

So the light at the end of the tunnel is that we have put our names down to adopt a new born baby. We have been told, though, that there could be a long wait. But that is fine with us.

There have been lots of joyous occasions during the past year. Getting to know Anna at a deeper level for whom my love has no bounds. However, it has also been a tough year and we've taken some severe emotional knocks. But we've endured them together, supporting each other, and perhaps that has made our love that much stronger.

On the music front, there was a particularly bright spot just before our first wedding anniversary when Anna's face beamed with pride. A Swedish group called ABBA won the Eurovision Song Contest with a song called *Waterloo*. We still do not have television here in South Africa, so we never got to see the contest but a few weeks later when the song was released in South Africa, I knew it was going to be our next duo project!

Scarlett, did you watch the Eurovision Song Contest? I wish Anna and I had been there in Brighton to witness Anna's fellow Swedish musicians win the competition. My understanding is that most winners have never gone on to become famous. I wonder if ABBA will be different? We shall see.

All my love, Michael.

Scarlett

One night when Scarlett was on night duty at the Red Cross War Memorial Children's Hospital she walked down the passageway and passed by the cardiology ward. Through the glass panels in the doors, she saw as she had done so often before, a man slumped in a chair sleeping next to the bed of one of the patients. Normally he would have a small blanket over his lap, but that night it had fallen to the ground.

Scarlett entered the ward, partially out of curiosity but also to help. She bent over and picked up the blanket, and carefully placed it back on his lap. The man woke, looked up at her and to her surprise it was Dr Chris Barnard. It was the first time she had ever seen him and despite his legendary status she remained unfazed.

'Thank you, Miss ...,' Chris Barnard commented with a faint smile.

'Mrs,' Scarlett replied. 'Mrs Rhodes.'

'Are you a new nurse here at the children's hospital?' asked Chris Barnard.

'Actually, I'm a doctor,' replied Scarlett. 'Just doing my night rounds and was curious who this gentleman was that slept in the cardiology ward three nights a week. And I must say that I'm quite surprised that it's you.'

Chris Barnard responded, 'I think it's only right that having operated on their hearts during the day that I'm here for them at night when they are most vulnerable.'

'That is admirable.'

'Actually, it is the work I do here at this hospital that I would like to be most remembered for,' the heart surgeon said as he looked around the ward of children, mainly from poor backgrounds. Returning his gaze to her face, he commented, 'Dr Rhodes, you have the most beautiful eyes.'

Aware that the famous heart surgeon could be quite a flirt, Scarlett brushed it off. But what he said next took her by surprise.

'And those beautiful eyes will be soothing and healing for the children in this hospital.'

'Thank you,' replied Scarlett.

'You know, Dr Rhodes, we're the privileged ones. You should use your position to pay back to society and to those who are most in need.'

'I'll remember that.'

And with that brief interlude, Chris Barnard closed his eyes and went to sleep.

1st January 1976

Dear Scarlett,

Unfortunately my parents were unable to attend our wedding. And due to logistical nightmares of trying to coincide leave, they had never met Anna, so I rectified that with a visit to Cambridge over the Christmas period. But first we made a detour to experience the Christmas markets in Germany.

Both Anna and I love Christmas. Anna's parents, Stefan and Ingrid, always visit us in Cape Town over Christmas, and we have special family time. We love playing Christmas carols together, Anna on the piano, me on the guitar. I try not to sing, so I whistle instead. An all-round festive occasion with much delicious food. My one wish would be for Stefan to deliver the message at the Christmas church service as he is such a good orator. Perhaps his Swedish accent helps to make him sound different and therefore so special.

But while Christmas in South Africa is a lovely occasion, there is an element that is missing. Yes we have Christmas trees decorated as we do in the UK, we send Christmas cards to family and friends with the usual Father Christmas pictures or snow covered chalets lit up with bright stars, we swig back eggnog on Christmas Eve and tuck into roast turkey for Christmas lunch, but ... it's hot! So, while most follow all the traditions of a European Christmas, there is an added African element that we cannot escape, the heat! As much as I have loved our Christmases here in Cape Town, I was looking forward to once again experiencing, if we were lucky, a white Christmas.

In Germany, instead of going to one of the more popular Christmas markets, we chose the quaint town of Rothenburg ob der Tauber in Bavaria. Strolling the streets, we felt as if we were living in a fairy tale. With half-timbered houses and their red-tiled roofs, the flower-filled window boxes and cobblestone streets, the medieval town that was surrounded by massive stone walls transformed into a winter wonderland before Christmas.

Sipping on mulled wine and eating traditional pastries and grilled sausages, it felt like we had slipped back in time to another era as Anna and I walked the narrow winding streets, the smell of gingerbread and roasted chestnuts wafting in the air. Thankfully, it was not in the era of medieval times when it was believed that a mystical messenger would appear and float through the skies carrying the souls of the dead while issuing messages of doom. Apparently, times have changed and that messenger is now friendlier and welcomed! The mood was truly festive as we spent the day marvelling at the handcrafted treasures in the stalls in the squares around the town hall.

Later in the evening as we slowly walked back to our hotel snacking on roasted chestnuts, we came upon a snow covered church, lights shining through the windows into the dark of night and heard the beautiful sound of a boys' choir singing *Stille Nacht*, as if sung by the angels. Anna and I stopped and whispered to each other that this was, 'Christmas in heaven!'

After spending a week in Germany, we travelled on to my home in Cambridge to spend Christmas with my parents and my sister Jean. It was such fun, and I'm so grateful that my family adore Anna as much as I do.

A highlight was attending King's College Chapel for the Christmas Eve service. You know how much Anna loves music, so I was thrilled to see her reaction to the beautiful singing from the choir of 16 men and 16 boy choristers, especially with its Christmas theme. As I sat there, I couldn't help gazing around and marvelling at King's College Chapel, its gothic splendour, amazing medieval stained-glass windows and above the altar *The Adoration of the Magi* by Rubens. I looked with new eyes at walls of intricate master building work rising to a ceiling that seemed to float as if it were weightless. This was a truly special place and I felt blessed to have attended the University of Cambridge. Back home we sipped on eggnog before retiring to bed. Filled with a kid-like excitement, I couldn't wait for the morning. Presents!

So, what did Anna give me? An LP record called *A Night At The Opera* by a group called Queen. I have to admit that I had not heard of the group. Anna took the record and played just one song from it on the record player in the lounge, *Bohemian Rhapsody*. Was that even a song? It was so long and seemed more like ... well, I don't know what! I'm not sure what my parents or Jean thought of it because they're a bit old-fashioned, but I loved it. What I didn't understand was the slight mischievous smile on Anna's face, until she finally told me that our next musical project together was to learn to play *Bohemian Rhapsody*, me on the guitar, she on the piano. Phew! That seemed daunting, but I was up for the challenge.

Between Christmas and New Year I took Anna on a tour of Cambridge and showed her this amazing university city. A place where I was privileged to live my youth and attend university. Of course, you've seen Cambridge so it needs no description from me. Even though it was cold, a treat was to go punting on the River Cam. We're still like two teenagers in love, so there was much fun and laughter.

Of course, it didn't go unnoticed by me that we punted under the very bridge that I first laid eyes on you. We also passed King's College and I pointed out to Anna where my bedroom used to be, the very room where I wrote my first letter to you.

So once again I sit at my desk in the home where I grew up and write my annual letter to you, looking back on the year gone by. Much of the time I spent up to my elbows in blood, desperately trying to save lives. It was a year spent waiting to hear if we are to become parents of an adopted baby. A year in which my love for Anna grew deeper than I would have ever imagined possible. And a year that ended with a splendid holiday that allowed me to connect the dots of my boyhood, for Anna.

My only regret is that due to leave restrictions, we could not extend our holiday to visit the country where Anna spent the first 15 years of her life. Since ABBA won the Eurovision Song Contest, Anna has been very keen to see them in a live performance. And it is such a pity because they are due to perform in Stockholm in less than two weeks. Perhaps another time.

All my love, Michael.

Scarlett

As Scarlett was tucking her daughter in bed, Robin, snuggling up to Cub, looked at a poster of Karen Muir on the wall next to her bed and asked, 'Who is the best ever swimmer?'

'Well, thinking back to the last Olympics,' Scarlett answered, 'I would have to say Mark Spitz.'

'But the best woman swimmer?'

'I'm not sure, Sweetie, but I think Karen could have been if given the chance,' Scarlett suggested, nodding her head towards the poster. 'To think that she's the youngest person to break a world record in any sport. And just three years older than you!'

It was two months before Robin's tenth birthday. She touched the poster and commented, 'Such a waste of talent.' Then she asked a question that cut straight to her mother's heart. 'What's the point of swimming if I'm never, ever allowed to compete at the Olympics?'

'Why don't we think about that another day,' Scarlett answered, trying to steer away from the inevitable tough question she had been expecting for a long time.

'I think you just don't want to answer me.'

'That's only partially true, Sweetie. But I don't really have an answer.'

'Mom, why is everybody so mean to South Africa?'

'It's complicated, way too difficult to explain to a child your age.'

'Try me. After all, it's something that is going to affect me deeply.'

'Well, Sweetie, we have, for want of a better term, an odd system of government where white people rule the country. They are the only people who are allowed to vote. And most whites, though not all, have better schools, better hospitals and better jobs.'

'Why is it like that?'

'That's the hard part to explain. You have to go back a long time to try to understand how it all came about, but it doesn't get away from the fact that it is what it is.'

'Then why don't they just give everybody the vote, so we can all be happy.'

'It's not as simple as that, Robin. Even amongst whites there are two groups of people, what they call parties. Every few years we vote and the party that wins makes the rules. And so far, it's the party that only wants whites to vote. The members of that party are probably afraid they'll lose their privileged way of life.'

'And which party do you and Dad vote for?'

'The one where everyone is equal. Obviously!'

'Then why were you punished by not being allowed to swim in the Olympics?'

'It's something I've questioned a million times, Sweetie. I've never been in favour of collective punishment. Just like when someone talks in class when you're supposed to all be quiet, and the teacher asks who the culprit is. When he or she doesn't own up then the teacher gives the whole class detention. That doesn't seem fair to me.'

'What's the point of banning South Africa from participating in the Olympics?' asked Robin.

'They hope it will change the white people's attitudes in South Africa so that everyone gets a chance to vote.'

'Do you think it will work? And I know this sounds selfish, but do you think it'll work quickly enough to give me a chance to swim in the Olympics?'

'Actually, I don't think it will work. I think it will just make our government angry, and then they won't want to change. I believe that each one of us should do our bit to change people's minds by talking or treating everybody fairly. That's why at the hospital I work equal time in both the white and black sections and treat each person with the same respect. And because the black section of the hospital is poorly equipped, Dad and I often donate supplies to help—'

'Even though you were banned from swimming in the Olympics?'

'Yes. Morally it's the right thing to do.'

Robin nodded her head and said, 'I do understand that, Mom.'

'So back to your original question, the small things we can do will take a long time to change the country, so I'm afraid I do not think it will change in time for you to swim in the Olympics. Sorry, Sweetie.'

Robin's eyes got moist as she asked, 'But I've read in the newspapers of other South Africans playing sports. Why is that?'

'That's true. Mostly the sports that are banned are those where you represent your country. It's a little easier for sports like tennis or golf where you play a tournament as an individual, but even they are experiencing more and more difficulties.'

'Are there any other countries where they don't allow blacks to vote?' asked Robin.

'There've been many but most have now changed.'

'Why can those countries change and South Africa doesn't?'

'It's only my opinion, but it was easier in those countries because there were more whites than blacks, so they knew their lifestyle would not be affected that much.'

'Were those countries punished when blacks couldn't vote?'

'Not as far as I'm aware.'

'Are other countries punished because they do other mean things?'

'No,' replied Scarlett. 'And that makes this even harder for us to accept.'

'Why don't they have a special team where you can still swim or run in the Olympics — but not for your country?'

'That's something I've wondered about a million times.'

Desperate for answers, Robin continued, 'Mom, I've learned at school that South Africa is very rich in diamonds and gold and makes a lot of money selling them to other countries. Why is that allowed?'

Scarlett shrugged her shoulders. 'Now, perhaps, you can understand why I said it was complicated.'

'It must have been very hard for you and Dad to be told you couldn't compete when you were already on your way to the Olympics.'

'It was. I was both angry and sad for a long time, especially since it had been my goal from when I was very young. When you think of all the hours of training I put in, only for the chance to be taken away from me at the last moment, it was very tough.'

'For me it's simpler,' said Robin. 'You've told me way ahead of time that I'll never swim in the Olympics, so what's the point of training? I guess I'll just have to become a doctor.'

'Why do you say that?' asked Scarlett.

'Because that's what you and Karen did.'

'But, Sweetie, don't you also swim because you love the sport.'

'I do love it, Mom. Love the water. Love the feel of it on my skin. When I'm in the water, I feel free. Free to let my imagination go and feel like I can do anything I want. Didn't you feel the same?'

'I did and I still do.'

'And that won't change,' commented Robin. 'But it's because I love the sport so much that I want to be the best and compete against the best. I want to try and win a gold medal and I'm willing to sacrifice a lot to achieve that goal, but if that goal is taken away from me, I don't see the point of training until I hurt, doing lap after lap until I'm exhausted.'

Scarlett could not argue with that logic, especially coming from her child. Hurting for her precious Robin, but without really knowing how to address the problem, Scarlett put herself on the line by saying, 'I promise you, Sweetie, that if one day you're good enough, I'll see to it that you get to compete at the Olympics.'

'How, when you couldn't do it yourself?'

'I'll move heaven and earth to get you there. If it means we leave South Africa, I'll back you all the way. Your part of the bargain is to get to that level where you are good enough to compete.'

'You would do that for me?' asked Robin, with both excitement and a small measure of disbelief in her voice.

'Yes! I just wish it were done for me, but by the time South Africa was banned from the Olympics I was probably too old to move to another country. Besides, my parents would not have supported that idea.'

'Would Dad?'

'I think I could persuade him. After all, he also trained all his youth to become an Olympian, only to be thwarted at the last moment. You leave it to me.'

Scarlett kissed Robin on the forehead. 'Sweet dreams. Dream of touching that wall like I did every day when I was growing up.'

§

After leaving Robin's bedroom, Scarlett headed downstairs to join Paul in the lounge.

'Robin is questioning the reason for training so hard when she knows that she'll never compete at the Olympics.'

'At such a young age? I would have thought she'd only wonder about that when she was older and only if it came to a point where she knew she was good enough to make it to the Olympics.'

'Paul, every child who swims competitively wants to be an Olympian.'

'I know that, but we also know that most lose that dream very quickly when they realize that they'll never be good enough.'

'But Robin is talented. Graham has confirmed that. Barring injury, if she puts in the hours, there's every possibility she could make it to Moscow. And she is astute enough to know that. But she's also astute enough to know that it's that end goal that drives one, and, without the lure of the pot of gold at the end of the rainbow, questions about the hours of sacrifice are valid.'

'Isn't it a moot point. South Africa will not compete at the next Olympics, perhaps not even for decades to come.'

A look of resignation swept across Scarlett's face. Something inside told her that now was not the time to talk about emigrating to another country.

§

The following day at the swimming pool, Scarlett brought up the subject with coach Graham O'Brien. 'Last night, for the first time, Robin questioned the point of such demanding training if she is prevented from achieving her dream of becoming an Olympian.'

'What did you say to her?'

'That we would emigrate to another country if that is what it took.'

'That's a drastic step. As I've mentioned before, Missy, she is supremely talented. But one small hiccup, an injury, a change in body structure, might mean that she never fulfils her current potential. And to emigrate to another country is a life changing move for what is still a small chance that she ever gets to a point where she could compete at an Olympic Games.'

'Whatever it takes, Graham. I had my dream scuppered and I won't let it happen to Robin. And no, I'm not living my dream through her. You yourself said that she is more talented than I was, so it's only fair that she be given the chance to compete at the highest level.'

Graham studied her thoughtfully, before asking, 'What is your ancestry?'

'As you know, my maiden name was Harrison and my mother's maiden name was Morris which I guess has an English origin. Why do you ask?'

'And were your parents both born in South Africa?'

'Yes. Again, why do you ask?'

'That's a pity. I was thinking there may be the possibility of fast tracking a foreign passport for Robin. What about Paul's heritage?'

Scarlett immediately tightened at this question. Very few people knew that Robin was not his legitimate daughter.

'On the father's side he comes from a long list of Rhodes that have lived in South Africa for many generations. I am not sure about his mom.'

'Will you investigate about Paul's mother?'

'Alright,' replied Scarlett, knowing that she would not.

'You say your mother's maiden name was Morris which is likely English. What do you know about her mother?'

'I'm not sure but I would guess from England too.'

'As you know, Missy, I'm from Ireland and what I've found over my lifetime is that an extraordinary number of people have some Irish blood in them.'

'I don't think that's the case with us. Besides, my mother was born in South Africa. Isn't it true that one can only get a foreign passport based on where your parents were born?'

'Well, that's just it. In most cases, yes, but there is a slight anomaly with Ireland. For some inexplicable reason they dish out passports to people whose grandparents are Irish including maternal grandparents. If your grandmother was born in Northern Ireland before 1922, I'm led to believe, there is the possibility that you could qualify for an Irish passport and my understanding is that you can then register Robin as an Irish national so long as it is done before she turns 16.'

'Graham, I think we're clutching at straws here but if that's what it takes I'll certainly find out.'

'And I'll contact Patrick Ryan at the Consulate of Ireland in Johannesburg, just to make sure that what I've told you is correct.'

§

Scarlett could not ask her mother about her ancestry, so she solicited the help of her brother Danny.

'Pretend that you're interested in our heritage,' Scarlett told Danny. 'Ask where Granny was born and, if possible, find out if Mama has Granny's birth certificate. If so, borrow it, if you know what I mean.'

'Sure, Sis!'

§

By quirk of fate, it turned out that Scarlett qualified for Irish citizenship. Her great-grandfather had been a policeman in England and was seconded to Belfast in Northern Ireland for one year of duty. It was there that Scarlett's grandmother, May, had been born. And Graham was correct. Scarlett could apply for Irish citizenship based on her maternal grandmother. That was confirmed when she received in the post her certificate called Foreign Births Entry Book which she read and reread as she held it in her hands as if it were a gold medal. On that basis she applied for and received dual citizenship with Ireland and an Irish passport. And on the grounds of Scarlett's status, both Robin and Paul received the same.

Delirious with excitement, Scarlett asked Graham if that meant that Robin could one day represent Ireland at the Olympic Games.

'I would say yes, though there may be a waiting period. For that, I'll ask Patrick Ryan.'

1ˢᵗ January 1977

Dear Scarlett,

Bohemian Rhapsody! Did I say I was up for the challenge? It took most of the first half of the year for me to keep up with Anna, but I am pleased to say that together we conquered the quest.

Then we faced another challenge. But more about that later.

With a Swedish tennis player, Björn Borg, doing so well on the tennis tour, Anna applied for tickets to go to Wimbledon. The biggest tennis tournament in the world is so popular that the only way to obtain tickets is to enter a lottery, and can you believe that she got a pair of tickets for the finals! That, of course, didn't mean that Anna was guaranteed of seeing her favourite tennis player as he would still have to make it to the final. A Wimbledon final is a once-in-a-lifetime opportunity so even though we were in the UK last Christmas, I booked a holiday for the European summer with a surprise or two for the love of my life.

Given that Anna's favourite film is *The Sound of Music,* my first surprise was a visit to Salzburg so that we could see all the famous film locations. When I told Anna, she was ecstatic.

First we hiked up the mountain to the meadow where Julie Andrews sang about the hills being alive with the sound of music. Then it was off to the city. We had been married three years then, but that didn't stop us from behaving like two teenagers who had just fallen in love as we toured the lovely Salzburg on rented bicycles, stopping off at famous spots that were depicted in the film.

In between much gaiety and laughter we held hands as we entered the enchanting Mirabell Palace Gardens, danced around the circular lip of the Pegasus Fountain while singing *Do Re Mi,* then hopped up the 'musical steps', using them as a musical scale just as Maria and the Von Trapp children did in the film.

Anna could not believe that I had booked a night at the Palace Leopold and on a gorgeous summer evening we strolled the lake terraces sipping pink lemonade and singing *My Favourite Things,* our favourite song from the film. Without either of us suggesting it — perhaps we have a mental telepathy — we edged closer and closer to the adjacent lake and thought that if Maria and the children could do it, then so could we, so we jumped into the water!

And can you believe, late that night, like two naughty kids, we sneaked out and roamed the estate and simply could not resist singing

Sixteen Going on Seventeen, as we danced around the famous gazebo. Young love!

Of course, we sang *So Long, Farewell* as we left Salzburg and headed off to London to go to Wimbledon.

Apparently a few years ago, Björn Borg caused quite a stir with teenyboppers going wild at Wimbledon, idolising him as if he were a rock star. Anna celebrated her thirtieth birthday this past year, so it was quite odd to see her, normally such a calm and composed person, also being caught up in the whole Borgomania thing. The funny thing, though, is that most of the members at Claremont Tennis Club, many players much older than Anna, are also huge Borg fans. I desperately hoped for Anna's sake that Björn would make the final so that she could get to see her hero.

Anna had heard that many tennis players stayed at the Gloucester Hotel, so we booked a double room at the same hotel. And just as well that it had air-conditioning because the summer of 1976 must have been the hottest on record. Before moving to South Africa I had spent 24 years in the UK and had never experienced anything like it. People were taking off their shirts, standing under fountains, eating ice-lollies and ice-creams, and behaving as if on a holiday at the French Riviera.

Finals day! Ecstatic that Björn had made the final, Anna was like a kid on the morning of her birthday. We caught the tube to Southfields station and walked to the All England Lawn Tennis Club where they hold the tournament called Wimbledon. It is a beautiful setting, one that conjures up images of a 'Great English Garden Party'. Soon we made our way to Centre Court and the first thing that struck me was how brown the grass was due to the heatwave. I am not sure Anna even noticed. Her mind was elsewhere.

Finally, Björn Borg and his opponent, Ilie Nastase, walked out onto Centre Court amid rapturous applause. My first thought was that the appeal of Björn to Anna may lie in some ancestral connection because he looked like some modern day Viking.

The match did not start well for her hero and although Anna was quiet, I felt her disappointment when Björn went 3-love down. But he picked up his game, and he won in straight sets, throwing his racket high in the air after the winning point. Nastase, to his credit, jumped over the net to warmly congratulate the new champion. When Björn Borg held the trophy aloft it glittered in the bright sunshine and next to me my wife was jubilant with excitement.

But that excitement soon changed.

That evening in the Gloucester Hotel, I climbed into our double bed while Anna took a shower. When she walked out of the bathroom in the nude and joined me in bed, I naturally expected some amorous adventure, especially when she quickly took my hand and put it to her left breast.

The excitement of that glorious afternoon turned to one of despair, at least for me, for under the surface of Anna's breast was a lump. I asked her how long she had known, and she told me she'd first noticed it a couple of weeks before we left for our holiday. When I asked why she hadn't told me before she said that she didn't want to spoil the holiday for me! Oh, Anna!

I was bewildered. I obviously know that Anna is a calm and easy-going person, but even I could not believe that she had withheld that information to allow me to enjoy our fabulous holiday, especially when it catered more for her interests — visiting the scenes from her favourite film, *The Sound Of Music*, a Wimbledon final that fortuitously had her hero winning the tournament, and later a visit to her homeland of Sweden. Even more bewildering was that she seemed on top of the world in our time in Salzburg and in London. I simply could not fathom that someone who only hours before had been so excited at Wimbledon could be the same person to reveal to her husband that she had a lump in her breast. And, she seemed so composed!

Despite her calm demeanour, I explained to Anna that most breast lumps are not malignant. Also, her young age was on her side. I then told her that we needed to go back to South Africa so that she could have a biopsy, that if the lump were malignant then the earlier it was treated the better. She listened attentively, but did not appear overly concerned. She asked me about the treatment if her lump was malignant and I replied most likely surgery and then chemotherapy. At the mention of surgery, Anna said that if it came to that then she wanted me to do the operation. I told her that it would be better to be operated on by a surgeon more experienced in breast surgery, that although I did some general surgery in the mornings, I spent most of my time in trauma. But she insisted that if the lump was cancerous, that I do the surgery. I compromised by suggesting that a surgeon experienced in breast surgery perform the procedure, and that I would watch over him. But she turned the tables, that I operate and an experienced breast surgeon could watch over me. Anna had never asked for much, so I relented.

What I didn't tell her was that the position of the lump in the top right quadrant, its irregular shape and the fact that it seemed fixed to the breast tissue, sounded alarm bells in my head. I got out of bed and started packing. Anna looked bewildered and asked what on earth was I doing? When I told her that we needed to get on a plane back to South Africa because the earlier we had the lump in her breast checked out the better, she calmly said no, that for a few years now she had wanted to take me to see her homeland of Sweden, and we were still going. But Anna, time is vital, I counselled, the earlier we have a checkup the better. But I also knew that one could not argue with Anna. She is the least argumentative person I have ever met, which makes most people conclude that she is a rollover. But it's the exact opposite. She is so sure of herself in such a tranquil manner that it is hard to go against her. She said that if the lump was benign, then it didn't matter if we went to Sweden. On the other hand, given that she was so keen to show me the country of her birth, if she did have cancer and was going to die, then now was her only chance to take me. There seemed to be a certain logic to that, I guess.

I didn't sleep that night. Anna slept soundly with her head tucked up against my shoulder. I couldn't help but think that there was a third alternative which was that if she did have cancer and was cured, then she could take me on a tour of Sweden sometime in the future. I wondered, too, if deep down she knew what I feared. As I gently caressed her hair throughout the night, I also wondered how she could be so calm.

We went to Sweden, visiting both Stockholm and Västervik, the city where Anna had lived until moving to South Africa. I tried hard not to show it, but the holiday was something of a blur with the dark shadow of Anna's potential predicament consuming my mind. What I do remember most was visiting the town where Björn Borg grew up, a place called Södertälje. The story goes that Björn's father won a table tennis tournament and the prize was a tennis racket which he gave to his son. The kid was not good enough to join a tennis club, so he practised against a garage door for hour upon hour to get good enough to join the local club. Of course, we had to find this famous garage door and, as it turned out, so did a lot of other people. For Björn Borg fans it had become some sort of pilgrimage to the birthplace of the tennis legend. It was quite odd seeing other people stopping off and staring at the now famous garage door. But it made Anna deliriously happy, especially when someone produced a racket and a ball and allowed her to hit a few rallies against her idol's garage door.

On returning to South Africa, I immediately arranged for Anna to have a biopsy on the lump in her breast and what I feared most turned out to be true. The lump was malignant. Anna still insisted that I do the surgery, so I gave in. I had done far more complicated operations but none made me as nervous as this one. As agreed, I did have a specialist breast surgeon watching my every move, and he seemed totally satisfied that all had gone well.

Anna then went on a three-month course of chemotherapy. It was tough for me, watching her beautiful blonde hair fall out and seeing her in a constant state of nausea, causing her to lose a lot of weight. Obviously it was tough on her too, but you wouldn't have known. Each day she would make and wear a circlet of fresh yellow flowers, similar to what she wore on her wedding day, a queen with her crown. But there were days when she tried to play the piano and halfway through a song was so weak that her fingers could no longer press down a key. It was a torrid three months but without a single complaint from Anna.

As I write this on the first day of 1977, Anna is in remission, but now the wait period starts. I question myself repeatedly. Did I remove all the malignant tissue? Had it spread before I operated on her? Has the brutal regimen of chemotherapy killed off all remaining cancerous cells?

Time will tell.

All my love, Michael.

Scarlett

Many parents and coaches will say that they get more nervous than the participant in a sporting event. The fact that Robin was swimming in the under 12 national championships a year younger than her fellow contestants did not make it easier for Scarlett. The woman who was deprived of participating at the 1964 Olympic Games in Tokyo and again in 1968 at Mexico City was secretly hoping, hoping that a good showing at this meet would give her an indication of what lay ahead for her daughter.

Robin entered all nine events on offer, the 50 and 100 metres of each stroke and the 200-metre individual medley. Sandwiched between these events were races in other age groups and also medal presentations.

By the time Robin was about to swim the 100-metre backstroke, she had already won all eight races that she had participated in, some comfortably, some close. But it was the 100-metre backstroke event that Scarlett was most interested in, her signature event prior to the 1964 Tokyo Games. She knew that for Robin, even at her tender young age, it would also be her best chance for victory in years to come.

Scarlett sat between Graham and Paul. She held tightly onto Paul's hand waiting for the contestants to come out of the call room. From experience, Scarlett knew that this moment was swimming's equivalent of purgatory. For some, the wait felt like hell. For Scarlett, it had been a space of serenity, a place where she would draw mental strength to separate herself from the rest of the field even before the race commenced. When Scarlett had walked out of the call room, she never saw the crowd, didn't even hear anything, for she was in the zone. She hoped that Robin would be the same.

Robin sat in the call room clutching Cub, her teddy bear, close to her chest until the swimmers were called. As they marched out to the starting blocks, Scarlett's heart fluttered like a butterfly. In a way she hoped to catch Robin's eye to give her one last nod of encouragement, but her daughter did not even glance in her direction. Clearly, she was in the zone!

The contestants lined up against the starting blocks, but all Scarlett saw was Robin in her black Speedo costume. On command, they pin-dropped into the water and took up the ready position. Scarlett squeezed Paul's hand until her knuckles turned white. The starter's gun fired and Robin pushed off the wall with her legs, swam underwater with a dolphin kick before surfacing ahead of the other swimmers and breaking into backstroke. By the time she turned at the halfway mark, she was a body length clear. Scarlett could hardly believe her eyes. In the second 50 metres her precious water baby pulled even further ahead as she touched the wall to win gold.

Scarlett wanted to jump, scream, dance, and go crazy, but such a show would be demeaning to Robin's competitors and their parents. Somehow she forced herself to suppress her unbridled joy and instead just stood proudly between Graham and Paul, clapping her hands.

When the three of them finally sat down, the coach had a few words to say to Robin's parents. 'Your daughter has something special. She has a unique talent. Scarlett, you were good. I never doubted that you would become an Olympian. I felt you could medal but that was never certain. As you know, there's never any certainty. There's a long road ahead for Robin and any one of several issues could raise its ugly head, but in her case I'm as close to certain as I can be. She's the real deal. She has your drive, Scarlett, but, and I am sorry to have to say this, she has more natural talent.'

'Graham, you don't have to be sorry. That's the best news you could have given me.'

Between two races of other age groups near the end of the meet, the medal presentation for the 100-metre backstroke took place. It was a quick affair but one that made Scarlett's heart purr as her daughter ascended the top tier of the podium to receive her gold medal. Little did she know that it was the last medal that would hang around Robin's neck.

1st January 1978

Dear Scarlett,

This past year has brought profound changes in my life. A lot of things have happened so it will be a long letter.

After Anna's chemotherapy ended, she rebounded. Her beautiful blonde hair started growing again, she got her weight back and resumed playing the piano. Often I would join her with my guitar, music bringing us so much joy.

Then the wheels fell off. At first, every few days I could see that Anna was not well, but she shrugged it off. Those episodes became more frequent. Soon it was obvious that her cancer had come back with a vengeance. What I had most feared, had indeed happened. The disease had spread throughout her body.

On our wedding anniversary in April, a glorious sunny day, we went up in the cable car to the top of Table Mountain, a first for us because we always preferred to hike up. I pushed a wheelchair to a sheltered spot where I laid out a blanket, and a frail Anna and I sat with our legs dangling over the edge of a rock face. As we had done so often before in both the Cape and abroad, we packed a picnic basket, this time with simple goodies — bread and cheese and wine.

Together, we quietly absorbed the grand views from the iconic mountain. Lion's Head and Signal Hill on the left, the City Bowl below us with Table Bay stretching out to the horizon, and Devil's Peak to the right. Beautiful places we had visited together over the last five years.

After I packed away our picnic, I could see that Anna was tiring, so I sat behind her, legs to one side and leant on my left hand so that my darling could lie against me for support. We didn't want the day to end for although neither of us voiced our thought, we knew this was the last time we would both look out at the world from this majestic mountain.

The following day I received a call from the adoption agency to say that Anna and I were to become the parents of a newborn baby boy. Due to the stress of Anna's illness, I had completely forgotten that we were still on their list. The news brought tears to my eyes, reminding me that Anna had desperately wanted to raise a family with me. Now it was too late and I declined the offer, quietly letting go of the son I would never know. Though we kept no secrets from each other, it served no purpose telling Anna this bittersweet news.

At the beginning of June, Anna's parents moved in with us and were a great help, lifting some of my heavy burden.

Two weeks later Anna took a serious turn for the worse and had to be hospitalised. She was fading fast but was still aware that the first Saturday of July meant the men's singles final at Wimbledon, and not just any Wimbledon but the centenary edition.

I lay next to her on the edge of her hospital bed and held her hand as we listened to the final between her hero Björn Borg and his arch rival Jimmy Connors. I say listened, because although South Africa had finally started broadcasting television the previous year, the powers that be had not yet grasped the importance of the big occasion, so we had to rely on short wave radio for the BBC commentary of the final. And what a final! It didn't start too well for Björn as he lost the first set, but then he kicked into gear and seemed to be steamrolling his way to the title. Then he lost the fourth set! Despite her weakened condition, I sensed the tension in Anna. Then her hero raced into what seemed like an insurmountable 4-love lead in the final set. Not to be. Jimmy came storming back, 4-1, 4-2, 4-3 and suddenly it was 4-all. Anna was shaking. Part of me wanted to switch the radio off, another thought that if she died of a heart attack then at least it was while listening to the Wimbledon men's singles final! But Björn did not disappoint, taking the next two games and the title.

Immediately afterwards, Anna asked me to take her home to her own bed. I knew why. Later that evening, lying next to her in our bed, it struck me that it was exactly a year before, on the night of the Wimbledon final that Anna had placed my hand on her breast and I had felt a lump. Cancer is such a cruel disease. Only six years before, President Nixon of the United States of America had declared war on cancer. Now it seemed to me as if the war was going to be a long one and, sadly, I wondered if it could ever be won.

For the next few days I never left our bedroom. Anna's parents brought us meals although Anna had no appetite, and the four of us spent many hours together, often with long periods without a word spoken. In all my years as a surgeon, I had never seen anyone so at peace with impending death.

On the Friday following the Wimbledon final, Anna reached out and took my hand. The warmth of life was draining fast as she felt cool to touch. But despite her perilous condition she looked as serene as ever as she spoke softly to me. 'I know you're going to be sad when I am gone,' she said, 'but please take comfort knowing that I will have gone to a better place.'

A lump grew in my throat as I realized that in those last moments she was thinking about me. And with that final comment she closed her eyes and my beam of light extinguished. Coincidentally, 10 years to the day that Vivien Leigh passed away, the actress who played the character after whom I named you, Scarlett from *Gone With The Wind*.

Anna didn't want a funeral. She wanted me to invite all our friends over for a party a few weeks after she was gone to celebrate her life. I never got to honour her wishes, but more about that later. Stefan, Ingrid and I did have a brief memorial at the cemetery where she was buried next to a grave that bore three small crosses, our babies. Both Stefan and I had our arms around Ingrid as Anna's father gave a beautiful eulogy. Afterwards, we had a few quiet moments during which a version of the words from a Don McLean song, *Vincent*, played through my mind. 'Anna, this world was never meant for one as beautiful as you!' My soulmate and I had loved performing that song together, but now she was gone and how sad we would never do so again.

I held it together for the sake of Anna's parents who left the next day to go back to White River, but that first evening alone I was lost. Our home felt so empty, as if it had lost its soul. I didn't know what to do. I thought I would cook a meal to take my mind off my loss, but what was the point of eating alone? I was desperate. So I took out my guitar and tried playing a song. It only made things worse. For me, music and Anna were inseparable. Without Anna, music had suddenly lost its appeal.

Sitting on a couch, still holding my guitar, in my mind I thought back over my life, how at school I was driven to get to university to study medicine, and at university I was driven to become a surgeon, especially a trauma surgeon where so often you try to tilt death in favour of life. Now, it seemed, medicine had let me down when I needed it most. I felt deceived. I felt angry. My anger festered and boiled until I stood up and shouted at it, demanded answers as I paced up and down our apartment until in a fit of pique I smashed my guitar against the shoulder of a dining room chair. Amidst the broken pieces, I sat down on that chair, held my head in my hands and sobbed. Yes, I was devastated that Anna had died, but I was bitter to my stomach that what I had devoted all my life to had allowed my precious wife to be taken away from me. The following morning I handed in my resignation at Groote Schuur. As I walked away from the hospital, I recalled Dr Chris Barnard's comment that great surgeons' marriages don't last. Perhaps, but it was not meant to be this way.

That same day I packed two suitcases and decided to drive and drive and see where the road took me. The only way from Cape Town is north, so that's where I headed, staying in B&Bs along the way. And that's why I never got to invite our friends over for a party to celebrate Anna's life. Perhaps some time in the future.

Although it wasn't my intention, a couple of weeks later I arrived at White River in the Eastern Transvaal, the town where my in-laws, Stefan and Ingrid Lagerström, lived. They were very pleased to see me and, like me, they had been having a tough time after their daughter's death, so we consoled each other for a few days, reminiscing and sharing stories about Anna.

I also told them that I had resigned from Groote Schuur and was on a road trip to try to find myself. My purpose in life. Stefan picked up on this very quickly and said that his church mission had once operated a hospital nearby that was recently incorporated into a state hospital, and they were always on the lookout for doctors. I said thanks, but no thanks. He then mentioned that his mission also operated a clinic in the bush somewhere between White River and Kruger Park. Perhaps, he said, there was an opportunity to still practise my skill but in a very rural area where I might find peace. I knew Stefan meant well, but my heart was no longer in medicine, and he came to understand. Finally, Stefan said that what I needed was a complete break in a completely different environment, and he highly recommended spending some time in Kruger Park. It's like no other place on earth, he said, and will be the tonic that will heal you. I took his advice and the following morning said my goodbyes.

I drove to the closest entrance, Numbi Gate, and asked if there was any accommodation available. Luckily it was after the winter school holidays, so I was in luck and, not knowing much about Kruger Park, I selected the closest camp which is Pretoriuskop Camp. I booked and paid for a week's stay. After that, depending on whether I liked it or not, I would make a decision to either continue to stay in Kruger Park, perhaps in another camp, or head off somewhere else in South Africa.

As I entered, something strange happened to me, but I will explain that in a moment. Firstly, some information about Kruger Park. Apparently, at the end of the last century, the president of the South African Republic, Paul Kruger, became concerned that hunting was taking its toll on the wild animal population, and with numbers decreasing at an alarming rate he set aside part of the eastern Transvaal as a wildlife sanctuary. That was the start of what is known today as the Kruger National Park. And it is huge! The same size as Wales!

So what happened to me? Well, it's quite hard to describe but, upon entering, it struck me that as far as the eye could see the countryside belonged to the animals of Kruger Park, roaming free and living as nature intended, and we humans were guests in their land. There are roads, some tarred, others made of gravel, and you simply drive along at a slow pace observing real nature, a plethora of animals, birds, reptiles, insects and natural bush and grasslands. Now, there isn't an animal around every bend in the road, though that does sometimes occur and can be quite frightening when a huge elephant looms in front of you, or exhilarating when you come across a pride of lions, but mostly you have to look carefully to spot the animals. It's like nothing I ever imagined. Certainly not an oversized zoo!

The first species I came across was a majestic kudu bull, a beautiful antelope that was feeding off leaves from a tree. And I thought, wow, this animal is not your family cat or dog, it is wild! I was intrigued watching him, but more intrigued that I was in another world, their world. After 20 minutes or so, I carried on driving and came across a herd of impala crossing the road. That was quite a sight. Perhaps I got too close because they suddenly started running across the road in these high-flying leaps. I was thrilled to bits. Just so that you know, I quickly realised that impala are a very common species, but they're a pretty antelope, the males with their lyrate horns and the ewes looking so graceful.

Then it was giraffe, a tower of them, and aptly named because my goodness they are tall! Picture books simply do not do justice to the height of a giraffe. I was fascinated watching their tongues twirl around a clump of thorns in a tree to extract a single leaf to devour. Given the size of a giraffe, I immediately concluded that it would take all day feeding on one leaf at a time to satisfy its need for sufficient nutrition. I felt proud of myself for concluding that because I was soon to learn that all the herbivores seem to eat all day!

Dotted around the park, anywhere from 30 to 100 kilometres apart are fenced off camps where visitors may spend the night in rustic chalets. I got the idea that they are purposely not too posh to give one the 'bush' experience, but also the whole point of the Kruger Park experience is to spend time outside of the camp driving around the park to observe nature.

It was late afternoon when I finally reached Pretoriuskop Camp. I booked in and drove to my chalet which looked onto a large grassy patch with a few rugged trees providing some shade. By the time I had unpacked my belongings, still only two suitcases containing all my worldly goods, I was ravenous having not eaten anything since breakfast. Alongside my chalet, people from a neighbouring unit already had a fire going for their braai, the colloquial term for a barbecue. The smell of mashed potatoes permeated the air which set off my hunger pangs. I was so ill prepared for my sojourn into the park that the only food I had was a packet of Marie biscuits which are nibble biscuits, only nice if you are not hungry! Although I was to find out later that the smell of mashed potatoes was not from people cooking up their supper fare but was an aroma given off by a shrub called the Potato Bush that was growing nearby, I was on the verge of setting off to scavenge some food from one of my neighbours, when someone knocked on my door. I was desperately hoping that it was a fellow visitor who had noticed my state of hunger and had kindly come over to invite me to join them for supper!

It wasn't a bonus meal. Instead, when I opened the door I saw a short thickset man standing there in khaki shirt and shorts. He uttered something that I did not understand, which prompted me to explain to him that my understanding of Afrikaans was still limited. Thankfully, he could speak perfect English, though with a heavy accent. He asked me if I was a doctor. Obviously I was taken aback by this question but answered in the affirmative. He then introduced himself as Kobus de Beer and explained that he was a game ranger, the green epaulettes and a gold-plated badge pinned to his shirt which read 'Game Ranger' confirming that. Okay, but the doctor thing? He said that the receptionist at the office had noted that I'd used the title of doctor on the form that I'd filled in at the office when arriving at the camp. Of course, that is not a crime, so why the game ranger visit? He then asked if I was a medical doctor. When I said yes, he asked if I would come with him to have a quick look at his son as he, to use Kobus's words, 'Did not look too well.'

A part of me was annoyed. After all, I was running away from anything to do with medicine. But that Hippocratic Oath ran deep in my blood, so I couldn't refuse. Kobus and I jumped into his pick-up truck — known in South Africa as a bakkie — and drove out of the camp and to his house not far away.

He quickly introduced me to his wife, Sandra, and then took me to his son's bedroom. This is Japie, the game ranger said. He repeated that his son didn't look too well but given that the month was August and nearing the end of winter, it was highly unlikely that it was malaria.

'Not looking too well' was an understatement! A quick examination revealed a severe headache and fever, symptoms of many diseases, of course, including malaria. I asked for a torch, which was handed to me by Japie's twin sister, Helena. Sensitivity to light, a rash on his torso and especially a stiff neck pointed directly to bacterial meningitis. I sensed the diagnosis didn't mean much to Kobus and Sandra, as they both wore an expression of well what about it? Some aspirin? See how he is in the morning? That was the first time I was to discover that a game ranger is made of sterner stuff than most. Sandra picked up on my anxiety when I told them that their son was seriously ill, that he needed to be hospitalized immediately. Not knowing the medical facilities in the area outside of Kruger Park, I asked where the closest hospital was and Kobus said in White River. A good decent hospital, I asked in a demanding voice? An increasingly worried Sandra quickly replied Rob Ferreira Hospital in Nelspruit. They said that it would take an hour and a half to get Japie to hospital, so I told to Kobus to make it in an hour, but to go via my chalet. Fortunately, the doctor in me still kept some broad spectrum antibiotics as a carryover from my recent days at Groote Schuur. I shoved them down Japie's throat, then Kobus and I, together with our patient hightailed it to the hospital in Nelspruit. I had been down this road before with my sister Jean, figuratively speaking, of course!

Being a Sunday evening, the hospital was quiet. I knew that time was the issue. Any delays would either mean death or serious irreversible damage. My first thought, perhaps unfairly, was that Rob Ferreira Hospital was no Groote Schuur, so I took control, causing some wide eyes along the way. I ordered a lumbar puncture, which confirmed my initial diagnosis, and that Japie immediately be put in intensive care with a regimen of antibiotics and cortisone. Although he resisted at first, I sent Kobus back to his wife and daughter and volunteered to stay with Japie. I promised that I would contact the camp manager at Pretoriuskop as soon as there was any change or important news to tell them.

Luckily I can sleep sitting up in a chair, so I dozed next to Japie's bed that night. The following morning after Sandra had dropped Helena off at boarding school, she came to the hospital. She became very tearful when she saw Japie in intensive care connected to a drip, and perhaps it was only then that she realized how close her son was to death. Sandra said that Kruger Park had a flatlet in Nelspruit for emergencies and that she would stay there while Japie was in hospital. The hospital was strict on visiting hours so Sandra could only visit for three short periods during the day. It must have been tough on her, waiting for hours on end for those precious visiting periods. I, on the other hand, managed to exert 'doctor privilege' and sat in that same chair for what seemed like an eternity, only vacating it for ablutions and thankfully meeting and talking to some specialists at the hospital. Japie went into a coma for three days, but fortunately pulled through and after two weeks was allowed to go home.

I relate this story because it led to a profound change in my life. When we got back to the De Beer's home, I mentioned that I needed to go and fetch my belongings at the camp and maybe re-book another week's stay. But Kobus and Sandra would have none of that. They were so grateful to have Japie home again, that they insisted that I stay with them as a way of thanking me. Of course, I didn't want to be a burden on them, but they insisted. So I gladly accepted their hospitality, especially since it meant I would probably get a decent meal every day, something I couldn't count on staying on my own!

Despite having slept a lot in that chair next to Japie's bed, I was mentally exhausted, so I went to bed early, and just as well because just before dawn there was an almighty honking noise just outside my window. I woke with a start. Unable to sleep with such a din, I got up, made myself some coffee and wandered out into the backyard to see what the commotion was all about. Egyptian geese! Beyond the fence at the back of the De Beer's house is a waterhole and two geese sitting there seemed intent on telling everybody for miles around that the sun was soon going to rise, and that meant that everyone else should do so too.

With a glow of light appearing from the east on my right, Sandra, a petite softly spoken lady, joined me at the fence. Still in her pink dressing gown, she greeted me and handed me a rusk. She also had a mug of coffee and a rusk. Having lived in South Africa now for nearly 10 years, I had heard of rusks but had never eaten one. They are an Afrikaans speciality, best described as a large rectangular biscuit, often made with buttermilk and other goodies such as nuts and raisins, that is baked, and then placed in a low warm oven to dry until hard and crisp. The secret is to dunk the one end of the rusk into your coffee to soften it, then let it melt away in your mouth and repeat this until it is finished, upon which you wished you had another because they are divine! Then you drink the coffee.

Sandra explained that this was her morning ritual. Get woken by the Egyptian geese alarm clock, and come out to look at the waterhole and the bushveld beyond as dawn broke. As the sun peered over the eastern horizon, the sky slowly lit up, with drops of dew on the veld grass shining like diamonds and the waterhole shimmering in the light. The air was fresh and the atmosphere heavenly. I could also get used to this routine, I thought, except, did the geese have to get me up so early?

As Sandra left to go and make breakfast, she did say that if I were to come out in the dark again that I should wear shoes. Why, I asked? Snakes! That gave me a bit of a jolt, I tell you! A timely reminder that I was in the middle of the bush in the wilds of Africa.

The next week I spent most of my time exploring the area around Pretoriuskop with all its gravel loops, then venturing further afield. As I write this letter, I'm still amazed that this different world exists, a world that I had heard about but never in my wildest imagination thought could be so big, so wild, and so filled with animals and birds of all sizes, shapes and colours. But they're real, going about their lives right in front of me! It has intrigued me no end. Best of all was that I got to see a pride of lions with little cubs. It may sound cliché, but a lion has become my favourite animal. I am stunned at how big they are, especially the pride males, so immensely powerful, and they walk around with regal aloofness as if they know they're the king of the beasts. Love them!

At the end of that week we had a braai in the back garden. I mentioned earlier that a braai is the same as a barbecue, except it's not. To explain, in South Africa braais are a big deal, especially amongst Afrikaners. In fact, there is a certain ritual about it, one with social norms. For starters there is always the master of the braai, in our case Kobus. Wood is the fuel of choice, and while Japie and I may have gathered the firewood, which is plentiful in the park, Kobus was the one who arranged the wood in pyramid form on a plough dish on legs and lit the fire. The activities around the fire are a man thing, the main activity being drinking and shooting the breeze, watching the fire burn brightly before turning into hot coals. And the choice of drink in the bush is beer.

Looking straight out from the De Beer's property, there are several marula trees growing in the bushveld before the land becomes covered with silver cluster-leaf trees to the east. But it is from these marula trees that Kobus collects small round fruit which ripens from green to yellow in the summer. Inside the thick skin is a hard nut surrounded by a white, juicy flesh that has a unique tangy flavour that Sandra uses to make juices, jams, jellies and marula pie. Kobus has other ideas. In his case the choice of drink in the bush is not just any beer, but his homemade marula beer. And lots of it!

The braai master will check on the fire and decide when the coals are ready to cook the meat. Meat! Africans, black and white, love their meat! Typically, this includes steak which may be dressed in a cream and garlic sauce, racks of spareribs, lamb or venison chops, sosaties which are generally made of cubes of lamb, beef, chicken, dried apricots, red onions and mixed peppers, all skewered together on a stick, and, of course, boerewors which is a long sausage made of ground up meat and spices, an Afrikaans speciality. All is grilled over glowing coals at the pace of the braai master

While the men do their thing around the fire, the women are in the kitchen preparing pap, which is a type of crumbed porridge smothered with tomato and onion sauce, plus they conjure up an array of tasty salads and vegetables. And, of course, desserts such as milktart and koeksisters.

Then everyone gets together outside to eat and drink, a social occasion lasting well into the night. That is a braai!

It was a chilly late winter evening as we tucked into our fare, feeling cosy as we gathered around the fire pit. The De Beer family had been wonderful hosts. As I looked at the four of them, all with the same honey brown hair, Sandra's with natural auburn streaks that glowed in the sunlight and always worn in a low French plait, the mother and children with the same sallow skin, Kobus with more of a tanned and weathered hide due to long hours spent in the sun, I thought to myself that they were a good family. But I felt I had overstayed my welcome and mentioned that it was time to move on.

Sandra asked me where I was going and I said that I had so enjoyed Kruger Park that I planned to stay longer and visit all the other camps. Of course, curiosity got the better of them and it was Helena who asked about my job, or the lack of one. I was reluctant to say much about my past, but eventually they pried it out of me and I told them about Anna's recent passing and that I had decided to give up medicine and just get in my car and see where it took me.

Well, that opened up a lively response, Kobus and Sandra saying that there was no better place to heal than Kruger Park. It was balm for the soul, they said, and I knew from the last week that there couldn't have been truer words spoken. And to heal, they said, it would best happen if they could look after me. That, of course, took me by surprise. They insisted that I stay with them for as long as it took me to get over Anna. At first, I wondered if it was because I had helped Japie in his moment of crisis, but the longer we chatted the more it became obvious that they really wanted to help out a person who was truly lost. Even Japie and Helena begged me to stay. And stay I did!

The prospect excited me, so much so that I dared to ask Kobus a big favour. I knew so little about nature and wildlife that I wanted to learn from the master, so I asked if I could accompany him when he went to work. 'You would be most welcome, my friend,' he replied. As he laid out some ground rules, that I was a guest and not an employee, that I must remain in the vehicle at all times, he seemed to be as excited as I was at the prospect.

And so began a new chapter in my life. Never in all my growing up years going to med school or working at Groote Schuur, would I have believed that I would end up living amongst wild animals in Kruger Park.

My lifelong night owl tendencies came to a sudden end as my Egyptian geese alarm clock changed me into an 'early to bed, early to rise' person. My early morning coffee and rusk moments with Sandra became our daily routine. Then it was off to work with Kobus. How can I even begin to describe a game ranger's work? The easy answer is a bit of everything. There is a standing joke amongst game rangers that if a problem arises in their section, the stock answer from the chief ranger is, 'Sort it out!'

And sort it out we did. Problems are always arising and Kobus is always sorting them out. And that is on top of all the normal duties, the main one being preserving the vegetation, for without vegetation there would be no herbivores, and without herbivores there would be no carnivores. And to preserve vegetation, a game ranger needs to constantly monitor those two elements — water and fire. In addition, he does game census, culling, relocation of animals, controlling disease, anti-poaching patrols, freeing animals from snares, fighting raging bush fires — which I can attest to is hell on earth — and even finding tourists that have gone missing. And all this amongst the wildest of animals, where close encounters with death are routine.

As we travelled in his bakkie from one corner of his section to another, I would pepper Kobus with questions, eager to learn as much as I could. Some of the questions in the beginning must have seemed trivial such as, 'Aren't you scared of being attacked by a lion or an elephant?' But Kobus was a good and patient teacher, even if some questions seemed plain dumb. After only a few weeks, all the rules he'd outlined at the start were broken, and I was not the guilty one. If we came across some spoor that he needed to track, rather than leave me sitting bored in his bakkie, he would insist I join him and his field rangers, and along the way he taught me a lot. I sincerely believe that if he weren't a game ranger he would make an excellent teacher.

A few weeks later, we were back in his bakkie after having just greased the windmill at Shitlhave dam. 'Before we break the rules again, perhaps I should prime you on what to do in certain potentially perilous situations,' Kobus said, reflectively.

So as we sat sipping coffee poured from a Thermos, I questioned him about some scenarios that had been concerning me. 'What happens if we come upon a lion?' I asked.

'Never run,' Kobus replied. 'Running will kick in an instinct for it to charge you.'

Okay, I thought, but had to ask, 'What happens if it does charge?'

'It will be a mock charge. Stand your ground and it will back off.'

'But what if it's a real charge?'

'That is not likely to happen unless it's a lioness with cubs that feels under threat.'

The words 'not likely' did not go down too well with me, so I asked, 'What if it does happen?'

'It's never happened in all my time as a game ranger, but if it did, I'd shoot it.'

'But I don't have a gun,' I protested.

'There is a maxim in the bush,' Kobus said, 'that it is best to stick close to the person who does have the gun.'

This information was getting my adrenalin going as my imagination ran wild. When I first met Kobus I had noticed deep scars on both his left arm and leg. I had some concern for my own wellbeing given that I now accompanied him on his daily work, so I asked him what had caused those scars. Kobus dismissed them as just an honour badge received in the line of duty. He obviously didn't want to talk about them.

I asked my next question. 'What if an elephant charges?'

'If it flaps its ears, raises its trunk and trumpets, then it's a mock charge.'

'And?'

'You stand your ground and shout at it.'

'That's it?'

'Yes.'

'So how will I know if it's a real charge?'

'Its ears will be flat against its head, the trunk coiled under its chest and it will be silent.'

'And what do you do then?'

'Get the bloody hell out of there.'

'And if you can't?'

'Then you shoot it.'

'And if you don't have a gun you stick close to the person who does have one, right?'

'You're learning fast,' beamed Kobus as he took a sip of his coffee.

'Buffalo?'

'Mostly they're fine, but the daggaboys are cranky and act like they have a permanent headache, so it's best you steer clear of them.'

'What's a daggaboy?'

'Old bulls that have left the herd, often in two's and three's but sometimes alone.'

'And what do you do if they charge?'

Kobus repeated that it is best to steer clear of them.

'Rhino?'

'The white rhino are fine. It's the black rhino that's the problem. They are demented and run all over the place when charging, changing direction as if trying to escape a swarm of bees buzzing inside their heads.'

'So what happens if one charges?'

'We don't have many black rhino.'

That, of course, didn't satisfy me, so I repeated the question.

Kobus replied, 'Climb a tree.'

'Okay, but what if there is no tree?'

'Then you climb the stairway to heaven!' chuckled Kobus.

After allowing Kobus his moment of humour, I continued my questions. 'Snakes?'

'All except one snake will retreat so there is no problem there.'

Of course my thoughts immediately turned to the one that doesn't retreat, so I asked Kobus about it.

'The puff adder,' Kobus replied. 'He's a lazy old sod.'

'And what do I do about it?'

'You wear boots and keep your eyes open.'

'What about hippo?'

'They feed on vegetation out of the water, often covering huge distances, but they feed at night so that shouldn't be a problem. But if ever you do come across one, don't get between it and the water or you will die.' Kobus said that last part emphatically. He then told me that more people are killed in Africa by hippos than by any other animal.

'So a hippo is top of the list to look out for?'

'No. It's the mosquito!'

'Really?'

'Yes!'

Kobus then told me that all animals have an instinctive fear of man and will retreat if allowed to. Only if they feel threatened will they attack, especially when they have young ones. So the key is to find a way to defuse the situation and retreat.

'Does a crocodile have an instinctive fear of man?' I asked.

'No.'

And?'

'Don't get too close.'

Okay, I thought, with a lot of apprehension.

I remarked to Kobus that in the short period I had been with him, I was aware that killing a number of animals was all part of a game ranger's work. Culling, animals that are injured by snares or poaching that have no chance of recovery, and even animals that may have become a threat to tourists or workers, so I asked if he'd ever had to shoot an animal in self-defence. And he said no. I found that quite remarkable, because game rangers often find themselves in very tense and tenuous circumstances. It is simply a part of their daily lives in the work they do. Many bear the result of encounters in the form of scars, but I did find out that in the history of Kruger Park very few had died as a result of a dangerous encounter.

With that lesson over, I continued asking Kobus questions over the next few weeks and the good teacher patiently taught me the ways of the bush. At first, the lessons were answers to rather simple questions such as what is the reason that vultures are circling above in the sky. And he explained that there could be a kill on the ground, therefore to look out for predators in the vicinity, but they could be catching thermals looking for a carcass. It soon dawned on me that this was a world of animals working according to their ways and the black and white answers demanded by humans were not always a given.

'What's the meaning of monkeys squawking in a tree?' I asked. Now, I'm not an unintelligent person, so when Kobus looked at me, askance, I felt like I had let my teacher down. But he patiently explained that it was a warning call. A predator was most likely walking past and it would be a good idea to watch which way the monkeys turned their faces over the next few minutes to see in which direction the predator was moving. That seemed logical which prompted me to add that I had noticed impala doing the same thing, all barking in the same direction giving an alarm call. The slight look of disdain changed to one of satisfaction. The student was learning!

Kobus's lessons got harder. Placing one's finger into elephant dung to test the temperature to see how far away the herd may be. Checking the trunk of trees for scratch marks made by a lion using it to sharpen its claws before going on a hunt. Then at the site of the kill, like a forensic detective, Kobus would explain from the pug marks exactly how the kill went down.

There was a lot that Kobus could not teach me because it quickly dawned on me that, through vast experience, game rangers develop an innate ability to read the bush, stuff that could not be taught, but a necessity if the game rangers were to last until retirement. It puzzled me how Kobus could look into the distance and amongst the camouflage of low-lying clouds see the smoke of a fire starting. And I was okay with that because I felt confident that over time I might, too, develop that same skill.

Standing next to Kobus's bakkie, I looked to Shitlhave dam in front of us. A hippo snorted. A crocodile lay on the far bank sunning itself. And from a tree on my left came the call of a fish eagle, the evocative bird call of Africa. Below the tree I spotted some movement. I nudged Kobus to look at what I had seen. A cheetah! The fastest animal on the planet! From its starting blocks it burst into blinding speed towards the water's edge where a warthog was kneeling down eating short scrubs of vegetation. It was all over in a blur and a squeal. Not only had I seen my first cheetah but also my first kill. I had mixed feelings, of course, but I knew about the circle of life in the wild.

There were many occasions when I could not accompany Kobus. Often he would have meetings at Kruger Park's headquarters in Skukuza, or he would be away for days and even weeks at a time on some project such as an anti-poaching campaign. In those times, I would often sit in the garden and absorb the surrounding nature, admiring the stunning bird life and also the smaller creatures. Lizards, chameleons, butterflies, squirrels, tortoises.

A humorous incident occurred the first day I spent on the two acre property. While exploring, I came across a black man working in the vegetable garden. I shook his hand in what appears to be a traditional African handshake — a three step action where you clasp someone's hand in the traditional handshake as in England, followed by locking thumbs while still clasping hands with your thumbs pointed upwards, and back to the traditional English handshake, all done in a smooth action — and introduced myself as Michael. The only thing he said was the word 'problem'. So I reasoned that I had not quite mastered the handshake and offered my hand again. But he looked confused and went about his gardening business. Later I mentioned this incident to Sandra, and she giggled before explaining that his name is Problem. She told me that many of the indigenous Africans have their normal African name and also what they call a European name, often alluding to the circumstances in which they were born. For example, Problem's mother may have had a difficult time giving birth, hence the naming of her child Problem. He, as with many other Africans in the area, comes from a tribe called the Shangaan people and speak Tsonga. To make life easier for me, I have decided that I need to become multilingual and learn both Afrikaans and Tsonga.

Dogs are a big part of a game ranger's life. Their value is endless, but apart from companionship they are excellent at sniffing tracks of poachers and also giving warning barks when they sense danger before a human can. The De Beers have a Rhodesian Ridgeback called Wagter which means watchman. Sometimes Kobus takes Wagter with him, but on occasions when he doesn't, I play with him in the garden. I have also observed how well-trained he is. Kobus and Sandra have taught him not to bother the general game that passes the property, but to give warning barks when there is an element of danger such as a predator or a snake. And he fiercely protects the fruit trees from troops of baboons and monkeys.

When Kobus was away, I would always accompany Sandra on a late afternoon walk in the bushveld, often with Wagter if he was not on duty. Sandra goes on these walks even if I am not there which I think is pretty brave of her. Late afternoon is a beautiful time in the bushveld, known as the golden hour when the sun casts its light from a low angle to make everything look golden. I noticed that Sandra always carried a gun, which made sense since we were out in the wilds of Africa, sometimes it would be a rifle but sometimes a hand gun. I never questioned why the difference. Guns are not my thing.

On these walks I found Sandra to be a beautiful human being. Apparently she was a city girl, visited the park as a tourist, had a puncture which Kobus helped to fix, and given her state of anxiety he invited her into his home, and she never left. At 35 years old she is a decade younger than Kobus and, given that she is softly spoken and petite, has adapted so well to the way of life in Kruger Park. In her spare time Sandra paints beautiful watercolours of the wildlife and picturesque landscapes of Kruger Park, many of which adorn the walls of their house. Game rangers are special, but so are the wives who create manicured gardens, sew and weave and decorate their homes with exquisite things, grow vegetables and fruit trees, make jams and jellies out of every type of edible wild fruit and berries, raise children under what can only be considered some of the most trying of conditions where snakes and scorpions in the house and even in the bed are often encountered, but most of all they are the stable rock behind a man who has dedicated his life to conservation in a place that is not for the faint-hearted.

On one of these walks, once I had got to know Sandra quite well, I asked about the scars on Kobus's left arm and leg, and mentioned that he had dismissed it as nothing serious and seemed unwilling to talk about it.

Following is Sandra's story:

'Game rangers are a different breed. The potential for mortal danger is ever present, but for them it is all in a day's work. In this instance, a lioness had been caught in a snare on the eastern border of Kruger Park, down towards the Crocodile River. Kobus learned from the game ranger in the Crocodile Bridge section of the park that the lioness had broken free of the snare and, given that lions heal quite quickly from their wounds, had decided to take a 'wait and see' approach. And the wound did heal. But over the next few weeks the lioness started losing condition, so the section ranger and a few field rangers decided to investigate and possibly anaesthetize her to assess the problem. Kruger Park has a policy of only intervening if man has caused the problem, otherwise they let nature take its course. Being a good shot, Kobus offered to help. Unfortunately the lioness had taken to spending most of its time amongst the reeds of the Crocodile River. And reeds and wild animals do not make a great combination for the safety of humans.'

I interrupted, telling Sandra that even with my inexperience I had already concluded that!

Sandra continued with her story:

'The Crocodile Bridge ranger and his field rangers were armed, but Kobus had only a dart gun to anaesthetize the lioness. They tracked her spoor to the reeds, but it was suicide to go in, so they camped the night nearby. Kobus told me that he could hear growls all night, distress growls. The following day they got sight of her in reeds that were less dense but Kobus maintained that the lioness was facing him head on, so he could not get a clear shot. She was clearly agitated, but given that he may not get another chance, Kobus indicated to the other rangers that they keep her focus while he circled around to get a better shot. But not everything in the bush goes to plan. After growling at the rangers she backed off and ran, unfortunately straight through the reeds and into Kobus. Despite her poor condition, the Crocodile Bridge game ranger told me that she threw Kobus around like a rag doll. There was no way they could shoot the lioness without putting Kobus in serious danger, so they fired shots in the air and shouted at the lioness. Eventually she let go and ran off. But Kobus was seriously mauled and the danger with a lion bite is sepsis.'

I'll add in here that Sandra then looked somewhat sheepish, explaining sepsis to a doctor, but truth be told game rangers and their wives probably know far more about it than we doctors do.

Back to Sandra's account:

'Kobus was rushed to hospital where the wounds were scrubbed clean and left open, but unfortunately infection set in. Despite strong antibiotics my husband went into a coma and a decision had to be made whether to amputate both his arm and leg. I insisted that they did not because it would be the death of him if he could no longer work as a game ranger. Thankfully, after several rounds of a combination of scrubbing, debriding infected flesh and antibiotics, Kobus eventually turned the corner and started to heal. With the loss of muscle tissue there was a fear that he may not be able to walk again, but he is made of stern stuff, and he pulled through, though not without the slight limp he has.'

I know that Kobus is a strong man, both physically and mentally, but even I was surprised when Sandra said that the first question he asked when he came out of his coma was how the lioness was doing!

Of course, having been told this story, I also wanted to know what had happened to the lioness. Sandra said that the Crocodile Bridge ranger had managed to dart her and discovered that the wire snare had pulled so deep around her throat that the flesh had started to heal around it, which is why they originally thought she was on the mend, but the wire was causing her difficulty in swallowing, so she wasn't getting enough nutrition, hence the loss of condition. But they managed to save her.

Why wouldn't Kobus tell me, I asked Sandra? She again explained that game rangers are a different breed. Despite being paid a pittance, they have a calling to protect and preserve their section of the park and, despite all the hardships, they see it as their duty — not heroics. Do you see him as a hero, I asked? Of course, replied Sandra. It would have been easy to just shoot the lioness. After all, there are a lot more of them. But they go beyond the call of duty. If the injury is caused by man, there is a deep sense in game rangers to right the injustice. Protect and preserve.

On our walks together, Sandra also taught me a lot. Different things from what Kobus taught me. To the east of the De Beer's house is a valley dominated by silver cluster-leaf trees, her favourite place to walk. Sandra showed me that Kruger Park is not just about the big animals. She educated me about the flora of Kruger, reminding me too how the landscape had changed from the golden colours in winter when I first arrived to the lush green foliage of summer. Over the months we witnessed many species of animals and it is the small ones that fascinate Sandra. Only once since we started on our walks together did we have an incident which according to her was mild, but very scary for me! Although Wagter issued a sharp bark, at first we didn't see anything. Then a lone elephant bull emerged from behind a bush ambling its way straight towards us. Sandra and I moved steadily out of its way but as it passed us some 50 metres away, it turned to face us and started flapping its ears, raised its trunk and trumpeted. It was as awesome as it was scary. My heart was thumping but Sandra stood still. I guess she remembered better than me the advice Kobus had given us. It charged a few paces, then backed off, but was still not pleased. Sandra stood her ground, so I decided that if she could do it, so could I, though not without adrenalin coursing through my veins. Something made me look at which firearm Sandra had brought that day and it was the hand gun! That didn't help my heart rate. The elephant charged a little further, so Sandra clapped her hands and shouted at the ever growing beast. I know that animals have a great sense of hearing, but I was not sure that her timid sounding voice was going to have much impact in warding off a charging elephant, so I bellowed, upon which the bull got the message that we were not looking for trouble but also didn't want to be charged at, and he trundled off. A very calm Sandra congratulated me and said that Kobus had taught me well!

The Pretoriuskop area of Kruger Park has a special beauty with enchanting koppies that dot the undulating landscapes. A koppie, by the way, is a large rocky outcrop which Mother Nature has decorated with a myriad of boulders and rocks, forming caves and crevices, and ledges and sheer faces, with little indentations where water pools and provides succour for a variety of trees and shrubs. Across the land are trees and grasslands and waterholes, a landscape that transforms with the different seasons and the ever-changing shades due to the angle of the sun from dawn to dusk. All of this makes for a beautiful territory to explore. And explore we did. Japie and Helena attended boarding school during the week in Nelspruit, but on weekends we'd all go camping, fishing and my favourite which is climbing to the top of a koppie to spend a lazy day gazing over the vast African land below in a world of complete freedom. Special times!

Two weeks before Christmas, we were having a braai — yes, another one — and I thanked Kobus and Sandra for their wonderful hospitality and especially for the recommendation that Kruger Park would be the cure for my deep sadness at the loss of Anna. Of course, I am still sad, but Kruger Park had soothed my soul, and I mentioned that I wanted to live permanently in the park but that I needed a purpose. Kobus immediately said that I should apply to become a game ranger.

'But that would mean having to shoot an animal,' I said.

'Yes,' he replied.

'But I can't do that!'

'Then you can't become a game ranger,' he said.

So I was at a loss.

A week before Christmas, Kobus and Sandra went off to Skukuza for the annual game ranger's party. I stayed behind and chose to sit outside with several bottles of Kobus's famous marula beer. It was a beautiful summer's day, the trees full of foliage and the wild flowers in bloom. Oddly, in a place that can suddenly wreak such terror when a predator makes a kill, it very quickly settles down to a most peaceful paradise that makes one think of aeons ago. In the mid-afternoon an elephant came by, placed its head against a marula tree and shook it violently to cause its ripened fruit to drop to the ground, creating a feast for the huge tusker. As the sun set in the west I could see in the distance a troop of baboons settling down for the night in a Jackalberry tree with much muttering and quarrelling as they chose their spots for the night. After the sun goes down in Africa, the twilight hangs in the air for a while, then suddenly darkness falls and the night creatures come alive with their own sounds. As I swigged from another bottle of marula beer, an eerie cackle of a lone hyena sounded and lingered in the air, signalling that the night belonged to the predators.

From the staff village in the distance I heard an amazing chorus of harmonious singing as only Africans can perform, accompanied by the rhythmic beating of tribal drums. They too, were having an end of year party, partaking of much jabula which is their homemade beer, also a Tsonga term that suggests a state of happiness. There was much jabula drunk that night and much happiness in the air!

Then late at night, while sitting under a chandelier of stars, suddenly I heard it. The roar of a lion. A roar so loud and so close that I felt it vibrating deep in my stomach. The true sound of Africa! Yes, this was Africa at its finest and I knew my heart belonged in this special place called Kruger Park.

The problem? I need a purpose.

All my love, Michael.

Scarlett

Sitting in the stands watching Robin doing time trials with Graham timing her, Scarlett did not require a stopwatch to know how fast Robin was swimming. It was as if after all her own years of training, she had a built-in timer. Lately, Robin's times had been a bit slower than usual. Scarlett brought this to the coach's attention.

'Missy, you should know better than anyone that as you grow there is an upward curve to getting faster times but that the graph is cyclical.'

Scarlett nodded in agreement.

Graham continued, 'There could be any number of reasons. Growth spurts. Menstruation. I would relax if I were you.'

But after several more weeks of slower time trials, as Robin got out of the water at the end of a session, Scarlett asked her daughter, 'How are you feeling, Sweetie?'

'Pruney!'

Pruney was an inside joke amongst swimmers, a reference made to how their skin wrinkled to resemble a prune. As with Scarlett, it was a good feeling for Robin, affirmation that she had been working hard.

§

That evening after Robin had gone to bed, Scarlett mentioned the slower times to Paul.

'What has Graham said?'

'Oh, the usual. A wavy upward progression. Having to adjust to a growing body.'

'Then why do you doubt him?'

'I don't,' stumbled Scarlett, before saying, 'but Robin looks like she's swimming tired.'

'Didn't we all go through periods like that?'

'I suppose so.'

§

Over the next few months Robin's times got slower, at a rate that was hardly noticeable to those who were not well versed in swimming.

One day when Robin exited the pool, Scarlett again asked her daughter how she was feeling.

'Fine, Mom. Why do you ask?'

'No reason.'

'Mom?' Robin prompted. 'Tell me.'

'It's just that your times are a little slow and you look a bit tired.'

'I'm fine. And don't you worry, I'll get those times down, especially with nationals coming.'

Pointing to her daughter's shin, Scarlett asked, 'Where did you get that bruise from?'

'The other day, dumb ol' me slipped and fell when climbing out the pool.'

§

When more bruises appeared, Scarlett decided to take a sample of blood to be tested.

As she inserted the syringe into Robin's vein on the inside of her elbow, Robin said rather testily, 'I know you're a doctor, Mom, but that doesn't give you the right to treat me like a guinea pig.'

'It's just a routine check,' Scarlett answered, though she knew differently. 'It's always good to check one's blood when growing up, especially if one is training to be an athlete. You've been looking tired lately so perhaps you're in need of a vitamin supplement.

§

Scarlett handed the vial of blood to the pathology lab at the Red Cross War Memorial Children's Hospital and waited anxiously for the results. They came two days later.

A lab technician knocked on Scarlett's office door, entered and announced, 'Dr Rhodes, your blood test results are back.'

'And?' asked Scarlett, anxious, her heart pounding.

'It's best you have a look at them.'

The technician handed over a sealed envelope and left the office.

Her hands trembling, Scarlett opened the envelope and quickly scanned the results. What she had feared most was true. Robin had leukemia!

§

Scarlett asked a fellow doctor to cover for her and drove over to Paul's practice. She waited patiently for Paul to finish with his patient, then slipped into his consulting room.

'Darling, why're you here? And you've been crying! What's the matter?' asked Paul.

Scarlett handed the blood test results to Paul and said in a very shaky voice, 'Robin has leukemia.'

Paul studied the results before taking his wife into his arms.

'It's not the death sentence it once was,' Paul consoled her.

'It's acute myeloid leukemia, Paul. Chances of recovery from that variant are small.'

'Maybe. But we'll get her the best treatment possible. And that, my dear, is right where you work. Robin's a strong kid. Just like you were. If anyone is to pull through, it will be her.'

Scarlett broke down, then sobbing into the crook of Paul's neck, she stutteringly questioned, 'Why does it have to be Robin? Why my precious darling?'

1st January 1979

Dear Scarlett,

I got sick! Actually, I died! Well, this is not a ghost writing to you, so I suppose that is hyperbole, but only a little.

I never get sick, not even a cold or flu. In fact, the last I can recall any medical intervention on my behalf, was my pathetic attempt at trying to stitch my eyebrow together in front of a mirror the first day that I laid eyes on you. But all that changed. It was as if all the illnesses that a normal person might endure over the years accumulated and attacked me in one cataclysmic storm.

Late February, I had been feeling a bit off colour for a couple of days, but still managed to go out with Kobus, while I mulled over what my purpose in life ought to be. One particular evening I went to bed a little earlier than usual and soon started to get the chills. Although I have never had flu, I am obviously aware of the symptoms and concluded that this was what I was succumbing to. Even though it was a hot summer's night, the chills worsened as the hours passed, so I started scrounging around the house for extra blankets, careful not to wake the De Beer family who by that stage had also gone to bed. Despite feeling weighed down by a ton of blankets, the cold shivers worsened, my teeth started chattering, so I curled up into a ball to try to build up some heat. I didn't think it was possible but I got even colder, as if I lay naked in the snow in the Antarctica. Not only that, I felt as if I had frozen solid because at some stage I was desperate to go to the loo but my limbs wouldn't move. It was a long night but in the early hours I started feeling quite a bit better, so much so that by morning I was up and watching the sun rise with Sandra at my side, enjoying our coffee and rusks. That was bizarre, I thought, but then forgot about it and got ready to go out for the day with Kobus.

When we came home that evening I was feeling a little weak, probably from the lack of sleep the previous night, so I thought, and went to go and lie down. When supper was ready and I had not appeared, Sandra told me that she popped into my bedroom and found me under a mountain of blankets, my face was blue, my teeth chattering and my limbs shaking uncontrollably. I could barely speak but somehow managed to say in a shaky voice, 'Flu.'

After what seemed like an eternity, the chills subsided but my temperature rose quickly to a burning fever. My head felt like it was being crushed by a ton of bricks. I also had the urge to vomit but without having eaten anything since breakfast there was nothing to come out. I felt desperately thirsty. Sandra brought me a glass of water but I couldn't lift my head to sip it as the ton of bricks just wouldn't allow me to move my head, so excruciating was the pain.

Perhaps not wanting to question a doctor's diagnosis of flu, Sandra waited several more hours before asking me if I was sure it was the flu. I couldn't answer. Only towards the following morning did the rampant fever abate but it was followed by profuse sweating. I managed to sit up in bed feeling somewhat better, when I heard Sandra say to Kobus just outside my bedroom that she was convinced that I had malaria, that I was seriously ill and that I needed to get to hospital immediately. Despite being drenched in sweat, I still felt it was a bad dose of flu and that the worst was over. But a determined Sandra was adamant and so the same trip to Rob Ferreira Hospital in Nelspruit that was done just six months ago for Japie was now done on my behalf.

Never doubt a game ranger's wife! A blood smear test indicated malaria, and not just any malaria, so without getting too technical it was the form of the disease known as pernicious malaria. In other words, the bad one!

I was put on treatment immediately but unfortunately did not respond, so the doctors then administered chloroquine intravenously. The disease plays out in cycles of chills, then fever, then profuse sweating. And this process repeats itself over and over again, if you're lucky, otherwise you die. Sandra told me that I would shiver so violently that she would pile up the blankets, put an oxygen mask over my face and then lean over me because she was worried that I would land up on the floor. After a few hours, the next stage would begin. The hot stage. Apparently my temperature would rocket sky-high, the ton of bricks on my head would return and I would go in and out of delirium, the stage lasting so long that Sandra saw resignation in my eyes indicating that I no longer had it in me to fight for my life. Then the third stage. The nice stage I can say in retrospect. A stage when you perspire so heavily that you feel as if you are drowning in sodden bedclothes. But at least I felt more amongst the living than the dead. An interlude, too, to sip on water to replenish what I had lost through perspiration. But the longer that stage plays out, the more it dawns on you that the chills stage is soon coming again and fear sets in. And so this process repeated over and over again for the next four days until finally the medication got a hold over those darn parasites.

But the ordeal was not over. I battled with kidney failure caused by a blockage of capillaries by parasitised red blood cells and if that was not enough a side effect of chloroquine is insomnia. By that stage I was physically and mentally exhausted, at my absolute limit, but could not sleep. And lying awake, I kept reliving the nightmare of the past week. It made those 18 hour day shifts at Groote Schuur feel like a walk in the park.

So, that was malaria! I wouldn't wish it on my worst enemy. I was in hospital for 10 days and during that time Sandra never left my side. It was much harder for her than for me when I had stayed with Japie six months earlier. I distinctly recall Sandra saying that I was lucky to be able to easily sleep in a chair because it was something she found impossible to do!

I arrived back at the De Beer's home weak and having lost a lot of weight, but good ol' Sandra's cooking and nursing got me back in ship shape condition and after two weeks I was almost back to my old self. And it was about that time that Kobus berated me, saying that I call myself a doctor, yet I failed to apply the dictum that in the bush influenza is malaria until proven otherwise. I asked Kobus if he'd ever had malaria, and he said no. When I asked him why not he replied that it was due to his homemade beer! 'With all that alcohol,' he said, 'I think a mosquito would be too drunk to pass malaria on to me!' I obviously don't believe in Kobus's malaria remedy, but I have to confess that I now drink quite a lot of his marula beer! After his scold, Kobus told me that he was very happy to have me back home. I was touched that he and Sandra regarded me as part of the family and believed that their home was also my home.

Despite their insistence, I was not sure how long I could carry on staying with them without discovering my direction in life. But all that changed in an instant when a few days later Kobus came home late in the evening and said to me, 'You've had the bush fright, now you can experience the bush flight.' Of course, I didn't understand what he meant until he explained that a tourist had got lost and despite the rangers checking every road in the area, they had still not located the tourist's vehicle. So early the following morning a pilot for the park was going to fly a helicopter to the Pretoriuskop area in a search and rescue mission, and I was invited to join him.

That night I was like an overexcited kid going to bed on Christmas Eve, unable to sleep and wishing time away. I had never flown in a helicopter. But to fly over Kruger Park would be stunning, to see the great wilderness that I had travelled over and over by car but this time from the air.

It was late summer so the sun still rose early, but I was ready long before sunrise. The helicopter arrived just as the sun rose. Kobus introduced me to the pilot whom he called Captain. That was it, no other name for him. I climbed into the helicopter with what felt like champagne bubbling through my veins. Kobus was to travel in his bakkie to monitor operations on the ground, but we would be in radio contact.

As we lifted off the ground the sensation was thrilling, especially as the sun was peering over the horizon and casting its early morning rays over the bushveld. We quickly covered the main roads around Pretoriuskop. There are many gravel patrol roads that are meant to be used by game rangers only, a rule that is sometimes abused by tourists wilfully or in error, so we covered those too. That took longer because there are a lot of patrol roads allowing the game ranger to access as many parts of his section as possible. We covered all of them except one. But more about that in a moment. Captain then said that it was possible that the tourist had travelled outside the Pretoriuskop section. However, based on the information given by the tourist's wife who had stayed back in camp, her husband was just going for an afternoon drive around the Faye loop, about a 12 kilometre gravel circular road that starts and ends near the camp. Captain felt that it was best to fly in grid sections over that area before extending outside the Pretoriuskop section of the park. And so we crisscrossed the Faye loop area several times with no luck. We were just about to go back south on the next stage of the grid when, very close to camp, I spotted a vehicle in an area I knew well, the valley where Sandra and I had walked so often, the valley dominated by silver cluster-leaf trees.

Captain radioed Kobus about our find, located a suitable landing spot which was not easy given the terrain and trees, and expertly landed the helicopter. The tourist's vehicle was on the one patrol road we had not previously checked, probably borne out of logic that it was so close to camp that the occupant could have just walked back home if his vehicle had a puncture or he'd run out of fuel. However, when we came upon his car there was nobody in it. Just then Kobus arrived in his bakkie and no sooner had he stopped when we heard someone shouting in the distance. There was a man sitting at the base of a silver cluster-leaf tree, shouting and waving.

It turned out that he had indeed taken the wrong road, wilfully or not Kobus did not question, and had run out of fuel. He sensed camp was close by and with darkness approaching he started running in that direction, slipped on a rock and fell. He tried to get up but could not exert any weight on his left leg and he thought he may have twisted his ankle. Unable to walk he started dragging himself towards camp, but when it got dark he decided it would be safer to lean up against a tree and spend the night there. He appeared to be in shock — from his injury, the fear of spending a night surrounded by predators that would have seen him as easy prey, and a reaction to being saved. I did a quick examination and said that in my opinion he had most likely broken his leg but that he needed X-rays for confirmation.

A discussion took place between Kobus and Captain and they decided to fly him to Rob Ferreira Hospital in Nelspruit, asking if I would accompany the patient on the flight. What a dumb question! Yes, I had recently been a patient myself at that hospital but my medical training and the chance to fly again in the helicopter overcame any memories of my bad experience. It turned out that he did have a compound fracture of his left leg, just below the knee, one that would require a metal plate, so he would be in hospital for a couple of days.

So what changed in my life? The helicopter! Yes, I had performed every possible kind of surgery in the trauma unit, where the life of the patient was literally in my hands, but nothing gave me the adrenalin rush of flying in a helicopter, albeit only as a passenger. On the way back to Pretoriuskop Camp, I asked Captain a thousand questions about flying. When over Kruger Park space, possibly sensing my newfound interest in helicopter flying, Captain let me take over the controls for just a few minutes. I mentioned a moment ago that nothing before had given me the adrenalin rush of flying in a helicopter. Update. Change flying in a helicopter to actually flying a helicopter!

When I got back to the De Beers, I was giddy with excitement. But nobody was home. The time dragged until Kobus and then Sandra returned. But I waited until supper to tell them about my breakthrough! In fact, the excitement written on my face must have been so palpable that they asked me what had happened that day to make me look like I had found the Kruger Millions!

I had found my purpose! I knew with absolute certainty what I wanted to do, and that was to become a helicopter pilot. I explained that I had decided to rent a flat in Nelspruit, find an instructor and take flying lessons for the next three months, every day, in fact several times a day. Both looked quite surprised but happy for me that I had found my calling. And both asked if I would be back, with pleading in their eyes. I promised that I would because I had a plan!

My Ford Anglia had given up the ghost, so the following day Sandra drove me to Nelspruit in hers, which I might add was not far from joining mine in the Ford Anglia afterlife. I rented a flat, bought myself a brand-new Golf Mk1 car, contacted the helicopter flying instructor recommended by Captain, and set about learning to fly one with the same zest I had when studying to become a surgeon. The flying instructor must have thought he had struck gold, not only due to the number of lessons I demanded but also because I was a very eager student.

After completing my commercial licence, I drove back to the De Beer's home and received a warm welcome. Firstly, a congratulations on my new car and then a demand to know what had transpired in the three months that I was away.

Sitting in the lounge with a welcome cup of tea in my hand, we had a small disagreement when I told them that the car was a gift for all their hospitality, my way of thanking Kobus, Sandra and the children. At first, they refused to accept it, saying that it had been a pleasure having me to stay. To which I replied that it also gave me a great pleasure to gift them the car and would not take no for an answer! Except in the case of my beloved wife, Anna, I can be quite stubborn in these types of arguments and I eventually got my way!

My next news was that I was now a qualified helicopter pilot with a commercial licence. Curiously, Kobus asked me why commercial, to which I replied that I wanted to work in Kruger Park as a helicopter pilot. There was a stunned silence.

'But,' said Kobus, 'we already have two pilots for the two helicopters that we own.'

'I know, I know,' I said, 'but when I flew with Captain three months ago he told me that there was such an overload of work that they could not keep up.'

Let me explain that Kobus would have been absolutely thrilled for me to join the team of pilots, but he was merely pointing out the practicalities, the biggest being that he didn't think there would be enough in the budget for an extra pilot especially when the park only possessed two helicopters.

And here is where I need to explain something to you that I have never mentioned before. You may have wondered how on a pittance of a salary earned at a state hospital, I could afford some of the things I have done while living in South Africa. The honeymoon, living in an upmarket apartment, holidays abroad. My parents are both professors at the University of Cambridge and earn very good salaries and, while they are very well off, I wouldn't call them wealthy. But my grandparents are. Old money, they call it. And for reasons that I don't quite comprehend they bequeathed my sister Jean and myself quite a vast sum of money when we each turned 21 years old. Now you know.

I explained my financial situation to Kobus and Sandra and, in my determination to be a pilot at Kruger Park, I had bought myself my own Bell JetRanger and was quite prepared to work for free. That stunned both of them. Eventually Kobus asked where it was and I said that it was being repainted in black and white stripes because I was going to call it the Flying Zebra. I could see I was slowly winning him over, but Kobus still had concerns and questions. Next, he pointed out that I had no experience flying in Kruger Park where on many missions it can be extremely dangerous. I realized that, I told him, and said I was prepared to start with simple jobs, such as ferrying materials, looking for lost tourists as we had three months earlier, until I had gained some experience. In the meantime, I would like as much as possible to accompany Captain on his more dangerous missions to learn from the master. Not that Kobus was the person to make the decision, but I was relying on him to go in to bat for me, so I repeated that not only would I work for free but I would supply my own helicopter. Knowing that Parks Board bureaucracy could simply turn down the offer on the basis that there was no advertised post, I suggested working as a reserve pilot on a subcontract basis, with no pay, making myself available if and when they needed me. The look in Kobus's eyes grew more positive, so at that point I delivered my clincher.

'What if that lost tourist had a more serious problem than a broken leg?' I asked him. 'What if he had a heart attack? What if an elephant pierced a tusk through a tourist's car and into the occupant's leg? What if a game ranger or field ranger was mauled by a lion?'

'I'm listening.'

'I have no doubt that Captain is a brilliant helicopter pilot and could swiftly evacuate those patients to hospital, but I have an added expertise. I can deliver first class medical care before evacuation. And believe me, time is often the critical issue between life and death. In fact, I am having my JetRanger refitted for medical evacuation.'

After the way I explained it to Kobus, he was convinced that the Park Warden would not only agree to such an offer but would be over the moon about it. But he said that he would approach the warden with my suggestion on one condition. What was that, I asked? He and Sandra wanted me to continue living in their home. They had become dear friends so that was hardly an onerous condition. The idea of living at a game ranger's house, my morning coffee and rusk routine, the outings spent climbing koppies at the weekend and braais in the bushveld, all that was heaven on earth. And now I had a purpose!

My contract as a reserve pilot started with a bang. Just the day after I had parked the Flying Zebra on a rudimentary concrete helipad constructed near the house, a call came through early in the morning from Kobus via the VHF radio transmitter. A field ranger's son, out with his father, had been bitten by a black mamba somewhere in the

Olienhoutfontein area. Could I deal with it? My heart started racing with excitement. There was a rider attached to his request. Even though I could hear the conversation, Kobus asked Sandra to explain to me about every snake being a black mamba. Of course, that confused me, so Sandra explained that snakes play a huge role in many of the black cultures in South Africa, often intertwined with their ancestors and witchcraft, and are something to be feared beyond reason. And the snake they fear the most, and with good reason, is the black mamba. Therefore, many would consider all snakes to be black mambas. Sandra did say, however, since the call came from a field ranger, in all likelihood it probably was indeed a black mamba.

Not to worry, I thought, I had the anti-venom for all the major snakes except for a boomslang. Knowing that a black mamba's bite is deadly, I quickly scrambled off to the Flying Zebra, got airborne and followed the N'Waswitshaka creek until, just before the Olienhoutfontein waterhole, I spotted some field rangers furiously waving at me. I found a suitable landing spot, rushed over to the agitated rangers who were all shouting at once about a black mamba and pointing to what looked like a teenager lying on the ground. The one field ranger who spoke a little English said something about the young boy's blood shaking, which sort of made my mind shake at the time, though I later found out that it was an expression that the Shangaan people use when feeling unwell. I did ask if they were sure it was a black mamba, but still not adept in Tsonga the only reply I got was, 'Black mamba!' The black mamba venom contains neurotoxins, which can be very fast acting especially if the fangs penetrate a vein, a bit slower if into the muscle. Essentially it shuts down the nervous system and paralyses the victim. And that process was well under way for the field ranger's son. I could see he was battling to breathe. I administered the anti-venom and with the help of the rangers placed him in the Flying Zebra, then flew off to Themba Hospital in White River and delivered the patient. For a brief moment, my mind flashed back to Groote Schuur, and I thought that this was where I used to take over. Now it was someone else's problem.

I visited Stefan and Ingrid, had lunch with them, and we shared our news, then I returned to the hospital and was satisfied that the kid was going to pull through. And then I flew back home. And felt very pleased with myself, I might add!

When Kobus came back home later that afternoon, he was profoundly grateful. He asked me if I was aware that I had saved the boy's life. I did know, but having worked those years in trauma, I was used to tilting the life and death seesaw to a favourable outcome, and had not thought much about it. And then Kobus said something that was somewhat surprising. He told me he'd never doubted my determination, but he'd doubted that a city boy could pull that off. He was really proud of me.

But I was more interested in the field ranger's son. Why was he not at school, I wanted to know? Kobus said it was one of the numerous cases in South Africa where a black kid had escaped the schooling system. He was totally illiterate, Kobus told me. Perhaps his father wanted him to herd his cows instead of going to school. Speaking of which, Kobus told me, the boy's father wanted to meet me and give me a cow for saving his son's life. That seemed odd to me, but cows also play a big part in the black cultures of South Africa.

I reasoned that at his age the kid could not be an employee at Kruger Park, and asked Kobus what he was doing out there with his father. The game ranger replied that the son wanted to follow in his father's footsteps and also become a field ranger. In the meantime, he was learning under the mentorship of his father. Instead of a cow, I asked if there was any way in which he could work with me? If it weren't for the field rangers who helped me get the boy into the helicopter, I would have battled. Kobus understood and promised to ask the father. I asked my friend if he knew the boy's name. 'Yes, it's Blessing!'

Over the next few months, Blessing and I flew many missions together. Small stuff, but useful stuff. Excuse the pun but the boy was a blessing for me and in return I made it my role to educate him as best I could.

In June, Kobus dropped a bombshell when he asked if I would help him do a census count. Each game ranger is responsible for counting the number of each of the main species in his section, the most important animals being elephant and buffalo. Although not seriously dangerous flying, it did require flying at less than 200 metres in altitude. A quick explanation about the risks of low flying. If a helicopter loses power, a pilot can put the machine into something called autorotation in which the rotors are kept spinning by the upward pressure of the air and drops the helicopter reasonably gently to the ground. But the critical factors are height and speed and let's just say that if one is too low or too slow, one enters what is called the 'dead man's curve' and it becomes difficult, if not impossible, to put the machine into autorotation. That term should explain that this would be my most difficult mission and it was a great fillip that Kobus's request was affirmation that he trusted me.

The census is done in winter when the trees have fewer leaves, making counting easier, and all went smoothly, I am proud to say. Part of the reason to count elephant and buffalo is to determine how many of each species to cull. For someone whose training was all about keeping people alive, the concept of culling did not appeal to me. But Kobus explained that as big as Kruger Park is, it is still too small to be a self-sustaining system and that the growth in elephant population leads to major destruction of the habitat and therefore to other species. If left to their own devices the elephants would eat the larder bare! Kobus blames the problem squarely on the shoulders of the human race for having squeezed the animal habitats into such small islands in a world of an ever growing human population. I am not sure if he meant it this way, but my goal of saving humans is leading him to have to kill elephants and buffalo!

I didn't argue but went for the ride. What I saw Captain do in his JetRanger would have defied belief if I had not actually seen it. He would locate a huge herd of elephants and scatter them. According to Kobus, they scatter in several directions but stay in family groups. To lessen stress in the herd, it is policy of the Department of Nature Conservation to cull whole family groups. So Captain would isolate a family, literally herd it towards a patrol road so that the culling operation would be out of sight of tourists, then approach the herd at under 10 metres, Kobus would fire two darts of scoline at an elephant, a drug that knocks them out, then Captain would increase altitude, circle, herd the group together again while Kobus would reload and then shoot the next two darts. I could see immediately that this was a very traumatic experience for Kobus, one that he carried out with grim determination. A ground crew would then go in and kill each elephant with a shot to the brain, followed by an 'insurance' second shot just to make sure it was dead, and the elephants would be taken to an abattoir to be sliced and diced with not a scrap going to waste.

As much as I detested the killing of the elephants, though I understood the rationale behind it, the helicopter flying was breathtaking. Captain had that machine flying in and out like a bumblebee and at such low levels. His skill was such that the family of elephants all dropped within a few paces of each other. I knew I had a long way to go. But I am okay with that. I am determined to reach his level.

At the end of the operation I praised Captain for performing a bold operation to which he replied, 'There are old pilots and bold pilots, but no old, bold pilots!' It was a sobering thought, something I promised to keep in mind when I got too exuberant about my helicopter flying.

And that, I guess, is what I did over the last year. Nearly died, but found a new purpose in life, getting an adrenalin rush each time I zoom off in my Flying Zebra and spending my off time with the De Beer family in what I have come to believe is the best place on earth, Kruger Park. Who would have thought that just over a year ago I was a trauma surgeon at Groote Schuur and because of Anna's passing I now fly helicopter missions over a game reserve! It's a strange ol' world!

All my love, Michael.

Scarlett

As the year progressed, Robin became progressively weaker and more frail.

'Mom, am I going to die?'

It was the question Scarlett was dreading and made light of it. 'Sweetie, we are all going to die'

'You know what I mean. Please be honest with me.'

With great difficulty, Scarlett looked into her daughter's questioning blue eyes and said, 'Honestly, I don't know.'

Robin nodded her head ever so slightly, appearing to be satisfied that she had been told the truth.

§

Robin stopped swimming completely to keep her strength up to face several bouts of chemotherapy, which eventually caused her to lose her hair.

'Sweetie, if you like I can get you a wig until you get better. The same long dark hair that you had.'

'Actually, Mom,' replied Robin as she lay in the oncology ward at the Red Cross War Memorial Children's Hospital, 'I want to be the same as everyone else here. Besides, I like to think we are all wearing our swimming caps!'

The easy going sentiment made Scarlett feel very proud of her daughter, but it was difficult not to be able to help as the disease ravaged through the young girl's body.

§

'Your birthday and Christmas are coming soon. Is there any special gift you would like?'

'Can you take me for one last swim?'

'Why do you say a last swim?'

'Mom, I know!'

Such a simple answer, spoken with such innocent understanding, yet it brought tears to Scarlett's eyes.

'You remember I asked you a few weeks ago if I was going to die. I know now that I am. I can feel it in my body, but more than that I can see it in your eyes.'

'Oh, Sweetie!' Scarlett responded softly.

'It's okay, Mom. But I would like one last swim. On my birthday.'

'Of course, my darling.'

§

On Christmas day, Robin's birthday, Paul and Scarlett brought cake, cool drink and a gift for each of the children in the oncology ward, to celebrate the special day. Later in the afternoon, Scarlett drove Robin from the hospital to Newlands Swimming Pool. It would normally be closed on Christmas Day, but Scarlett had her own key. She opened the car door, took out the wheelchair and gently placed her frail daughter into it.

Scarlett briefly disappeared into the change rooms to get into her costume, then wheeled Robin to the swimming pool where she had spent much of her life. She lifted her daughter from the wheelchair and placed her sitting on the edge of the pool. After entering the water, Scarlett reached up and embraced her emaciated daughter who was still in her nightgown, drawing Robin to her breast.

Mother and daughter. Two water babies.

As Scarlett walked in the pool she slowly bounced her daughter up and down as if on a merry-go-round in an amusement park, much as she had when Robin was a baby.

'Would you like to go under the water?' Scarlett asked.

'Yes please.'

Scarlett bobbed Robin's head under the water and she rose with a smile from ear to ear, again just like she had when a toddler.

'Mom, how about one last backstroke?'

Scarlett held her daughter under her back, while Robin tried, almost pathetically, to kick her legs and rotate her arms.

Finally, the young girl was exhausted and said, 'I'm tired now.'

Scarlett lifted her daughter to sit on the edge of the pool and stared deeply into Robin's blue eyes. Both were quiet for a while, Robin exhausted physically, Scarlett emotionally.

'That was the best birthday present I've ever had,' said Robin with a faint smile.

'It's not your last swim, Sweetie,' Scarlett said to Robin. Still standing in the pool she gave her daughter a hug and whispered in her ear, 'You'll be swimming with the angels. And you'll be the envy of them.'

§

At the hospital that evening, Scarlett tucked Robin into bed and laid Cub next to her.

'Goodnight, Sweetie!'

As Scarlett turned to leave, Robin called in a soft voice, 'When you bury me, please will you bury Cub with me?'

Scarlett nodded her head, and hurriedly turned to leave as the tears started to stream down her face. Those were the last words she heard her daughter speak. At 10.15 pm that evening, Scarlett got a telephone call to say that Robin had passed away. Dead on her 13th birthday, Christmas Day.

1st January 1980

Dear Scarlett,

Sandra and I have a baby! Okay, since Kobus and I are best friends, that is going to require some explaining!

In early July, during the winter school holidays, Sandra, Japie and Helena, together with Wagter, spent a week with Sandra's parents who live in Barberton, which is not too far from Nelspruit. On the Sunday that they were due back, Kobus asked if I would like to join him for a walk. He said that he had often seen a particular koppie from a helicopter while doing a game census, and said that it was time he climbed to the top of it. Well, by now my answer should have been obvious as climbing those koppies is one of my favourite pastimes!

We drove on a patrol road alongside the N'Waswitshaka creek until we neared the particular koppie that Kobus had earmarked, then set out on foot, got to the bottom of the koppie and started our climb. So that you understand, there is no footpath that you can follow to the top. You simply have to navigate on the fly. We had ascended a third of the way up, reached a ledge and, with Kobus in the lead, were about to climb over a boulder and continue our ascent when we heard a growl, a reverberating growl that reached deep into the pit of my stomach. To our right, lying in front of a small cave was the unmistakable tawny coat of a lioness. And she was not happy. She had crouched low to the ground, her ears were pulled flat against her head, a snarl crinkled her face as she growled and her tail was swishing like a windscreen wiper.

In dangerous situations, experts talk of the fight or flight syndrome. Someone forgot to tell them there is a third option and that is fright! Never in my life had I been so scared. You may recall when I first joined Kobus patrolling his section of the park, I asked him a thousand and one questions, one of which was what to do if you came across a lion. He replied that one should never run. Well, there was no chance of that happening because my feet were glued to the ground with fear! In fact, my whole body was so spiked with adrenalin it turned me into a statue. There was another reason that neither of us could run. The ledge we stood on was narrow, and while we faced the lioness only a dozen or so paces away, immediately behind us was a cliff which, if we fell off, would mean instant death. We were trapped! An angry lioness in front of us! A death fall behind us! A boulder to our left which, if we were to climb over would mean turning our backs on the lioness — not a good idea!

And, unfortunately, the route that had led us to this spot meant having to go closer to the lioness if we were to reach the entry point to the ledge! There were simply no escape options!

At the first growl, Kobus slowly lifted his arm to signal to me to stay put. That gesture was unnecessary as I was frozen on the spot. Kobus then spoke gently to the lioness in a tone signalling that we meant no harm, 'Easy girl, easy girl.' During his soothing conversation I distinctly heard the click as he released the safety catch on his rifle. Even with my limited experience in the African bush, I knew we were in a perilous situation that would not have a good outcome.

As we stood there, unable to move, the lioness became increasingly agitated. She charged a couple of paces, then stopped and retreated, possibly the one and only chance she was giving us to get out of her comfort zone. And get out fast! For reasons I didn't understand at the time, Kobus slowly took a step forwards. Then with a deep earth-shattering growl, the lioness charged, Kobus fired and the cat landed at his feet, dead. The lioness charge and the loud bang had me shaking like a leaf, and it took a moment to sink in that it was all over which caused some deep nervous breathing on my part.

A forlorn looking Kobus then sat on the boulder that had blocked our journey to the top of the koppie, a dead lioness at his feet, looked down at the ground with his head in his hands and wept uncontrollably. I didn't know what to do, so I just stood there, a million thoughts and emotions blazing through me. Several minutes went by, Kobus still weeping. Finally, he stopped, stood up, looked at me and uttered the word 'sorry'. He then stepped over the dead lioness, walked away from me towards the route we had taken to get to the ledge and mumbled, 'I'll be back.' And with that he was gone.

I suddenly felt bereft without Kobus. I looked nervously at the lioness and concluded that she was indeed dead, then checked in all directions for any sign of approaching danger. With none to be found, I sat on the same boulder that Kobus had vacated, stared down at the dead lioness, and pondered my friend's reaction as my adrenalin eased. Of all animals, a dead cat looks the worst, something so sleek and athletic, now so lifeless. It was a sad sight to see the lioness lying on the ground, blood pooling beneath her, but surely in all his years Kobus must have killed many animals before. I had witnessed it. Culling. Supervising the shooting of rogue elephants. Putting down various animals that had been caught in snares that were beyond the chance for rehabilitation back into the wild. Even shooting for the pot. Why this uncontrollable weeping from a man who is as tough as one can get, here in the African bush?

Two hours later, Kobus returned with a wooden box which I recognized as the tool box he always kept in his bakkie, the box now empty, and also a blanket that he kept for an emergency if ever he got stuck in the bush during a winter's night. Without a word spoken, he folded the blanket a few times and lined the wooden box with it, then went inside the cave and returned with a bundle of fur, a lion cub, placed it in the box, then another and another. Still without saying a word, he picked up the box and started the journey down the koppie with me following him.

When we reached his bakkie, Kobus placed the box on the ground, opened the passenger door, placed the box on the passenger seat and closed the door. Then he walked around to the driver's side, opened the door and started the engine. Without having to be told, I got the message and jumped onto the back of the bakkie. Off we drove, back to the De Beer's home, my mind searching in all directions. As we entered the gate it was clear that Sandra and the twins had just arrived home. Kobus greeted each one of them, then walked over to me and again uttered the single word 'sorry', then walked off to the house. I never saw him again that day.

Sandra, Japie and Helena all went into the house, but I stayed behind leaning against the bakkie, knowing that Kobus was in an extremely fragile emotional state. Every so often I peered through the passenger window, but could not see the three lion cubs as they were so deep in the box. My mind kept going over the day's experiences, as I tried to process all we'd been through.

Half an hour later, Sandra emerged from the house and made the comment that she again had some orphans to look after. She made no reference to Kobus. Instead, she opened the passenger door of the bakkie and asked if I would carry the tool box into the house. As I walked with the box in my hands, I peeked in and saw the cutest little balls of fur you could imagine. A bittersweet moment of carrying three lion cubs in my hands but knowing that their mother was dead.

Sandra's comment about again having to look after some orphans referred to the many animals she had become a surrogate mother to over the years. She would rear them as best she could, get emotionally attached to them, and then at some point as they learned to hunt or fend for themselves they would leave the house for longer and longer periods until they became fully independent and wild. Her orphans included amongst others a slender mongoose, a serval, a honey badger and a vervet monkey. The latter was the only one that could not be returned as it was missing both legs and an arm, victim of a snare. But with careful nurturing, the monkey survived and can you believe that it would hop around upside down on one arm, contentedly exploring the garden as if such a life was normal. That was, until it disappeared. Probably taken by a leopard, Sandra told me. That, of course was an indirect way of telling me that despite the property being fenced, nothing could prevent a leopard from entering it. Another reminder that I was in the wilds of Africa!

Inside the house, Japie and Helena joined us, marvelling at the lion cubs, but Sandra looked at them solemnly, saying that not only would the cubs sense that something dramatic had occurred in their young lives but, without knowing when last they had fed, it was vital to give them nutrition. But what? I could see her mind ticking over when Japie, who had just read the book, *Born Free*, suggested that we consult the book to see what the Adamsons had done with Elsa. He quickly flipped over the first few pages, then excitedly shouted that the formula used for Elsa was diluted unsweetened evaporated milk, fed from a baby's bottle. And, that later, Joy Adamson added glucose and cod liver oil. I wondered out aloud how old our cubs were and Sandra relayed that Kobus estimated they were about five days old. Japie then revealed that Elsa was quite a bit older, and we all wondered if the formula should be adjusted, although it was not much of a formula at that stage because all we had was the evaporated milk. Sandra suggested that we get through the night with what we had, and send someone for glucose and cod liver oil in the morning. Also, we wouldn't change the formula at this stage because that was all we knew. A more immediate problem was how to get the milk into the cubs. We had no baby's bottle and being a Sunday evening, the shop at Pretoriuskop Camp would now be closed.

I felt that I had contributed very little, so felt proud when I suggested that we use an eye dropper. Our mood picked up and with each one doing his and her bit, we sterilized an eye dropper from a bottle of eye drops that I kept and made up some lukewarm formula. The moment of truth. The twins and I all looked on as Sandra, her maternal instinct kicking in, lifted the first cub, placed it on her lap and put the dropper to the cub's mouth. There was a collective dismay when the cub refused the eye dropper. Sandra then squirted a few drops on her little finger and placed it to the cub's mouth. The liquid appeared to disappear, so she repeated the process. Then she tried placing the dropper in the cub's mouth again and we all breathed a sigh of relief as the liquid in the dropper disappeared. It was a laborious process, but eventually the cub seemed sated.

We decided that Helena would hold the first cub in her lap as we didn't want them to get mixed up in the box and re-feed a cub that had already been fed, while starving another. And so all three cubs had their meal. On closer inspection, we discovered that there were two males and a female.

With all three fed, Sandra placed the cubs back in the box, concluding that they would feel less frightened if they sensed each other's presence. While the cubs captivated the twins, I followed Sandra to the kitchen and asked her if Kobus was alright. She told me that her husband had already gone to bed, feeling utterly distraught. He had failed to spot any spoor which would have indicated that a lioness was in the area. She repeated what Kobus had once told me, that he had never shot an animal in self-defence before. That he prided himself in always managing to defuse a dangerous situation, something that I had learned occurs quite frequently for a game ranger. Sandra also said that her husband felt responsible for putting me in danger. It was only then that I realized that his reason for taking a small step towards the lioness was to protect me by placing himself in the first line of defence. And I'm sure that in his mind his slight movement towards her was taken as a sign of aggression.

I felt awful and told Sandra that as usual, in my insatiable desire to learn more about the wild, I had distracted Kobus by asking numerous questions. Also, as we landed on the ledge, I'd pointed out the beautiful view on our left, diverting his attention away from the cave, so was hugely responsible for what followed. But she said that Kobus would not see it that way. He was the experienced game ranger and took all the blame squarely on his shoulders and there was nothing I could do or say that would change his mind. The best way forwards would be to give him time, time to regroup and sharpen his focus. But that he would get there.

In the meantime, Sandra told me, the pressing problem was what we were to do with the three lion cubs. When I mentioned that she had raised many orphans before, why not three lion cubs, Sandra explained that all the other wild and wonderful creatures she'd cared for were smallish animals and, apart from the vervet monkey, had eventually adapted to the wild and left to join their own kind. She said that was impossible for a lion, that even though a lion has a built-in instinct to hunt, it has to be taught by its mother to actually kill, a process that can take a minimum of one and a half years. And there was an even bigger problem. The Kruger Park authorities did not allow the keeping of wild animals. Smaller ones were sometimes overlooked, but a lion was different as they posed a threat to human life and ultimately Kruger Park would be responsible for any injury or even death to a human. But what were we to do with three helpless cubs that were now orphaned, caused by human intervention. That last comment of Sandra's pierced like a dagger right into my heart, as I still felt responsible for distracting Kobus.

Sandra took the three lion cubs to the bedroom she shared with Kobus. I battled to go to sleep, going over in my mind how much I was to blame for the predicament in which we found ourselves, and in the early hours of the morning I decided to make myself a cup of tea. As I walked to the kitchen I saw the light in the lounge was on and found Sandra feeding one of the cubs. She looked exhausted, saying that she had reared twins before but not triplets! The cubs were constantly making little sounds to express their hunger. No sooner had she finished feeding the third cub when the first made mewing demands.

I made us both a cup of tea and sat a long time with Sandra attending to the new orphans. Eventually I suggested that she go to bed and let me take over, but she refused, saying that she was experienced at this, having been through it before, both with her own children and with all her other orphan animals.

I eventually went back to bed and by the time I woke up Kobus had already left for work, and would be away for three days attending meetings at Skukuza. That day we managed to get a baby's bottle, a lot more evaporated milk, and both glucose and cod liver oil. At first each cub was reluctant to take the bottle, but after Sandra tried the trick she used the previous night, it was back to the feeding regimen, one that felt like an all-day affair with both Japie and Helena helping out.

At bed time Sandra looked exhausted, but when I suggested taking over the night shift she was adamant that I go to bed. She is a petite woman with a soft voice, but she can be quite determined, especially when it comes to maternal duties.

When I woke the following morning, Sandra was nowhere to be seen. I wondered if maybe, being so tired, she had overslept, even through the Egyptian geese alarm clock. I knocked on her bedroom door, slowly opened it and saw Sandra sitting up in bed crying as she cradled one cub. I had seen that look many times before. The two male cubs had died, she said, confirming what I'd already guessed. When she was calmer, we chatted and deduced that the constant feeding meant there was something wrong with the formula.

We couldn't make use of the VHF radio transmitter as the conversations were heard by all staff in the whole of Kruger Park, and without knowing what lay in store for the remaining cub, Sandra wanted to keep it secret at that stage. So she decided to phone Kruger Park's veterinarian, swear him to secrecy and ask his advice. Then she told me that she had named the remaining cub, Kike — pronounced Kee-Kay — meaning female in Swahili.

Sandra called the vet as soon as the office opened. Our suspicions were correct. The two males had died of malnourishment, the vet explaining that a lioness's milk is extremely rich to allow her to leave her cubs for extended periods so that she could go and hunt for her food. If the mother doesn't eat, she can't produce milk for her cubs. He recommended that we use any commercial substitute for dog's milk dissolved in full cream cow's milk, and add egg yolk and cream. I rushed off to White River, only to find that no shop stocked the dog milk substitute, but I found it in Nelspruit and bought several tins plus the other ingredients.

Kike's demand for milk reduced on this new formula, but she still looked like her life was hanging by a thread. Only by the Wednesday evening when Kobus returned did she start to look like a lion cub. Not only that, but lion cubs are born blind and when Kobus walked into the lounge Kike opened her eyes for the first time. Kobus had already heard the news of the male cubs from the veterinarian, but when he saw Kike his eyes lit up. It was a huge relief for me as it seemed as if he had put the tragic events of Sunday in the past.

After supper, there followed a long discussion about what to do with Kike. Kruger Park's policy is to let nature take its course, so if an abandoned lion cub was found, then as cruel as it may seem, a game ranger would be compelled to leave it and it would most certainly die through starvation or predation. But this case was different, since human intervention had created an orphan called Kike. So with this argument Kobus made his case to the Director of Nature Conservation and Research that we look after Kike until a solution could be found. And until that solution was found, the cub would be documented for research purposes. I will never know exactly how that conversation ran its course, but needless to say that a lot of emotional guilt was expressed that may have swayed the Director to overlook policy, because permission to keep Kike on a temporary basis was granted.

It was a decision that was to transform our lives. The reason? Lions are sociable, and young lions expend endless amounts of energy, demanding constant attention. Kike's eyes were still covered by a blue film which, Sandra told me, meant that her vision was still blurred. But that didn't deter the cub from exploring the house and bumping into everything at ground level. With Kobus at work all day and both Japie and Helena back at boarding school in Nelspruit, it was left up to Sandra and me, unless I was on helicopter duty, to look after Kike. While exhausting, it was a laugh a minute as she made her way around the house looking as if she were in an inebriated state.

An initial concern was how Wagter was going to interact with the cub, but after an initial fright, apparently borne out of the smell of lion, it proved no problem. Wagter assumed a status higher than that of a small lion cub and was very tolerant of the bumbling idiot!

At four weeks old the blue film disappeared and revealed an alluring set of amber eyes. Scarlett, I have written about your mesmerizing eyes, but you now have competition, though in a different kind of way. More than her mews or groans, Kike had a way of speaking to us through her expressive eyes that could assume a myriad of emotions, eyes that were going to tug at our heartstrings over the next few months. Looks of utter joy when she suddenly spotted you, contentment when she was satiated from her formula, sadness when you were about to leave, sheepishness when she knew she had done something foolish, a doleful look when she had done something wrong and was scolded with a stern tone of voice, mischief in her eyes when she was conjuring up something she knew she shouldn't, inquisitiveness when there was something new to be discovered, and a look of utter bewilderment when something backfired and she did not know why. But most of all, her eyes were warm and soft with love.

Our way to communicate with Kike is by talking to her as if she were a person. To this day I am surprised at how well she understands us, which I am sure is by the tone of our voices. But she does know her name. Call her, and she is all over you in an instant because she just loves to be hugged and cuddled.

Even at such a young age, Kike would stalk and hunt down everything in existence in the house. Incredibly there was this built-in instinct for her to take cover behind a couch, creep forwards ever so slightly until something triggered in her mind that it was time, time to rush at her prey, be it the leg of a chair, Sandra's leg, my leg or a very tolerant Wagter.

After a couple of weeks it became obvious to us that her prey species needed to be expanded, so Kobus constructed a timber box with a hinged lid that was to become Kike's source of prey. A small pot, a wooden spoon from the kitchen, a stuffed toy lion cub and a tennis ball from Japie, an old Barbie Doll and a hand-me-down hairbrush from Helena, and, can you believe it, an old towel. And there was one other toy which I will tell you about later. These items either became her siblings or her prey species of impala, wildebeest, zebra, warthog and all the other animals that lions hunt in the wild. I say her siblings, because I have been very lucky to have seen a pride of lions with young cubs during their play hour when they stalk, trip, chase and hunt each other in what seems like a never-ending perpetual motion game of tag. It is just so incredible to see the built-in instinct to hunt and the amazing athletic ability of lion cubs. I had a cat as a pet while growing up in Cambridge, but a lion cub is a cat on steroids!

It was no different for Kike. She instinctively attacked her toys, pawed at them, mauled them, flung them up in the air and rolled around with them. The Barbie doll soon lost its head but that just made up another toy for her to play with. Soon she turned the house into a war zone. Two toys or prey species stood out. The tennis ball because a ball has a mind of its own, rolling around, which set Kike off in a wild chase of this 'live' animal. The other was the towel. Quite often on her own, but sometimes with a bit of teasing from me, I have to confess, Kike would become smothered by the towel and it was a scream watching her walking and jumping blind as she tried to prise herself loose from this monster of a prey species that had dared to cover her. And when she did escape it was often with a look of, 'What the hell was that?'

Kike was exhausting, and given that lions often come alive at night, we reserved her best toy just before we went to bed to exhaust her into submission so that we could sleep. And that was a simple piece of string! One of us would quickly drag the length of string in a zigzag fashion across the lounge floor which kicked in an instinctive action to hunt it down. But catching a moving piece of string is not easy, and so this game would go on until it exhausted the precious cub. Kike would always end the day by going to lie on Sandra's lap, suck on her finger and fall asleep. And only then could we all go to bed!

When Kike was two months old, we had a scary moment. I walked into the lounge, sat down and noticed that Kike was not there. Wagter had duty that day and was off with Kobus. I asked Sandra where Kike was, and she replied that she thought the cub was with me, to which I said that I thought Kike was with her. That in itself was not much of a worry as Kike could easily have been hunting something in the house. But after a while when she didn't appear from behind the couch to ambush one of us, we got a bit concerned. We both got up and went our separate ways searching the house, calling her name. To our horror, we came up empty-handed. At that stage Kike had not been let out of the house. We wondered if she had found a way to get into the yard, so we dashed outside, calling for her, looking everywhere, but no lion cub was to be found. Panic set in. Had she crept into a bushy shrub and been bitten by a snake? Had an eagle swooped down and taken her? Sandra and I were beside ourselves with fear, a measure of how much Kike had crept into our hearts. We returned to the house at a complete loss as to what to do when we heard faint growls and mews. But where could she be? It turned out that she was in her toy box! What relief! She had obviously climbed in and the hinged lid had closed down on her! For the rest of that day we never let her out of our sight, and gave her extra attention to build her confidence. But she seemed none the worse for her toy box experience. Perhaps just one of her cat lives lost, another eight to go!

Looking for Kike outside made us conclude that it was time for our child to start exploring the yard. She was cautious at first and followed Wagter wherever he went, trotting on her oversized paws. Lions are territorial by nature and a month later she was soon exploring by herself, getting used to the new smells and expanding her territory which would eventually extend to the boundary fence of the property. And she slept in her own box on the patio next to Wagter's kennel.

One Sunday when Kike was three months old, Kobus was about to place various cuts of meat on the glowing coals of a braai when he threw a lamb chop to Kike. She pounced on it, flicked it with her paw and chased after it and eventually clutched it with her paws and started licking it. Lion's tongues are rough like sandpaper, so she obviously got a good taste of the meat. This was a tasty toy that got more licks than any other toy, a toy that she eventually chewed on and ultimately became a disappearing toy. And so, another stage of her development as she became a meat eater.

And not just meat given to her. It was at moments like these, at a Sunday braai, when she would suddenly jump up onto your lap while you were peacefully sitting in your chair, place her paws around your head and start licking your face. I'll say it again, a lion's tongue is rough and those were rough moments for the flesh on our faces, but all was forgiven when you knew that she was being so adorable and loving.

Cats have amazing imaginations, and so everything outside became a new prey species to hunt, which didn't do much for Sandra's and Problem's prized garden. So two new outside toys were introduced. The first was a car tyre that Kobus hung from a tree. This was an obvious attraction because it moved, and if something moves a lion will investigate. It was incredible to see how much fun such a simple toy gave Kike who would jump and strike at it, her alert eyes following its every move until at just the right moment she would pounce on it, often hanging on as she swung through the air.

The second outside toy was equally appealing to her. Sandra tightly rolled up many rags into a ball and then stitched several layers of hessian around them to form a big soft ball. As I said, balls have a mind of their own. A simple touch and they roll, and there is nothing like movement to kick in a lion's instinct to attack. And so Kike would swipe at the hessian ball, run after it, attack it and roll over and over with the ball, then come back to us with a look of, 'Huh!' Of course, that had us howling with laughter.

And there were two toys that Kike invented for herself. Anyone and everyone who visited the De Beer home got ambushed and pounced upon. The second was more intriguing. The De Beers have a fishpond next to Sandra and Problem's garden. Movement is a magnet for lions, but water is a no-no. So Kike had us in stitches as we watched her standing on the edge of the pond pawing at a fish. Being quick, the fish would dart out of harm's way. But every so often the instinct to catch a fish was so strong that Kike forgot about the water and plunged into the pond, only to instantly reverse with a look of utter disgust on her crinkled up face. In this regard Kike has a short memory because to this day the movement of the fish still attracts her, and so this amusing scene still plays out every day, but she has yet to catch a fish!

Over time, I have learned about the social hierarchy in a lion pride. I often wondered where Kike felt she was in our pride. One day while the family were sitting outside, Kobus threw the hessian ball into the air. Both Kike and Wagter jumped up to capture it. With Kike's greater agility and athleticism she was able snatch it out of the air and covet her prize. Wagter barked and snarled at her, which immediately caused Kike's eyes to assume that doleful look when she knew that she had done something wrong. By now Kike had the strength to stand up to Wagter and cause serious injury, but he was quite safe because she didn't have a vengeful bone in her body. They soon made up and became inseparable friends again. It was then that I asked Kobus what she felt was her status. He said that I was the dominant pride male which surprised me somewhat, but Kobus told me that she was always extremely obedient with me, possibly because a stern, 'No!' in my voice would put Kike in her place. Sandra was the mother, the provider of food and Kobus said that Kike sensed an emotional caring in her manner. A softie with a soft voice that Kike would sometimes test by being too physical, but express real remorse in her eyes when she realized that she had been too rough. Japie, Helena and Wagter were her siblings whom she adored. In lion prides, cubs can be at various stages of growth when from different litters and Kike probably thought Wagter was from her own litter.

'And you?' I asked Kobus.

He said that he had no idea. 'Maybe a nomad male,' he added with a chuckle. 'And as you know, nomads in the wild can challenge and take over a pride, usually killing the existing cubs. So she knows her place with me,' Kobus said with a smile. My friend then held out a small piece of impala steak and called Kike who jumped into his lap and set upon devouring both the steak and Kobus's face with huge licks of both. And I thought, more like a lovable uncle than a nomad!

Kike would often join Sandra and me at the fence looking at game that came to drink at the waterhole. At first just the sight of the lion cub caused the herbivores to bolt, perhaps through some primeval memory or the smell of lion or perhaps they wondered if the cub's mother was around. But eventually they wised up and took no notice of her. And I often wondered what they thought of this bizarre arrangement of humans, a dog and a lion on the other side of the fence. I, too, was intrigued by how Kike viewed herself and asked Kobus if she thought she was a human, a lion or a dog. He said that he hadn't a clue. He did say that certain eagles, when taken from a nest, will believe that they are human after only two weeks and no matter how hard one tries, the eagle will never see itself as anything other than human.

But an interesting event happened a couple of months later that may have given me a clue to Kike's thoughts. Late one Sunday afternoon, just as Kobus lit the fire for a braai, he looked up at the expanse of bushveld in front of the property. I couldn't see anything. But Kobus had that instinctive sense of something happening in the bush. Suddenly he saw it. A lone sable bull emerged from behind a shrub and slowly walked to the waterhole. It was a magnificent specimen with huge horns that arched backwards, each to a smooth point. Sable is a rare sighting but this was even more special since Kobus said it was the first he had ever seen from their property. Kobus, Sandra, Japie, Helena and I edged closer to the fence, ever careful not to startle it.

The sable bull got down on its knees to drink and then stood up. Tall and proud. From the look of awe on the faces of the De Beer family I sensed this was an exceptional sighting. Just then Kike and Wagter appeared alongside us. They had been playing in the front garden. On arrival, they too, must have sensed something out of the ordinary, their eyes looking intently at the bull but making no sound.

Suddenly at exactly the same moment, Wagter let out a short bark and Kike lay flat on the ground. To Kobus the bark was an alarm bark, so he immediately scanned the bushveld that lay in front and only after a few moments he saw a lioness on the right of the sable, some 30 metres away, its head peering just above the tall sour grass that now looked golden in the dusk. The cat then adopted that characteristic look of keeping low to the ground, its head flat as it sighted its prey in front of its nose. A typical stalk pose. Kobus looked to the left of the sable and saw three more lionesses spaced apart, their heads barely visible.

Using the grass for cover, the lioness on the right stalked closer and closer, belly almost on the ground. When she was close enough and the bull turned his back on her she charged, and charged at lightning pace. A lion hunt was playing out before my eyes in panoramic view. I was mesmerized. The sable bolted but unlucky for him directly into the three catchers that quickly brought the bull down, one of the lionesses getting a bite hold around the prey's throat. While being suffocated the sable kicked its legs wildly, but eventually the kicks diminished as it succumbed to death. The lioness that had given the sable the kiss of death stood up panting, then emitted soft calls while the other three cats tucked into their meal. Soon five cubs not much bigger than the size of a house cat emerged from the thicket and came trotting towards the kill. By now the sable's hide had been ripped open and the cubs climbed all over the kill to find the best spot to feed.

Up until then, none of us had uttered a word. This was raw and savage, but at the same time supremely athletic and to be admired. I looked to Kike who was still lying as flat as she could on the ground, eyes intent on what was happening before her. At nearly six months, she was older than the cubs but a lot smaller than the lionesses. I wondered what she was thinking as she had never before reacted like that towards any other animal. Was it possible that she felt an instinctive similarity to the cats in front of her?

Suddenly the peace was shattered as two male lions rushed in and with earth-shattering growls, chased the lionesses and cubs off the kill. Within a pride, lions are one of the most affectionate animals that I have ever seen in Kruger Park. They are constantly rubbing heads together, often lie on top of each other, something even the grumpy males do. But all that goes out the window when there is food. Lions have no table manners! It really is a bun fight, especially if the prey is small or at the beginning of the feast of a large prey animal. Only when they seemed satisfied that they'll all get a fair share, do they calm down to enjoy their feast. Kobus explained to me that the role of a male lion is to raise a pride and protect it from all dangers, so it made sense that they maintain their strength by eating first. Without them, the pride could well be in peril. It is their reward for often fighting to the death to defend the pride. Slowly the cubs returned to the kill and given that there was plenty of meat, the males tolerated them. That gave the lionesses confidence to join in the fray.

Soon it was pitch dark and, as we returned to the fire, Kobus asked if I would take over, resurrect the fire and start cooking the meat. Then he promptly went inside the house. I was stunned. Nobody, but nobody takes over the job of the master of the braai! I looked to Sandra for confirmation, wondering if I had heard correctly. She explained that he needed a moment alone. Sable are so close to extinction and so rare, that it would be very emotional for him to witness what we had just seen.

'He feels that us humans have caused sable to get to such low numbers, but he understands the circle of life and he'll soon cheer up, especially when he gets hold of a prized set of sable horns,' Sandra said.

'They are beautiful horns but would they mean that much to him?' I wondered.

Sandra said that game rangers do not want much in the way of material things, but they do collect odd things from the bush that become prized possessions, even an odd shaped stick. We both laughed at that.

With the wood coals glowing, I placed some thick impala steaks and homemade boerewors on the fire. Given what we had just witnessed, I asked Sandra if she had ever before seen a kill take place in front of their property.

'No, not in the ordinary sense,' she said. 'But an elephant was killed in an unusual circumstance. Late one afternoon, dark clouds built up, so we took our braai under cover on the back veranda knowing that there was about to be a cracker of a storm. As night fell, tongues of lightning struck all around and on each occasion revealed the silhouettes of elephants in front of us. It was eerie, almost as if we were seeing grey ghosts of the night.'

I was intrigued with this story.

'The following morning,' Sandra continued, 'we found one lying dead just beyond the waterhole, obviously struck by lightning. And then the most emotional scenes played out in the following days. Later the herd of elephants returned and each in turn would reach out to the fallen elephant with its trunk making deep rumbling noises. Eventually, they moved off. Later that day a pride of lions found the dead elephant and began feasting on it. The next day the herd of elephants returned and chased the lions away and repeated their actions of the day before, nuzzling the dead elephant with their trunks. This repeated every day, lions eating, getting chased off, then the same emotional behaviour of the herd of elephants. Eventually the dead elephant got reduced to bones. And still the herd returned, and each time an elephant would pick up a bone and walk some distance before dropping it in the veld. It was strange behaviour, but one that made me come to understand elephants as beautiful and intelligent creatures characterised by a highly developed social structure and a deep bond that links its family members.'

I did not sleep well that night. In part because of the amazing hunt that I had witnessed, but also because I could hear the crunching of bones and ripping of meat accompanied by the growling and roaring of lions very close by. Plus hyenas and jackals were making their presence known with their cackling and barking which got louder and louder through the night, as they closed in.

My coffee and rusk routine was a little different the following morning. Sandra and I stood watching the skeleton of the dead sable with only one lioness using her multi-barbed tongue to lick the ribs clean of any meat, the others lying about with bellies so huge that they appeared in pain. Hyenas and jackals were close by, circling, in anticipation of their turn. Every so often a jackal would chance its luck by darting in to steal a scrap but a snarl from the lioness sent it scurrying back.

Suddenly Kobus emerged on the scene, opened the gate and, clapping his hands loudly and shouting, he chased the lions away. Well, in the case of the cubs, more a waddling away with their bellies swaying exaggeratedly from side to side and nearly touching the ground as they tried to keep up with mum. Before the hyenas moved in, Kobus retrieved his trophy of a pair of sable horns, something that he would treasure for years to come.

Then all hell broke loose as a pack of marauding hyenas descended and ripped the remaining carcass with their powerful jaws while emitting a cacophony of cackles. The daring jackal darted in to steal a meal and, later that day, vultures descended from the sky for a final clean-up operation. I stood there, amazed at how just 12 hours earlier we were admiring one of the most beautiful antelopes in the park, now the sable sustained several animals, birds and microorganisms, and would soon be returned to the earth which would in turn nourish trees and shrubs and grass, and the whole cycle would repeat itself.

It has been quite a year. A lot of thrilling work done in my Flying Zebra, embraced with love and care by the De Beer family, but mostly one that has been dominated by Sandra and me raising the newest member of the family, Kike.

All my love, Michael.

Scarlett

Walking down the aisle of Rondebosch Congregational Church, Scarlett, dressed in black, clung to Paul with one hand and in the other she clutched Robin's teddy bear close to her chest. As they reached the front pew, Paul sat down while Scarlett walked on to the coffin, opened the lid and gently placed Cub alongside an angelic looking Robin.

The church was packed, the funeral service attended by all the children and her teacher from her first year class at Rustenberg Girl's High School, and also the entire swimming team from the Dolphin Swimming Club. The burial at Pinelands Cemetery was a private affair. Afterwards, Scarlett asked Paul if she could be alone.

She sank to her knees and knelt with her legs tucked under her on the green carpet that lay on the one side of the burial plot, a single red rose in her hands. Unusually for that time of year, the sky was covered in dark graphite grey clouds. For a long while Scarlett stared ahead in a daze. Finally, she focussed on where a headstone would soon be erected and read in her mind what she would have engraved in the marble, a quote from Shakespeare, 'Now boast thee death, in thy possession lies a lass unparalleled.'

Looking skywards, a faint drizzle started and mixed with tears streaming down Scarlett's face as she said aloud, 'Swim with the angels, Robin! Swim!'

She stood, threw the red rose down onto the coffin, then turned and walked to the car where Paul sat waiting. Not a word was spoken on the way home.

§

That evening, Scarlett lay on the couch, next to Paul, her arms wrapped around him, her head resting on his chest.

'Do you think I made a mistake not wanting another child?' asked Scarlett. 'A child with you?'

'No, darling. From the beginning I could see that Robin was your entire world.'

'But you're in my world.'

'In a different way, yes. But I'm your husband whereas another child would not measure up to Robin. In fact, it would have been wrong to have another child. Besides, Robin was mine too. It's not about biology,

Missy, it's about love. In Robin, we had an angel. That was more than enough for me.'

Scarlett reached up and kissed her husband.

'Today, my dear,' continued Paul, 'is not about whether we should have had another baby. Rather, it's about why our child was taken from us so early. Parents aren't meant to bury their children.'

'Do you think we could still have another child? I'm young enough.'

'Why don't we think about that another day.'

§

Three weeks later, Scarlett gazed out of the window of her consulting room at the children's hospital. Immediately in front of her was the Rondebosch Common, a place where she had jogged many times. Beyond that her old school, Rustenberg Girls' High. To the left, Newlands Swimming Pool, further ahead the University of Cape Town hugging the slopes of Devil's Peak, and to the right, Groote Schuur. Of course, her own home was in Rondebosch. It suddenly dawned on Scarlett that her entire life had existed within her view, a privileged existence. Deep in her mind she could hear Dr Chris Barnard. 'You know, we are the privileged ones. You should use your position to pay back to society and to those who are most in need.' Scarlett made up her mind that it was time to make a change.

§

Two weeks later, sitting opposite Paul at their dining room table, Scarlett took a sip of red wine and said, 'I've been thinking.'

'Uh oh!'

'Why do you always say that?'

'Because it usually means a big change in our lives.'

'Well, you're right about that, except that this is not just a big change but a complete change.'

'Like what?'

'Well, now that Robin's gone, I think I'd like to go and live somewhere else.'

'Have you had a bit too much wine?'

'I'm serious. This place holds too many memories for me.'

'Okay, I'm listening.'

'I've been researching and I've found a hospital in White River in the Eastern Transvaal called Themba Hospital, originally run by Swedish missionaries. There's an old run down clinic about a 20-minute drive away that they want to rejuvenate to deal with rural children, those in dire need of care.'

'And what about the practice?' asked Paul.

'Lease it out. It's a growing practice, and if we don't like White River, we can always come back.'

Scarlett could see that her husband was somewhat stunned.

'Paul, we've lived here all our lives. Let's take a leap and do something different. Live in a different place. Work for a missionary clinic instead of a private practice. We've had such privileged lives. Elite schools. Swimming clubs. Attended one of the best universities in the country. As doctors, we're seen as being better than others. Why don't we give back to the community? Offer our services for free, live a simple life out in the bush, and, quite frankly, do more challenging work.'

Realizing that Scarlett was desperately seeking a change in life, probably wanting to escape the hole that Robin had left behind, Paul agreed. 'As long as we have our practice to come back to I think it's a fine idea.'

§

One Saturday in February, a Stuttaford removal van, packed with the Rhodes family's possessions, pulled out of their driveway on the long haul to White River. Paul and Scarlett were to drive up the following day. They would spend the night at Danny's house before setting off at dawn for the long drive.

Over the whirr noise of the vacuum cleaner, Scarlett heard a knock on the front door. She opened it. And was stunned.

'Mama!' she cried.

At first, Scarlett was not sure how to react. What possible reason could her mother have for arriving on her doorstep the day before she was leaving Cape Town? But when her mother held out her arms and mouthed the simple words, 'I'm sorry,' Scarlett returned her embrace, holding on tightly as 14 years of deep pent-up anger, confusion, longing and sadness melted away and were replaced with a feeling of pure happiness and love.

As they separated after a long hug, Scarlett's mother asked, 'Can you ever find it in your heart to forgive me?'

Noticing Danny standing behind their mother and Paul suddenly appearing from inside the house, Scarlett did not answer the question her mother posed.

'Mama, this is my husband,' Scarlett introduced them. 'You remember Paul from old swimming days.'

The two shook hands warmly.

'Mama, there's nothing in our house. I can't even make you a cup of tea.'

'Not to worry, Sweetie,' said Mrs Harrison, using the same expression that Scarlett had used for Robin. 'Danny tells me that you're leaving Cape Town and I wanted to see you before you went to try to make things right.'

'Why don't we all go to my house?' Danny suggested.

'Actually, if it's okay with you, Danny,' Scarlett proposed, 'can you take Mama and me to Kirstenbosch Gardens. I think we need some time to ourselves.'

'Sure, Sis.'

'And could you pick us up later? Perhaps Mama can join us for supper.'

Mrs Harrison quickly said, 'Kirstenbosch Gardens sounds lovely, but I'll have to be home before supper.'

It was a stark reminder for Scarlett that her father still ruled the roost in the Harrison's home, but it also made her aware that it must have taken a lot of courage for her mother to come and say goodbye.

Acclaimed as one of the most beautiful gardens in the world, Kirstenbosch National Botanical Garden is nestled at the eastern foot of Table Mountain in Cape Town. Scarlett and her mother sat down at an outside restaurant.

'Lunch? Or tea and scones?' Scarlett asked.

'I think just tea and scones, Sweetie.'

While they waited for the order to arrive, Scarlett took her mother's hand and asked with some trepidation, 'Why, Mama?'

'I'm not sure I even know how to answer that,' replied Mrs Harrison in a quiet voice.

Scarlett looked across the table at her mother. She had aged beyond the 14 years they had been apart. She was still beautiful, but she looked tired, someone who had carried a huge burden.

After a moment of quiet, Mrs Harrison continued. 'Your father has a hold over me that I've never been able to break. He's old school. Truthfully, so am I. I felt I never had a choice.'

'But you did, Mama.'

'Yes and no. When we got married, I vowed to obey him. That vow was not an idle one.'

'But he asked you to choose between himself and his daughter.'

'He did, and he should never have put me in that position. There ought to have been a way to accommodate both. But he wouldn't have it any other way.'

There was a long moment of silence, Scarlett searching for understanding, her mother desperate to be understood. With a subdued demeanour, Mrs Harrison continued, 'Sweetie, don't ever think I made that choice easily. I've wrestled with that decision for as long as I care to remember. It made my life miserable. Cried myself to sleep many times, especially on occasions like your wedding day and Robin's funeral. Every Christmas day on Robin's birthday was the saddest of times.'

'Did you ever think of leaving him?'

'Yes. But despite his unforgiving attitude towards you, he was also a good man. He provided well for me, and for you, and Danny. I did love him. I do love him. And I vowed to love him and be with him so long as we are both still alive.'

Again there was a long moment of silence, each trying to make sense of a situation that had caused them a lot of suffering for 14 years.

'Why now?' asked Scarlett.

'When Danny told me that you were leaving, it was a wake-up call. I couldn't bear the thought of never seeing you again. With you living nearby, I felt there was always a chance of reconciling. In fact Sweetie, I did see you twice since that dreadful night.'

'You did?' Scarlett asked, shocked.

'I managed to sneak out and hide at the back of the church when you got married and then again at Robin's funeral.'

'Mama,' Scarlett cried out, 'why didn't you show yourself? Be with us?'

'I didn't want word to get back to your father.'

'Did Danny know?'

'Yes. He arranged it.'

'But why wouldn't he have told me?'

'I asked him not to. Perhaps I was wrong but I didn't want to disturb the status quo. It may sound strange, but Danny being a conduit between the two of us has been my greatest source of comfort. As meagre as it was, I felt you and Robin were in my life because of him, the things he would tell me. You have a good brother.'

'I know. I feel the same about him keeping me up to date with you. It was a small comfort to know I wasn't completely out of your life!'

'Sweetie, you asked why now? Even as the years went by, I never gave up hope. That while I missed you so desperately, there was still a chance that things would turn out okay. And then, when Robin recently passed away, I was shocked to the core. All that hope and belief that I would meet my grandchild one day came to nothing. It suddenly dawned on me that I had paid a terrible price, but also caused you terrible pain. So when

I heard you were leaving Cape Town I took a stand and that is why I'm here today.'

'How are you going to deal with the outrage from Papa?'

Mrs Harrison looked wistfully at Scarlett before answering, 'Frankly, what has made today a little easier, at least I hope so, is that he has—'

'What, Mama?

'Mood swings. He can go through months of being on a high, elated even, talking about selling up and travelling the world. Then it switches around in an instant, and he goes into a state of utter despair and sadness. And those periods seem to be getting longer and longer. He can sit for hours on end just staring into space.'

'Has he been seen by anyone?'

'No.'

'It sounds like he is manic depressive,' diagnosed Scarlett. 'He really needs to see a psychiatrist.'

'He flatly refuses to see anyone.'

'Is there a way that I can help? Despite our past, I would be happy to stay behind for a few days and have a look at him,' offered Scarlett before injecting a bit of humour as she continued, 'though I expect that might put him into severe and permanent depression!'

'Thanks, Sweetie, but at this stage I need to navigate returning from this outing without causing a major eruption. Let me sleep on it.'

As much as she wanted to help, Scarlett knew how delicate the situation was at home and how courageous her mother had been to come to say goodbye to her. So all she said was, 'Please call if you need any help and also keep me updated.'

Mrs Harrison took one last sip of tea, then said, 'Tell me all about Robin. First of all, why did you name her after me?'

'It was my way of linking the two of you. I thought you would like that.'

'Sweetie, when Danny told me, I felt so honoured. I felt I didn't deserve it after the way I treated you.'

Scarlett then walked around to her mother's side of the table, put her arms around her and looked intently into her eyes before saying, 'Earlier today you asked if I could ever find it in my heart to forgive you. Mama, I made a mistake but it turned out to be the biggest blessing in my life. I now fully understand the predicament you were in, so there's nothing to forgive. Let's make a promise that the pain of the mistakes we have made will give us the resolve to bring us even closer together than might otherwise have been possible.'

Mrs Harrison nodded her head, then requested again, 'Tell me about Robin.'

'There's probably not much to tell you, Mama, because I think she was another me. Looked the same, driven, a better swimmer—'

'I find that hard to believe!'

'Come, Mama. Let's go for a walk around these gardens, a beautiful setting to tell you about your beautiful granddaughter.'

Holding hands, mother and daughter wandered for over two hours around Kirstenbosch Gardens as Scarlett regaled her mother with stories about Robin.

§

Paul and Scarlett were to sleep the night at Danny's house before embarking on their journey to White River early the next morning. In the late evening before Danny took his mother back to her home, Scarlett took her mother's hands and looked intently into her eyes. 'Mama, we must keep in touch. Please write to me and I promise to do the same.'

'I will, Sweetie,' Mrs Harrison said.

'I don't know if we'll have a phone in White River but I'll make a plan and call you regularly. You'll have to be at Danny's house so Papa doesn't answer the phone. But we'll get some arrangement going.'

Scarlett's mother nodded her head

'And you promise to visit me!' exclaimed Scarlett.

Mrs Harrison again nodded her head before tearing up and saying, 'I'm sorry!'

Scarlett, herself on the edge of tears, embraced her mother and simply said, 'I love you, Mama!'

§

The following morning Paul and Scarlett drove to White River, travelling through the day and night. The journey took them through the wine estates of the Cape, through the town of Beaufort West in the semi-desert Karoo, a town where Dr Chris Barnard was born, onto Bloemfontein and Johannesburg, both cities where they had competed in swimming competitions, and finally east to White River which was situated in the lowveld just west of Kruger Park. The journey was exhausting, but they hoped to beat the removal truck so that they could organize the unpacking of their belongings into the house they were to live in.

The arrangement that Paul and Scarlett made was that they were to work *pro bono* at a clinic associated with Themba Hospital in White River. In return, they would get a free house which was right next to the clinic, located about a 20-minute drive outside White River. They met the missionary associated with Themba Hospital, as arranged, in the middle of the town of White River.

'Hello, Mr Lagerström,' Paul greeted his new boss, holding out his hand.

'Please call me Stefan.'

After a brief chat, Stefan Lagerström handed over the keys and gave Paul and Scarlett a hand drawn map showing them how to get to their house.

'There is no phone there, so the best we can do to keep in touch is via two-way radio,' Stefan informed, handing over a walkie-talkie. 'Good luck!'

Paul and Scarlett drove north for a short while outside White River, then turned right and started along a dirt track in the direction of Kruger Park.

Paul, who was driving, asked his navigator, 'Are you sure we took the correct turn?'

A somewhat disconsolate Scarlett replied, 'Well I hope I have made a mistake because this looks rather rough terrain.'

After 20 minutes of bumpy driving, the dirt track came to an end. In front of Paul and Scarlett were two buildings, both prefabricated and dilapidated.

'Do you think this is it?' asked Paul.

Scarlett stared in disbelief. Was this to be her home? Her work place? Had Paul given up working at his medical practice and had she given up her job at the Red Cross War Memorial Children's Hospital to live and work here in this isolated place?

'There's one way to find out. If the keys fit, then yes!' said Paul.

The keys did fit. One building was to be their home, the other the clinic. They climbed a few stairs onto a concrete veranda and entered their new home to discover three bedrooms, one bathroom with just a shower and basin, a lounge and a kitchen. There was only a double bed in the main bedroom, nothing in the second and third bedrooms, a moth-eaten couch and two armchairs in the lounge, and very few utensils in the kitchen.

'Paul, where's the loo?' Scarlett asked when they inspected the bathroom.

Her husband shrugged his shoulders and shook his head.

Scarlett tried the tap in the basin and sighed, 'A miracle! We have water.'

'Possibly not hot water,' Paul said, bringing Scarlett's world crashing down, 'as there's only a single tap. But there are two stopcocks in the shower, so let's keep our fingers crossed.'

'The loo, Paul? I need to go!'

Paul went over to the clinic to see if a toilet existed there, but no such luck. On his way back to the house he noticed a small building bordering on the bush and then returned to tell Scarlett the bad news.

'A long drop near the bush?' Scarlett cried.

'Just remember, Missy,' Paul said, mimicking her, 'we're the privileged ones. And we're here to pay back to society and to those who are most in need.'

'You don't have to rub it in,' said Scarlett, but with a face of abject misery questioned again, 'A long drop?'

'Yes, and if you're desperate you can try it now.'

'Will you accompany me?'

No sooner had they arrived at the long drop when Scarlett complained, 'Paul, there is no loo paper.'

'And we don't have any. I'll fetch a paper serviette from the car. In the meantime you do what you need to do.'

'Leave the door open. It's dark in here.'

As Paul returned with a couple of serviettes, to his utter amazement he saw Scarlett jump up from the toilet, turn around and smack herself on her bottom leaving a bloody splat on her bum cheek.

'Missy?'

'There are mozzies down there in that black hole. Waiting, just waiting for you to plant your tender white backside on the seat to create a juicy target for them!'

'We're the privileged ones!'

§

The house was dusty but that could wait for another day. Paul and Scarlett unpacked their belongings from the car, putting most of them in the bedroom where they were to sleep and a few edibles in the kitchen. Neither were hungry. But both were tired from the long journey and wanted to go to sleep.

'I'm desperate for a cup of tea before bed!' exclaimed Scarlett, as she stood up from the couch.

'Remember, Missy, if you have a cup of tea now, you will have to visit the long drop in the middle of the night.'

Scarlett looked horrified. She sat back down and her eyes teared up.

'Don't say it, Paul! Not now!'

'Missy, we'll get through this,' Paul said, comforting her. He sat on the arm of the couch and put an arm around her. 'It'll be tough in the beginning, a steep learning curve, but we'll find a way. Just remember how strong and determined you were to become an Olympic swimmer. You'll use that same strength to overcome the challenges that lie ahead.'

Scarlett wiped her eyes with the back of her hand and nodded in agreement.

'I hear you,' Scarlett replied. 'But seriously, it's easy for you but what am I going to do if I want to go to the loo at night?'

Paul shrugged his shoulders before saying, 'I think you're going to have to learn to pee standing up.'

'Paul!'

'In case you think I'm joking, I'm not! There's no way you can go to the long drop in the middle of the night. You're going to have to do what I'll do and that is stand on the veranda and pee into the night sky.'

Scarlett nodded her head resignedly before agreeing. 'Maybe. But I think I'll forego that cup of tea I was dying to have.'

'No you won't. We have had little to drink today and that cup of tea will calm you.'

Paul got up from the couch and went into the kitchen. There was no kettle, so he looked at the stove, turned a dial and heard a hissing sound. A gas stove, he concluded. He suddenly wondered about electricity for the house. Paul looked around and didn't see any electric sockets which set off a mild panic until he noticed a light switch. He flicked it on but no light emanated from the single electric bulb dangling in the middle of the kitchen. 'Maybe there's a mains switch that needs to be switched on,' he thought.

Back to the stove. Neither Paul nor Scarlett had ever used a gas stove. Paul turned a dial on again and heard a hissing sound and could smell the gas.

He walked back into the lounge to tell Scarlett the news that there was only a gas stove.

'Just leave it, Paul. We can deal with it tomorrow.'

'No. I am treating this as a test of our resolve,' Paul said in a determined voice. 'We are going to have a cup of tea and if need be you are going to learn to pee standing up! The big question is, do we have any matches?'

'Not that I am aware of.'

'Well, think then. How are we going to get a naked flame? Surely we're not going to have to rub two stones together!'

They both looked at each other like two city slickers dumped in the middle of Timbuktu.

After a moment of brainstorming, with little practical knowledge he had about living in the bush, Paul felt proud of his eureka moment. 'I've got it,' he said. 'I'll use the cigarette lighter from the car.'

Using another paper serviette, Paul managed to get a flame using the cigarette lighter, got the gas stove going and produced a cup of tea using powdered milk.

§

Paul and Scarlett went to bed just as the sun was setting. The bed was old and lumpy and musty. And it was hot! And innumerable mosquitoes were in full attack mode. They tossed and turned and tossed and turned, then just lay on their backs.

Neither had said a word until around midnight, Paul voiced, 'Are you thinking what I am?'

'If you mean 'what the hell have we done?' then yes! And what's more I need to pee!'

'I need to go too, so I'll join you.'

Standing on the edge of the veranda, Paul did his business while Scarlett watched, wondered and worried.

'Well, what do I do?'

'Missy, don't go and squat in the garden. Who knows what might be out there?'

'And?'

'Slip your panties off, stand on the edge of the veranda just like I did, make a parting of the ways and let rip.'

Scarlett followed Paul's instructions but nothing happened.

'What's the matter?' asked Paul after what seemed like a long time.

'I'm bursting but it's not coming out,' replied Scarlett. 'It's as if it's shy! Turn your head away.'

'Missy, I've seen you pee a million times!'

'This is different.'

Paul gave Scarlett a sharp smack on the bottom.

'Hey!' exclaimed Scarlett. 'What—'

Suddenly it happened.

'You were just tense,' Paul said as he came up from behind to embrace his wife. 'Look at that flow. You should be proud of that. And you'll get better at it.'

When Scarlett's pee trickled to an end, she burst out laughing saying to Paul, 'Never in a million years did I ever think that I would be in the middle of an African bush peeing like a man.'

§

Eventually both fell into a broken sleep. At 6 o'clock in the morning a noise from the kitchen startled Scarlett. She looked over at Paul but, given the night they had experienced, she didn't want to wake him just yet, even though it was now light. So she built up the courage and carefully stalked down the short passageway towards the kitchen.

In the kitchen she saw the back of a person, a black woman poised over the stove. For a moment Scarlett just stood there not knowing what to do or say. The woman then poured hot water into a teapot which she placed on a tray and turned around to see Scarlett.

'Good morning, madam,' the black woman greeted.

'Good morning,' Scarlett greeted hesitantly. 'Who are you?'

'I'm the girl,' the black woman responded.

'What girl?'

'The girl for the house,' the woman responded as if it were the most normal thing to say, and a bit perplexed why she was being questioned.

'I don't quite understand. Are you a maid for this house?'

'Yes, madam, the girl.'

Although Scarlett's family never had a maid while she was growing up in her parent's house, Paul's parents had three maids in their mansion, one of whom had doubled as a nanny for Robin when she was young. And although Paul's parents never called their maids using the term 'girl', Scarlett was aware that many people in South Africa did.

'What's your name?' asked Scarlett.

'Beauty.'

'Beauty, what do you do here in the house?'

'I clean the house, do the washing and I cook for you.'

'Who told you to do that?'

'The boss.'

'And who is this boss?'

'He's living that side,' Beauty told Scarlett, pointing in some vague direction.

'In White River?' guessed Scarlett.

'Yes, madam.'

'And what's his name?'

'It is a Stefan.'

'And he is your boss?'

'Yes.'

'And he told you to come and work here at this house?'

'Yes. He told me to come here and work as the girl.'

'And when there is nobody living here then what do you do?' Scarlett asked, intrigued, since the house had not seen a broom in months.

'Then I go and work on the other side.'

'In White River for Stefan?'

'No, but he gives me another job. Any job where he needs me. He says you are coming today, so I must come and be the girl for this house.'

'And where do you live?'

'On that side there.'

Scarlett clearly didn't know where all these sides were, so she stopped that line of questioning and instead asked, 'Who is the tray of tea for?'

'It's for you, madam, and for the boss.'

'For me and Stefan?'

'No, madam, for you and your husband. You must be in bed.'

'In bed?' asked a confused Scarlett.

'Yes. In the morning I bring you tea when you are in bed. You must go back to the bedroom, so I can bring you your tea. For you and the boss.'

A somewhat perplexed Scarlett led Beauty back to the bedroom where Paul was still asleep.

'Madam, you must get back into bed so that I can give you your tea. And you must wake up the boss while I open the curtains.'

Feeling as if she were in some sort of twilight zone, Scarlett got back into bed and tugged on her husband's shoulder to wake him up.

Paul took one look at his wife and exclaimed with shock in his voice, 'Scarlett! You look like you have chicken pox!'

'So do you, my dear. They're mosquito bites.'

'Good morning, boss!' announced Beauty in a cheerful voice as she drew the curtains open.

'Whoa! Who's this, Missy?' Paul asked, sitting upright.

'Apparently we have a maid who works at this house,' Scarlett told him.

'Really?' Paul queried. 'Under whose direction?'

'Stefan, she said. Perhaps we can clear it up with him. But now we have to stay in bed so she can bring us our tea. Her name is Beauty, by the way.'

Beauty laid the tray on Scarlett's lap and then said, 'I make your breakfast now, but there is no food.'

'Beauty, we'll go and buy food in White River today and see Stefan. Today you can just help clean the house.'

'Okay,' Beauty said obligingly, before adding some valuable advice. 'These spots,' she said, pointing all over her own face, neck and shoulders, 'there is a mosquito net in the cupboard.'

§

Before going into White River, Paul and Scarlett took a peek inside the clinic. It was pitiful with scarcely any supplies. They managed to meet up with Stefan Lagerström at a prearranged spot in town before their removal truck was due to arrive.

'Stefan,' Paul greeted. 'Many questions!'

Stefan Lagerström smiled and replied, 'I was expecting that!'

'The clinic has very little in the way of supplies. It would be impossible to run it based on what's there.'

'I understand,' replied Stefan. 'I was not going to equip the clinic with anything until I was sure you were actually going to arrive. I expect you got quite a shock yesterday.'

'That's an understatement!' said Paul.

'I have to be honest with you, Paul and Missy. It's not going to be easy. No doctor lasts very long there. The house is a shambles. And I guess you've met the long drop?'

'You could have warned us about that,' Scarlett said sharply.

'Then I doubt you would have come.'

'Oh, you are right about that,' Scarlett said with a certain degree of sarcasm. 'Stefan, how do you expect a woman to go to the loo at night?'

'I suggest you get a potty.'

'Or just pee like a man!' laughed Paul. 'You did a good job last night!'

Scarlett punched Paul on the arm for revealing that information and changed the subject by asking Stefan about the medical supplies and equipment.

Stefan said, 'I expect that you have brought some basic equipment, thermometers, blood pressure kits and so on. Regarding supplies, the best we can do is to give you a limited amount of analgesics, bandages and plasters, and maybe some disinfectant.'

'That's it?' an incredulous Paul asked. 'How do you expect us to run a clinic with less than what is in the medicine cupboard of a normal home.'

'A normal home to you, Paul. The patients you'll be dealing with will often have gone to either a diviner or to a herbalist, what Europeans call witchdoctors. If they aren't healed they'll come to you and a simple analgesic to alleviate pain will be like manna from heaven.'

'This so-called witchdoctor stuff, is it big and will there be a conflict of interest?' asked Paul.

'Yes on both counts, so you need to tread carefully and whatever your beliefs are you need to show respect.'

'Is there any protocol preventing us from getting our own medical supplies at our own cost?' asked Scarlett.

'Goodness, no. With our limited budget anything extra will be most welcome.'

'Then, Paul, we'll need to pay for new stock.' concluded Scarlett. 'Running a clinic with what we saw this morning would be going against our own ethics.'

'I agree.'

'I appreciate that gesture,' said Stefan. 'I have a son-in-law who is a doctor, and he may be able to help you get medical supplies at cost price. If you give me a list of your requirements, I'll ask him to see what he can do for you.'

Scarlett addressed her boss, 'Stefan, this morning we were woken by Beauty and—'

'Oh, her,' laughed Stefan Lagerström. 'She is a wonderful woman.'

'That may be so, but I don't think we need a servant to run our house.'

'Oh, yes, you will! Trust me, Paul and Missy, you'll be run off your feet at the clinic. Beauty will be a godsend for you. You may not like the idea now, but she will be a great source of strength for you. Apart from a normal maid's work, she is invaluable getting the generator going, fixing it up and firing up the boiler for hot water. She might just be the magic pill that keeps you from resigning in the next few weeks or months.'

'That sounds like an omen,' remarked Scarlett.

'Well, I'm hoping that Beauty and Precious will keep you sane so that you last longer than all the others who have tried to become bush doctors.'

'Precious?' asked Scarlett.

'Yes, she is a nurse who will be assisting you. She only has a crude form of training, but she'll be invaluable for translation. And I would appreciate it if you taught her medical practices along the way.'

'Where is she now?' asked Paul.

'I'll give her the go-ahead to join you when you have your opening day.'

'Which is when?'

'That's up to you. If you want to purchase supplies, get the clinic building spruced up a bit, get some idea of a system that you might want to run, then you let me know and I will send Nurse Precious along.'

'Where will Beauty and Precious be living?' asked Scarlett.

'You may not have noticed but there is a room attached to the house with an outside entrance and that is where Beauty will stay. There's another room attached to the clinic for Precious.'

'And where do they normally live?'

'Goodness knows. They will point somewhere and say on that side, but I have never known where all these sides are. So they will go home to whichever side on the weekends. I am aware that you are doing this *pro bono*, but I'd like to think that you keep to official hours which is all day Mondays to Fridays. No doubt some patients will pitch up on weekends, then it's up to you whether you see them. My advice would be to travel the Eastern Transvaal. There are some beautiful sights and, of course, there is Kruger Park so close to you.'

'Lastly, Stefan,' Paul said, 'our removal truck ought to be arriving at midday, but there is no way it will be able to travel on the dirt track to our new home.'

'Don't worry. I'll lend you a pick-up truck or bakkie, as you call it, and you can transport your belongings in shifts.'

'Thanks.'

'Oh, if it storms during the night, and it will,' Stefan suddenly announced, 'expect both Beauty and Precious to join you in your bedroom. They are petrified of thunder and lightning. And of snakes.'

'Snakes!' Scarlett cried.

Stefan walked away chuckling, but Paul called him back and asked with some concern, 'What other creatures are we to expect?'

'You have to understand,' the missionary tried to explain, 'you live in the middle of the bush. It is wild out there. We're close to Kruger Park and although the park is fenced off, you do get spillover.'

'Lions?' asked Paul with some trepidation, not really expecting the answer to be yes.

'There are no wild lions outside of Kruger Park but occasionally some escape. Usually after a few days the game rangers will track them down, dart them and take them back to the park.'

'And?' asked Paul, a little worried.

'Occasionally an elephant breaks through a Kruger Park fence, but again the rangers will deal with them. Just don't plant any citrus trees because that acts like a magnet for them.'

'And?' asked Paul, getting more worried.

'There will always be leopards lurking because you can't keep them contained. You won't see them, but they will see you. So don't go wandering too far from the house at night. Remember, most wild creatures are afraid of humans. They will retreat and only attack if they feel threatened. The exception is a leopard that is old and has lost its teeth. It will be looking for easy prey and that could be a problem. We've never had an incident, though if you keep a dog for a pet then expect that every so often you will lose one. It's best they are kept inside at night.'

'What else could be a danger?' asked Paul, quite agitated.

'Inside your house you mostly have to look out for spiders, scorpions and snakes.'

'Snakes!' exclaimed Scarlett.

'Not many. Occasionally they will come into the house for warmth. But they won't attack you. I do suggest that you turn your shoes upside down every time you put them on and tap on them just to make sure a scorpion hasn't made itself a new home.'

'What about the dam in front of the house?' asked Paul.

'You'll spend most of your evenings watching the sun set over that dam. I'm hoping that the unique beauty you find in the African bush will seep into your soul and dissuade you from leaving.'

'That sounds good, but I was wondering if there was anything to be concerned about.'

'We haven't had a hippo for a while but if you are walking in the vicinity of the dam and you see a log moving then walk the other way because it will be a crocodile. And crocodiles aren't afraid of humans.'

Paul and Scarlett looked at Stefan warily. They had a distinct feeling he was enjoying himself at their expense. Someone experienced living in the bush and putting a little fear into the city slickers.

'As I said, I know it won't be easy, especially at first,' consoled Stefan. 'Most of the wild creatures I've mentioned, fear humans. You will have the odd close shave but you'll get through it. Your biggest concern is that this is a malaria area, so try not to get bitten by mosquitoes. Looking at your faces and arms you obviously weren't successful last night so be sure to use the mosquito nets provided.'

'Hmm!' muttered Scarlett. 'We only found out about them this morning from Beauty.'

'Good for her. Trust her because she will be your rock. Don't worry about your mosquito bites. Most are more irritating than harmful and being doctors I am sure you are aware that it is only the female anopheles mosquito that transmits malaria. They usually try their luck at dusk and dawn and tend to bite around the ankles. So when you are enjoying your sundowner each evening overlooking the dam, make sure you use an insect repellent like Tabard.'

And with that last advice, Stefan Lagerström again walked away chuckling.

Paul looked at Scarlett. They both were a little shell-shocked. To add a bit of levity, Paul said, 'Remember, we are the privileged ones.'

'That's getting a bit tired, Paul,' Scarlett said with a degree of irritation.

§

On returning to their home, laden with food supplies, Paul and Scarlett noticed a black man hunched over with his back to them near the steps of the veranda.

'Hello,' greeted Paul.

The black man turned around and stood up. He was shirtless and barefoot and looked as if he was in his fifties.

'Hello,' he replied in a heavy accent, also raising a hand filled with weeds to embellish his greeting.

'Who are you?' Paul asked.

'I am the boy.'

'What boy?' asked Paul, prompting Scarlett to think, oh dear, here we go again.

'The boy,' the black man said again.

'What's your name?'

'Professor.'

Scarlett giggled as she walked past the two men. The black man's English was very poor, and she knew there would be a conversation that was going to go nowhere.

Inside the kitchen, Scarlett asked Beauty, 'Who is the gentleman outside who calls himself Professor?'

'He is the boy.'

'Okay,' Scarlett said guardedly, 'but what is he doing here?'

Beauty, whose English was considerably better than Professor's, replied. 'He is the garden boy. He comes one day a week to make the garden look nice.'

'And his name is Professor?' Scarlett asked purposely to see if it elicited a reaction of mirth from her maid.

'Yes,' replied Beauty, but with no indication that such a name was odd.

Scarlett went out to the car to fetch the food supplies, passing the two men who were deep in a conversation where neither understood the other, and returned with several packets which she dumped onto the kitchen counter.

Beauty saw this and said, 'No, Madam, it is my job to bring in the groceries.'

Scarlett replied, 'Okay, but I will help you.'

'No, Madam, your job is to work in the clinic. My job is to make the food and clean the house. And to fetch the groceries.'

'Well, the clinic hasn't started yet, so today I will help you with the groceries.'

During the next week, Paul stocked the clinic with medical supplies at his own cost, and then relayed a message to Stefan that the clinic was ready to open for business. Word went out that they would officially reopen the following Monday.

Beauty woke Paul and Scarlett early on Monday morning with their tea. They showered and dressed quickly, then ate a decent breakfast cooked by their maid. There was excitement in the air. Their first day at the clinic.

They walked over to the clinic building with a spring in their steps. Upon arriving they saw a black lady standing at the front door of the clinic building.

'One patient,' commented Paul. 'I guess the bush telegraph is a bit slow.'

'Hello,' greeted Scarlett. Paul did the same.

'Hello,' said the black woman.

While Paul unlocked the door, he asked, 'Have you come to see a doctor?'

'No,' laughed the black woman. 'I am the nurse.'

'Precious? Nurse Precious?' asked Scarlett.

'Yes.'

They shook hands, introducing themselves, and the nurse told them she would be working every Monday to Friday, and she would be staying in the room at the back of the clinic but on the weekends she would be going home .

'Where is home?' asked Scarlett.

'Oh, it's that side,' replied Precious, gesturing in some vague direction that could have meant anywhere.

As they entered the clinic, Paul asked Precious, 'You're here because Mr Lagerström told you we were starting today, but does anyone else know?

'Yes.'

'And will anybody come today?'

'Yes, they are already here.'

'They are? Where?' asked Scarlett.

'Outside. They made a line on that side,' Precious said, her hand pointing in some general direction.

Paul went outside, walked around to the side of the clinic away from their house and saw a queue of people that stretched into the bush and beyond.

He returned to Scarlett and said, 'I don't wish to alarm you but we have a queue of patients that extends as far as the eye can see. I shudder to think how long it is but expect a busy day.'

Paul asked Precious, 'I see the patients all in a line. How long is the queue?'

'Too long.'

'Okay,' Paul replied, not entirely satisfied with the answer. He then asked, 'Where are they coming from?'

Precious answered, 'From that side.'

Not wanting to go down that avenue again, Paul asked, 'Why are they in a line that goes into the bush? Why not gather here in the clearing outside the clinic?'

'It is going to get hot today. The trees give them shade.'

'Mental note to self,' Paul said aloud, 'we need to get some benches and maybe build a thatched gazebo for shade.'

Paul then asked, 'Precious, is the queue just this long because it is the first day and nobody has had any attention for many months?'

'No, it will be like this every day.'

'Scarlett, for your own sanity, do not go outside to see how long the line of patients is.' He then turned to the nurse and said, 'Your first job every day is to go down the line and decide which the most serious cases are, the emergencies, so that we can deal with them first.'

'Yes, boss.'

'Precious, you don't have to call me boss. My name is Paul.'

'Yes, boss.'

Paul realised that it was futile to get the nurse to change the way she addressed him. Perhaps it might come slowly, he thought.

'Maybe you can go now, and bring those who need attention the most to the front of the queue.'

'Yes, boss.'

A few minutes later a young boy arrived at the door looking rather forlorn.

Paul brought him in, sat him down on a chair opposite his desk and asked, 'What's the matter?'

The boy did not answer.

Paul repeated the question and still got no answer. So he stood up, walked over to the boy and pointed to his head, to which the boy nodded, then Paul proceeded to point to various areas of his body, eventually ending at the boys bare feet.

At that point the boy said, 'Mamba.'

Scarlett, who was about to take in a second patient, overheard. She murmured to Paul, 'Surely not. He would be dead by now!'

'Mamba?' Paul questioned.

The boy replied in his mother tongue, 'Yebo.' That meant yes.

They were at an impasse. So Paul tried again, pointing to the boy's head. 'Is it sore here?'

The boy nodded. As Paul continued pointing to various body parts, the boy said mournfully, 'Nyoga.'

'What the heck is nyoga?'

'I think we need a translator,' Scarlett said, and went to call Precious.

The nurse came in and spoke to the boy in Tsonga. 'Nyoga is a snake,' she told Paul.

'Well, he did say mamba. But surely he would be dying or dead by now,' said a worried Scarlett.

'Many of us call any snake a mamba,' Nurse Precious said. 'Our culture is very scared of snakes, especially the black mamba, so when someone gets bitten by a snake they will often say mamba.'

'Do they believe it is a black mamba?'

'Some do. They think all snakes are black mambas. Others know that there is a difference but will still call a snake a mamba because we are so scared of them.'

Paul looked closer at the boy's left foot and spotted two distinct puncture wounds that suggested the boy was telling the truth. He had been bitten by a snake. There was no swelling or deterioration of flesh. He asked Precious what symptoms the boy had, and she replied that he had a headache.

The thought temporarily flashed through his mind that he was now a bush doctor and must dispense treatment like one. Back in Cape Town, he would have done all sorts of tests but instead he gave the boy an aspirin, put a few more in a small envelope and asked Precious to tell the boy that he should take one at night and again the next morning, and if any other symptoms arose that he should return to the clinic.

§

That evening as they sat on garden furniture on the veranda after having a good home cooked meal prepared by Beauty, Paul said, 'Remind me that we're going to have to get snake anti-venom.'

'It's already on my list, not just for our patients but for us too.'

'Are you really worried that we may get bitten?'

'Yes!' said Scarlett. 'Our first patient today was someone bitten by a snake.'

'You're not more worried about malaria?'

'No!' replied Scarlett emphatically.

'I never realized you were so scared of snakes.'

'Well I am!' Scarlett said firmly. 'So I've done a bit of research into snakes and their venom.'

'When? We've only been here just over a week.'

'Well,' said Scarlett rather sheepishly, 'when Stefan mentioned snakes it gave me the heebie jeebies, so when we bought our groceries I snuck in a booklet about snakes of the lowveld.'

'And?'

'There are plenty of them here and some are pretty nasty. I know we probably learned about the different types of snake venom at med school, but that's a long time ago.'

'Remind me.'

'Well, the different venoms cause different reactions. The black mamba, which we learned today is every snake, has a neurotoxic venom that affects the nervous system and leads to death due to respiratory failure. Then there are those snakes such as a puff adder and the Mozambique spitting cobra that have a cytotoxic venom. That destroys tissue which often leads to amputations. The third one is the haemotoxic venom that causes internal haemorrhaging and, if it isn't treated, will lead to death. The boomslang has that venom. Fortunately it's a slow-acting one because they only keep a supply of that anti-venom in Pretoria. At least there should be time to get it flown in, though I don't know about here.'

'I'm assuming that boy today had a mildly venomous snake bite.'

'Yes, there are quite a few snakes that are either mildly venomous or not at all. So, the ones we need to look out for here are the black mamba, the puff adder and the Mozambique spitting cobra.'

'Okey dokes. Remind me to get some anti-venom for them.'

'Paul, are you not afraid of snakes?'

'I'm not unafraid, but I think that if we are cautious and aware, then we'll be fine.'

Scarlett didn't seem convinced.

'The other thing we need to do,' said Paul, 'is to utilize Precious as an interpreter, at least until we learn Tsonga. Excuse the pun, but she will be precious to us in that regard.'

§

Over the next few months, with the help of Professor in the garden, Beauty in the house and Precious in the clinic, Paul and Scarlett also slaved away on weekends painting the house and clinic, arranging their furniture and decorating the house with paintings they had bought locally to reflect the beauty of the lowveld, and creating a garden to be proud of.

As Stefan Lagerström suggested, they also used the weekends to travel and explore the Eastern Transvaal, taking in the natural wonders that surrounded them. Blyde River Canyon, God's Window, Bourke's Luck Potholes, Pilgrims Rest and, of course, Kruger Park.

In the clinic, the learning curve was steep. Despite their medical knowledge and experience, the challenges were huge. They disinfected and stitched wounds caused by a variety of sources, and treated numerous cases of influenza, malaria and tuberculosis with antibiotics and various vaccines.

§

At the end of the year, Paul and Scarlett spent two weeks on holiday in Cape Town staying part of the time with Paul's parents and the other with Danny, who was now a teacher at Rondebosch Boys' Preparatory School. Scarlett's mother was able to join them on many occasions.

On Christmas day, Scarlett invited her mother and Danny to have Christmas lunch at the Rhodes family home. After lunch, Scarlett asked her mother to join her in visiting Pinelands Cemetery.

After placing a vase of flowers in front of the headstone on Robin's grave, Scarlett asked her mother, 'How's Papa?'

'I'm afraid, Sweetie, that he has deteriorated fast this past year. He is in severe depression most of the time and there's a part of me that thinks he may have the start of dementia.'

'Is there any way in which I can see him and try to help?'

'I'm afraid not. He may not recognize you and if he did it will most likely set him back. I'm seriously thinking of putting him into a care home.'

'Well, let me at least help you find a decent one.'

'I would appreciate that.'

After a few quiet moments standing next to Robin's grave, Mrs Harrison read aloud the inscription on Robin's headstone, 'Now boast thee death, in thy possession lies a lass unparalleled.' With sadness in her eyes, she said, 'I will go to my grave regretting that I did not stand up to your father sooner. It robbed me of the chance to know my granddaughter.'

'You never know, Mama. Danny is in a serious relationship. Maybe you will get to enjoy a grandchild sooner than you think. And what about me? I'm still young enough.'

'But you live so far away.'

'I do, Mama, but it was my calling to go there and I've experienced a deep satisfaction giving back to the underprivileged community. Paul and I have created a lovely little home. If Papa goes into a care home, there is no reason why you shouldn't visit us for long periods at a time. I'm going to ask Danny to bring you to visit in the mid-year school holidays. That time of year is so beautiful in the lowveld.'

'I look forward to it.'

1st January 1981

Dear Scarlett,

The new year started with a gnawing feeling in my gut. For Sandra too. Until then, Kike had been kept under wraps, so to speak, but with her ever-exuberant pouncing and attacking visitors, all an act of play, I might add, word got around that a young lion resided at the De Beer's home, word that would inevitably get back to the Director of Nature Conservation and Research. We knew the status quo could not continue. The problem was what to do with Kike?

Following Kobus's advice, Sandra and I started taking Kike on walks in the valley of the silver cluster-leaf trees to introduce her to the wild. Recalling how Kike had reacted by lying flat on the ground at the sable kill, I was intrigued to see how she would react to other animals we encountered, especially lions. Did she believe herself to be a lion?

Every animal we came across on those walks got the Kike treatment. She would chase after them. In the case of smaller animals like impala, she would run after them, scatter them, and then return with a smug look on her face. At her young age, and with no training from her lion mother, there was no chance that she would ever actually catch anything. Encounters with the larger species, elephants, rhinos and such, were a lot more scary. Kike would chase after them only to be rebuffed and charged at herself. But she is an agile cat and would escape the angry elephant or rhino. Having escaped she would try again and again to chase them. For her it was all a game. For Sandra and me, well we were just hugely relieved when at the end of each walk a living Kike returned home with us. Whatever the future held for our beloved lioness, these walks provided invaluable experiences.

On weekends, the De Beer family and I took Kike along when we went fishing or camping or climbing koppies. That meant she had to ride in the back of a bakkie which she loved, but the problem was that a small section of the road we had to travel on before we could get to the private game ranger's patrol road was also used by tourists. I say problem, because the more people who saw a lion riding on the back of a bakkie, the more word would spread about Kike and the Director of Nature Conservation and Research would step in and order that something be done about our orphaned child.

On these patrol roads, every time Kike saw an animal she would jump off the moving bakkie and charge in hot pursuit of some unsuspecting and I guess bewildered creature in Kruger Park. But over the next few months, I noticed that Kike would always lie low if ever we came across any lions, something that still intrigues me.

Those were heavenly times. Who gets to walk a lion in the bushveld as Sandra and I did so often in the late afternoon, and who gets to explore the great wilderness of Kruger Park with a lion walking at your side as we did on weekends as a family?

At the beginning of July, I treated Stefan and Ingrid to a trip back to their homeland of Sweden. When I visited there four years ago with Anna, my mind was in a trance, so I've always wanted to go back to see where she lived her formative years, and going with her parents gave me a special connection to Anna.

We spent a week in Stockholm which, even though I am now very much an outdoor bush person, I found to be a lovely city. Although Stefan and Ingrid did not play tennis, they knew of Anna's love for the game, so we found a bar to watch the Wimbledon men's singles final. Incredibly, about half an hour before the final started, all the streets in Stockholm became deserted, everyone either at home or a tennis club or a hotel or a bar to watch their favourite son, Björn Borg, attempting to win a modern day record of five consecutive titles.

The bar was packed. I'm not sure if watching Björn in a Wimbledon final with a bunch of other Swedes was a good idea. So famous did his final with John McEnroe become that you may know about it, but the collective nerves had my heart racing like the rest of the Swedes. I, too, was desperate for Björn to win. After all, he was Anna's favourite. And so we lived and died through a fourth set tiebreaker where from 5-all every second point was either a match point for Borg or a set point for McEnroe. It was nerve jangling stuff and despite Swedish people having a reputation for being stoic, you can imagine the reaction when Björn lost that tie-breaker 18-16. The tears, the looks of abject misery, the swilling of beers to drown their sorrows, it was all quite a sight.

Oh, but how little faith they had in Anna's hero. He dug deep and eventually won the title in a close fifth set. Pandemonium set in. And how do I know that this meant a lot to the Swedish people? Because even though Stefan and Ingrid are teetotallers, both asked for a stiff drink after the match! I was so pleased for Anna, and I briefly wondered if, knowing that I was watching the match in Sweden, she had joined the tennis gods to help orchestrate this masterpiece.

Before moving on to Västervik, the Lagerström's home town, we took a detour to Södertälje where I proudly showed Stefan and Ingrid the garage door where Björn practised all day and every day to become the champion that he now is. And, I mentioned that Anna had also played against the wall on our trip to Sweden.

Visiting Västervik with Stefan and Ingrid was special as they filled me in on Anna's childhood years. I felt some closure after my last visit to her home town.

Then we spent ten days in the Archipelago off Stockholm, camping, hiking, cycling, swimming, fishing, kayaking — every outdoor activity that one could imagine in a setting of 30,000 islands.

On our way back to South Africa, we stopped off in Cambridge so my in-laws could meet my parents for the first time and, with the help of Stefan and Ingrid, I finally managed to persuade Mom and Dad and my sister Jean to visit my beautiful adopted country, South Africa. They promised to do so this July, so I am really looking forward to that! While in my childhood home, I heard the latest release by ABBA, the group Anna had grown fond of, a song titled, *The Winner Takes It All*. It dawned on me then that I had not heard any music since Anna had died. Yes, I had heard the symphonies of birds and insects, which I love, but not the type of music that Anna and I had listened to or performed together. I made a conscious decision that when I returned to South Africa, I would get back into music. In some ways it seems anathema to listen to or play music in Kruger Park with so many natural sounds emanating from the bush making their own music. But maybe I could steal just a little time each day for myself to indulge. When Anna died, the music in me died too, but it was time to resurrect a passion we shared.

My 'back to music' intention didn't quite happen, but more about that in a moment. I could not believe it but when I arrived at the De Beer's home, Kike was waiting there at the gate as if she knew I was due back. Her greeting was joyous, rubbing her head against my legs, standing up on two legs to grab my face between her front paws and 'lion kiss' me, accompanied by soulful grunts and groans. And the reception from the De Beers was equally welcoming, but I knew immediately that not all was well with Sandra. Her hazel coloured eyes betrayed a sadness.

When we had a moment alone, Sandra told me that Kobus had received an official letter from the Director of Nature Conservation and Research reminding him that it was against Kruger Park policy to keep a wild animal and demanded to know what we were going to do with Kike. And so my music took a backseat as all our energies were devoted to trying to decide what to do with a lioness that, despite all our attempts in the first six months of the year, didn't know that she belonged to the Panthera leo species.

There were demands on our part too. Kike could not be put in a zoo. She had to be a free lion, even if not a wild lion. The next few months involved searching or visiting every conceivable avenue to find Kike a new home, but just when we were on the verge of success, something scuppered our attempts. After three months another letter arrived from the Director of Nature Conservation and Research. Eventually, through a convoluted route, word got through to us, apparently via the legendary George Adamson that there was a game park that bordered Botswana where a man by the name of Samson, can you believe it, may have the ideal park that would suit both Kike and our wishes for her.

Those four months were a torrid time for us — not only because of the difficulties we experienced in finding Kike a suitable home, but also knowing we were about to lose a special and beloved daughter. So we made the most of it spending as much time as possible with her. All of us. Kobus, Japie and Helena, but Sandra and me most of all. Kike was maturing fast but never lost her *joie de vivre* spirit. And as much as possible, the time we spent with her was in the bush, because that is where she belonged.

Three weeks before Kike was to go to her new home, Samson came to spend time with us to have Kike get used to him. He looked like a lion! An old lion! In fact, he looked like George Adamson of *Born Free* fame! Not too long after he had arrived, Kike started to express an interest in Samson. That was unusual. As gentle and loving as Kike was, it usually took much longer for her to warm to anyone new in her life, almost as if she would only allow someone to enter her circle of trust once she was sure her human family trusted that person!

Samson had an incredible calmness about him. He allowed Kike to adapt at her pace. It was quite clear that he possessed a deep love for lions and had a special affinity for them. A true lion whisperer! Over the three weeks, Kike treated Samson as the equal of Sandra and me. In a private moment with Sandra, we both agreed that Kike could not have had a better person with whom to start a new chapter in her life.

Samson explained to us that Kike would be slowly introduced to other lions at his park, and he would start a process of de-familiarising her from humans so that she would come to know herself as a lion and hopefully one day produce a litter of cubs. Eventually she would have a huge open space to roam with her fellow lions and lionesses, a space that would also have several game species. He said that she would be a free lioness but would probably always be dependent on being fed by humans. Lions in the wild can live a very harsh existence, and as much as both Sandra and I wished that Kike could be a true wild lioness, selfishly we were pleased to hear that she would always be taken care of.

Samson left to return to his park. He had advised that we should not see Kike again for at least a year, so he wanted us to have one last full day alone with her. It was to be an emotional day, but I tried my best to make it as enjoyable as possible. Unfortunately, in the morning Sandra had to make final arrangements, sorting out permits, so in the early dawn I took Kike for a walk in our favourite valley. Kobus needed Wagter for work purposes that morning, so it was just Kike and me, meandering through the silver cluster-leaf trees which were now more beautiful than ever with their flowers looking like baubles on a tree, which was fitting with Christmas just around the corner. Kike, of course, stalked and charged anything that moved, at one point scattering a huge herd of impala ewes and their young lambs. This was the first time I had ever walked alone with Kike, and by alone I also mean without Wagter. I have to confess that my heart beat a little faster when Kike chased after the impala and went out of view. It beat even faster when after 15 minutes she had not returned. A myriad of thoughts went through my mind. Had she caught one? Had she got lost? Was I ever going to see her again? And what on earth was I going to tell Kobus and Sandra? Fortunately, much to my relief, she returned with an expression on her face as if to say that she was proud of her achievement and what did I think of that? Expletives were not in the language that Sandra or I had ever used in talking to Kike, so I was not about to start now, but if only she could read my mind!

Then something strange happened. November and early December is lambing season in Kruger Park when impala ewes drop their little ones. The theory is that if they all give birth at much the same time, while predation is high the sheer numbers of lambs born will result in a significant number that will survive to ensure the continuation of the species. Of course, the huge number of impala in Kruger Park is testament to that theory working. An impala ewe will usually leave the herd when labour starts and give birth in private before rejoining the herd. Not long after Kike returned we came across a ewe giving birth. The birth process was too far underway for the impala to run off and at first I was deeply concerned that Kike would chase after her. But she didn't. Instead, we both watched the lamb being born. Afterwards the mother ate the birth sac and licked her newborn, with each lick of her tongue encouraging it to get up and stand. I looked to Kike but her eyes were fixated on the birth process taking place in front of us. I am fully aware that one should not apply human thinking to an animal, but I did wonder if there was some maternal connection that had so engrossed Kike and stopped her from chasing the impala. The lamb soon got to its feet, wobbly at first, growing in strength over the next half an hour, and walked quite confidently as its mother took her newborn back to the herd. That is, of course, if there was still a herd and the impala not scattered all over Kruger Park because of that scoundrel called Kike!

After lunch, Kobus took the rest of the day off and the whole family and I, together with Kike and Wagter, spent our last moments with our adopted child by climbing to the top of Shabeni koppie, a place where we had spent our most enjoyable moments over the last year and a half.

It was a glorious summer's day. We reached the summit of Shabeni by mid-afternoon and sat together watching over the vast landscape below us. As we had done so often before, we absorbed the beauty and the serenity of this special view. The view from the iconic Table Mountain in Cape Town is spectacular, but this is just as special. So completely different. One looks over an ocean, the other over a sea of golden bushveld grass in the winter, now green with wild flowers in bloom in the summer. Unless we spotted some animal in the landscape below, a herd of kudu, an elephant appearing then suddenly melting away behind a clump of trees, a giraffe's head popping up over an acacia tree, or a klipspringer standing motionless on a rock nearby, we mostly sat in silence, absorbing this wonderful landscape that Mother Nature had painted.

Late in the afternoon, Kike, lay on her back next to me on my right, Sandra and Kobus to the left of me and the twins together with Wagter beyond them. As I stroked her white belly, I thought about the incredible affection that Kike had shown over the last year and a half and concluded that if given the chance a lion can truly be a man's best friend. At some point Kike sat up and joined the rest of the family sitting in a row on the edge of the rocky outcrop gazing out in the distance. Suddenly she looked up. Ever alert, she had spotted a Bateleur eagle soaring in the sky. I watched her as her inquisitive eyes followed the acrobatic eagle. Then suddenly she got up and left us to go and sit on a boulder nearby. At some point I turned around to see her draped over the boulder with a backdrop of blue sky. She looked regal and for the first time I saw her as an adult lioness, one that was waiting for her king as she scanned the landscape below that would one day be their kingdom.

I turned to Sandra on my left and noticed that she, too, was looking at Kike. Our eyes met, and we both felt a bond of deep satisfaction that we had raised a queen.

On the western horizon a small gathering of wispy white clouds had formed over the distant hills. And as the sun set behind them, the clouds radiated magical colours that changed from liquid gold to pinks and reds, and finally magenta and carmine. An African sunset in all its glory. But one that was setting on a special chapter of my life lived with Kike.

You may have heard of the expression 'walking the green mile', someone heading towards the inevitable, often execution. Well, Sandra and I drove the green mile, hundreds and hundreds of them the following day to take Kike to her new home and not a word passed between us.

We started driving in the middle of the night in a borrowed vehicle suitable for transporting a lion and reached our destination around mid-morning. It was a very emotional goodbye, obviously, but made worse because a forlorn-looking Kike betrayed that she knew something different was about to happen in her life. And, unlike with a human, we could not explain why. A last hug with a rubbing of heads and with tears flowing we said our goodbyes. After losing Anna, it was the hardest moment of my life. Sandra and I hugged each other before I opened the door for her to climb into the vehicle at which point she said, 'Don't worry, you'll see her again soon,' a comment which puzzled me since Samson said not for a year, at least!

Again, not a word passed between Sandra and me on the way home. Once we reached the open road with me navigating through blurred teary eyes, we held hands to comfort each other. Sandra and I had truly lost a dear friend.

Desperate to take my mind off this final goodbye, I noticed that there was a radio in the vehicle, switched it on and instantly recognized the song, *Imagine*. I had always thought it a beautiful song, one that Anna and I had often performed together. Then the news came on and I tuned out. I had not listened to the news in over four years. Then just before the top of the hour the channel again played *Imagine*. I wondered why, a wonder that deepened when this occurred each hour. Just before reaching Numbi Gate to enter Kruger Park in the late afternoon, the puzzle was solved when after another rendition of the song the announcer said, 'In memory of John Lennon who was murdered a week ago today.' I cried out in shock which prompted Sandra to ask what the matter was, our first conversation since we left Kike. I repeated what the announcer had just said, that John Lennon had been murdered. And she asked who John Lennon was! I'm not sure if I was more stunned about the murder of John Lennon or that Sandra did not know who he was. I explained to her, John Lennon of the Beatles. Oh, yes, she said, she seemed to vaguely recall the Beatles from her schooldays. It was only then that it finally dawned on me how secluded one can be from the outside world when living in Kruger Park. The Third World War could come and go and one might not even know about it. As we went through the gate it also struck me how much I had come to love my home in the bush, a place where I had found complete peace in the solitude offered by the magical place that is Kruger Park.

There was, however, a little niggle in my heart as the song *Imagine* reminded me of the fun Anna and I had playing and listening to music.

With Christmas just around the corner, perhaps it was time to buy myself a gift, a guitar.

Even though I'm now 37 years old, I woke up on Christmas morning as excited as a little kid. Excited to be getting a guitar that I had bought for myself. We had invited Stefan and Ingrid over and I gave each of them and the members of the De Beer family a gift that I had purchased in Sweden, then played and sang a few Christmas carols with everyone joining in. Sandra then took my hand and led me to the mantelpiece and peeled away a cloth covering that revealed a gift from the De Beer family to me. Sandra had painted an absolute masterpiece of Kike, our beloved queen sitting on that boulder on top of Shabeni. I then knew what she meant by soon seeing Kike again. The painting now hangs above my bed, allowing me to relive the beautiful memories of the time we had together as I fall asleep every night. A special gift in more ways than one.

And so, my dear, another year comes to an end.

All my love, Michael.

Scarlett

In May, Paul and Scarlett were sitting on the veranda sipping sundowners after an exhausting day at work. The setting sun created a magical glow over the dam, and the orchestra of night creatures started its concert.

'You know, Missy, I used to tease you that we were the privileged ones, but look at this. I think we really are the privileged ones now.'

'It is idyllic,' agreed Scarlett.

'And to think that all those years living in Cape Town, we were blissfully unaware of the South African bush in all its splendour.'

'There is one thing I miss, though,' said Scarlett.

'And that is?'

'The last time I swam was the day Robin died. I so miss the water. And I've been thinking, why don't we book into Kruger Park and spend a night at Pretoriuskop Camp. I've heard that it has a natural rock pool.'

'Then let's go this weekend. I'll make a booking.'

Euphoric at the prospect of swimming again, Scarlett smiled at her husband and said, 'Thank you. I'd like that.'

§

Scarlett got up and went into their bedroom to undress to take a shower before eating what Beauty had cooked them for supper. As she entered the room, she spotted a snake slithering out from under her pillow. Luckily as it lifted its head and spread its hood, Scarlett quickly turned away to call Paul, cringing as she felt the spray of venom hit the back of her neck.

'Yes!' shouted Paul who came running to his wife, sensing urgency in her voice.

'Turn around,' ordered Scarlett, 'or you might get it in your eyes. There is a snake on our bed coming out from under my pillow. It spat at me but luckily I turned around just in time and the venom hit me on the back of my neck. It's beginning to sting.'

Paul took Scarlett into the bathroom and washed the back of her neck. 'You have a slight scratch or perhaps an insect bite of some sort and maybe that's why you can feel a stinging sensation. If it were in your eyes you could have gone blind but I don't think much venom could penetrate through a scratch. I think you'll be fine.'

'That's all well and good, but the snake's on our bed.' And with a bit of sarcasm, 'You know, where we sleep!'

'I'll call Stefan and ask his advice. You go and find Beauty and ask her opinion.'

Walking into the kitchen, Scarlett spoke to Beauty, 'There's a snake on my bed. What do we do?'

'Eish! No madam!' And with that Beauty hightailed it out of the house.

When Scarlett joined Paul out on the front veranda, her husband said that he had just spoken to Stefan. 'He said the snake is known as an M'fezi in local lingo.'

'That doesn't help!'

'A Mozambique spitting cobra. He surmised that given the time of year, it's either looking for food before hibernation or is trying to find some warm place to settle for the winter.'

'Oh, that's comforting,' Scarlett said in a sarcastic voice. 'Looking for food where I sleep or hibernating under my pillow. What other useful advice did he have? Invite it around for supper!'

'No. He suggested that you keep an eye on it, but from a distance so that if it disappears we know where to look for it. My job is to put on a pair of glasses or sunglasses to avoid getting sprayed in the eyes, and then get a fork-pronged stick to prod it along and shoo it out the house. He said that in the process it may pretend that it is dead, but not to try to kill it as you are more likely to get attacked and bitten and their bites can be fatal.'

'You don't have sunglasses,' Scarlett said. 'But there is a fork-pronged stick in the cupboard. It's been there ever since we got here so maybe others have gone through the same experience. I'll get a transparent plastic bag from the kitchen while you keep an eye on the snake.'

When Scarlett grudgingly returned, she handed Paul the plastic bag and stood in the doorway of the bedroom, keeping her distance while making sure the snake stayed in view.

The snake was slate grey on top with a belly that ranged from salmon pink to yellow with black crossbars on the throat. 'It is a beautiful specimen,' commented Paul.

'There's no such thing as a beautiful snake!' responded Scarlett, in agitation. 'And please hurry before it disappears.'

Paul turned his back on the snake and rummaged around the cupboard to find the stick, then after piercing a few ventilation holes in the plastic bag, he placed it over his head and went snake hunting. Scarlett would have found it funny if she hadn't been so terrified. Paul managed to flick the cobra onto the ground where it pretended to be dead. That made it easier for him to nudge it out the front door.

As he closed the door and turned around, Scarlett sank onto the couch in relief. 'With the plastic bag over your head sucking in and blowing out, and you carrying a fork-pronged stick, you look like a monster from a horror film!' she said.

As Paul removed the plastic bag, he said, 'Good idea of yours, this bag. Look where it's discoloured from the snake spraying its venom. Right where my eyes were.'

In reaction, Scarlett gave a nervous laugh, bordering on hysteria.

'Remember, Missy, we are the privileged ones!'

With that comment Scarlett threw a cushion at Paul and, as accurate as a cobra, it hit him square in the face.

'But what if it has a mate?' asked Scarlett.

'I'm fairly sure it hasn't,' replied Paul, though he knew there was no good reason for his answer.

'Well I'm fairly sure I won't have a mate tonight because I am sleeping in another bedroom!'

§

At the weekend, Paul and Scarlett entered Kruger Park at Numbi gate, the gate closest to where they lived. They had done many day trips before, usually on a Sunday when they would take a lazy drive to Skukuza, have lunch and return later that day, enjoying the wonderful sights along the way.

But this time it was different. They were going to spend the night in Kruger Park for the first time and at a camp that had a natural rock pool. From Numbi gate they climbed a long steep hill and at the top turned right onto a gravel road. They toured around some mountain outcrops, spotting some baboons on the rocks, a herd of kudu in the bushes below, but when they headed down the dirt road towards Pretoriuskop Camp they came across a pack of nine African wild dogs, a rare find. Paul and Scarlett watched them run around full of mischief, emitting squeaks, chirps and hoots reminiscent of many of the birds in the area.

After the dogs disappeared into the bush, Paul and Scarlett drove a little further on and came to a stop at a T-junction with the tar road that joined Numbi gate to Pretoriuskop Camp. A bakkie passed in front of them, travelling in the direction towards the camp.

Both Paul and Scarlett looked at each other with confused wonder before Scarlett asked, 'Did you see what I think I saw?'

'If you mean a lion on the back of the bakkie, then yes!'

'Do you think that man driving the bakkie knows he has a lion on the back of his vehicle?'

Paul just shrugged his shoulders.

The camp was a minute's drive away. As soon as they entered the gate, they went to reception to book in.

Scarlett's curiosity got the better of her. 'I'm sorry to interrupt, but I have to ask,' she said to the receptionist. 'We just saw a man driving past in a bakkie with a lion sitting on the back. Do you—'

'Oh,' replied the receptionist in a nonchalant tone, 'that would either be the game ranger or his doctor friend. They have a young lioness that they have raised from a cub, but we're not supposed to say anything about it.'

It was now late in the afternoon and, as Paul and Scarlett emerged from the office, a herd of impala walked in single file through the entrance gate and into the camp.

'That's odd,' Scarlett said. 'If impala, then why not a lion?'

'Missy, it seems as if there is already a lion in the camp, albeit a tame one.'

'Hmm! I hope it's tame.'

§

No sooner had the Rhodes couple unpacked their few belongings in the chalet, when Paul started a fire for a braai. He and Scarlett sat around the fire, sipping from glasses of wine and absorbed the beauty of the African bushveld at sunset. Just then the herd of impala appeared and started grazing in the large open patch of grass in front of their chalet.

After eating boerewors and a spread of salads, Paul and Scarlett continued to sit around the glowing coals enjoying the African bush ambience, the dark night sky lit up by a myriad of bright stars. Suddenly they heard a splash some distance in front of them.

Somewhat startled, Paul fetched his torch and said he was going to investigate. Scarlett followed him, reluctantly. The two of them walked across the expanse of lawn where the impala had grazed earlier in the evening and came upon a gate in a fence. A notice attached to the gate indicated that beyond was a swimming pool.

Paul shone his torch towards the pool and a man's voice came back saying, 'Don't worry, I'm just teaching my lion to swim!'

Paul looked at Scarlett in bemusement and said, 'Well, at least we found where the pool is for our swim tomorrow.'

§

The following morning the sound of lions roaring woke them just before dawn which gave them a chance to go for an early morning drive on the Faye loop that circled the camp, a drive that brought sightings of buffalo, zebra, the rare tsessebe and, of course, the ubiquitous impala. Back at camp, Scarlett wolfed down her breakfast, put on her bikini, covered herself with a sarong and headed off with Paul to the rock pool. She quickly laid down her towel, removed her sarong and entered the cool water. Her first swim in over a year. Although the month of May was in autumn, the predicted temperature for the day was hot, resulting in Scarlett and Paul spending most of the morning either swimming or sunbathing on the rocks that overlooked the natural pool.

Around lunchtime Paul suggested, 'I'll go back to our chalet and bring back a few snacks for lunch.'

He had been gone only a short while when a sunbathing Scarlett heard the gate open. Thinking it a bit too soon for Paul to be returning with lunch, she glanced around and saw Michael Gibson and Japie de Beer enter the pool grounds and dive into the pool. She lay back to continue sunbathing and dozed off. Paul returned, sat down beside her and set out a few snacks and drinks. After a morning spent swimming and lazing in the sun, Scarlett felt ravenous. She and Paul quickly devoured a selection of cheese, crackers, biltong and glasses of red wine.

Between mouthfuls, Scarlett whispered to Paul, 'I'm sure that man's voice is the same one we heard last night, You know, the one who said that he was teaching his lion to swim.'

'Well that kid doesn't look much like a lion to me,' replied Paul

'I wonder if he is the game ranger or the doctor friend that the receptionist mentioned, the ones that have raised a tame lion.'

'I wouldn't know, Missy, but I think we ought to hurry so we don't get back home too late.'

§

During the July school holidays, Danny drove his mother to visit Paul and Scarlett in their home outside White River.

Scarlett was anxious. What would they think of their humble home?

'Thanks, Danny. I appreciate you bringing Mama,' Scarlett said, hugging her brother. 'I know it's a long drive.'

'Wow, Sis, you sure have upgraded from Cape Town!' Danny teased, which earned him a punch on the arm.

Scarlett took her mother's hands into her own, looked deep into her eyes and said, 'Mama, it means so much to me that you have come to visit us.'

Paul and Scarlett gave Mrs Harrison and Danny a tour of their modest house and well-manicured garden, and then a brief look at the clinic.

'Mama, I only get three weeks of leave a year and would like to use two of them to visit you in Cape Town at the end of the year. So for this first week of your two week stay, Paul and I will have to work in the clinic. You are welcome to join us or you and Danny can go sightseeing. But next week we'll be free to take you anywhere you want. There are so many beautiful places here in the lowveld, especially Kruger Park. Our time will be all yours.'

'I'll be glad to help you out,' said Mrs Harrison. 'I would dearly love to see close up what has drawn you to this neck of the woods.'

'Then,' Scarlett said guardedly, 'there is the issue of the toilet. It's a long drop on the edge of the bush over there.'

'Oh, dear!' exclaimed Mrs Harrison, somewhat surprised.

'We do have a potty for you to use at night.'

'Goodness! Is that what you and Paul use?'

'Um, let's just say we get by.'

'Way to go, Sis. A real upgrade from Cape Town!' laughed Danny, getting another punch on the arm.

Scarlett's mother squared her shoulders and said, 'I'm game for anything you can throw at me.'

§

The following morning it was business as usual, Paul, Scarlett and Nurse Precious dealing with patients who filled up the benches under the thatched gazebo, with the balance extending in a long queue that disappeared into the bush. And Danny and Mrs Harrison did their fair share, lending a hand when they were needed.

At the end of the week, Scarlett's mother said, 'Sweetie, I had my doubts about you coming here to get a clinic off the ground, but I should never have doubted your determination. For the last five days I have marvelled at what you and Paul are doing for the community. There may be specialists at Groote Schuur doing more ground-breaking work than you, but surely not as rewarding as the sheer number of people you help in this desperately poor community. I am very proud of you and Paul.'

'And I concur,' added Danny.

'Thanks, to both of you. It means a lot to me,' said Scarlett with a look of appreciation on her face.

§

On Sunday, the four took a leisurely drive from Numbi Gate to have lunch at Skukuza in Kruger Park. On the way they popped in at Shitlhave Dam where they saw waterbuck, prompting Danny to comment that the white ring around their backsides provided a perfect target, and at Transport Dam they were lucky enough to see a pride of lions come down to drink.

'Wow!' exclaimed Danny. 'The real thing!'

They spent half an hour observing and marvelling at the pride, watching six little cubs the size of a house cat, all in playful mood.

'That is quite a sight,' said Danny. 'To think I've lived in South Africa all my life and had never seen a lion. Have you ever seen a leopard, Sis?'

'No, but I've heard them. So have you.'

'What do you mean?'

'At our home. That sawing sound you hear at night is the resident leopard.'

'But that's not in Kruger Park!' cried Danny.

'No. Leopards are hard to contain. And they are so adaptable they can live almost anywhere. But they are secretive and mostly nocturnal so you never get to see them. However, they see you.'

'Now you tell me. And after I've been going to the long drop during the night.'

'I gave you a potty.'

'Sis, I am not going to use a potty! I don't believe you and Paul use one, so what do you do?'

'Least said, the better!'

At Skukuza camp the foursome sat down at a table on a deck overlooking the Sabie River. They saw crocodiles on the far bank, a few hippos in the water grunting now and then, and a bushbuck on the near side of the river, almost camouflaged by the dappled shade of a sycamore fig tree.

Danny perused the menu. Brown bean soup for starters, followed by fried fillet of hake and piquant sauce, a main course of grilled pork chops with apple jelly together with vegetables in season, an assortment of cold meats and salads if you were still hungry, granadilla ice-cream for dessert, and finishing off with cheese and biscuits, and tea or coffee.

As they finished, Danny announced, 'Not a bad meal given that we are in the middle of the bush. I wonder—'

He was suddenly interrupted mid-sentence as a helicopter flew overhead.

'Look, Mama!' exclaimed Danny. 'You said you wanted to see a zebra. You've gone one better, a flying zebra!'

Scarlett gazed up at the helicopter until it disappeared over the horizon. 'I am not sure if it is the same one, but we occasionally see a black and white striped helicopter flying above our house.'

§

After two weeks, it was time for Danny and Mrs Harrison to return home. Scarlett gave then both a hug and a kiss. 'Mama, please give Papa a kiss, and when you do, think of it as coming from me.'

'I'll do that.'

'Thanks. And I'll see you again in Cape Town at Christmas.'

Epilogue

A week into the new year, Michael and the De Beer family were about to sit down to enjoy the fare of another Kobus braai, when a call came through the VHF radio transmitter. A redirected message from Rob Ferreira Hospital prompted Kobus to say, 'I'm sorry Michael, but you and the Flying Zebra are needed urgently.'

Michael radioed through and was given news of a car accident just east of the Blyde River Canyon.

'Would you like some help?' Kobus asked.

'And miss your Sunday special?' exclaimed Michael, teasing Kobus who always cooked a little extra and a little special on a Sunday.

'You've tagged along with me a lot the last few years. Now it's my turn to see you in action. But I'll bring along our meat.' Kobus said, 'Sandra, please pack us the sosaties.' Then turning to Michael he said, 'You get the Flying Zebra up and running and I'll go and fetch Blessing.'

Michael took a direct route towards Blyde River Canyon and as he neared the canyon he followed the road. The accident was not difficult to find, but the landing was going to be a challenge, especially since a number of cars had blocked his ideal landing spot. By now Michael had amassed a significant number of flying hours and after circling three times to indicate that the stopped cars must give him space, he managed to land the helicopter on the road adjacent to the spot where a car had smashed through a crash barrier on a hairpin bend in the road. All three men exited the helicopter and peered down a precipice. A car had landed 10 metres below on a rock ledge, lying at a 45 degree angle and perilously close to falling off the mountain face.

Michael climbed into a rescue nappy and, using a winch, Blessing slowly let him down until he landed on the ledge below. He took a quick look to see why the car was tilted at a 45 degree angle, finding that after hitting the ledge the car had rolled towards the edge but was stopped by a boulder. He noticed an occupant, a woman, in the front passenger seat which was closest to the precipice that Michael had abseiled, and another person, a man, lying in front of the car in a pool of blood, obviously having smashed through the windscreen. Thinking it more likely that the woman was in a better condition, he decided to concentrate on that patient.

'Neck brace,' Michael shouted, and one came hurtling down courtesy of Blessing. 'Winch hook,' Michael shouted next.

Connecting the winch hook to the cable, Michael reached towards the open window of the car, careful not to lean too heavily against the car lest it fall off the cliff. He placed the hook around the frame of the front vent window.

'Kobus,' called Michael, 'ask someone to park his car up against the helicopter, preferably with a tyre resting on the skid.'

'At your service.'

A kind onlooker obliged, though he looked rather worried as he slowly came to realize that this was to prevent the helicopter from toppling over.

Once this was done, Michael asked Blessing to slowly pull the cable taut but not to right the car.

With the cable tight, the helicopter anchored by the onlooker's car, Michael climbed onto the side of the car, leaned through the window and secured a neck brace around the woman's neck, quickly determining that she was unconscious but still alive. That done, he gave instructions to slowly retract the cable which righted the car. He then unhooked the cable and sent instructions to lower a stretcher.

Michael then rushed over to the body lying on the ground in front of the car. There was a deep gash in the man's neck that had caused the pool of blood. He was still breathing. Barely. From all Michael's experience in trauma, he knew it was a lost cause and after a few minutes the man's life ebbed away.

Despite the condition of the car, Michael was grateful that he was able to prise the door open. He undid the seat belt, picked the woman up and laid her on the stretcher. He did a very quick check of her vitals. Alive but unconscious.

After raising the stretcher, Blessing sent the cable down for Michael to attach his nappy to, and he in turn was hoisted up to the road.

After Michael started the helicopter, Kobus asked, 'What about the man lying down there?'

'He's dead. Time is crucial for this patient. There is no point in risking her life just to bring back a dead body. I'll deal with him later.'

As fast as the Flying Zebra would allow, Michael flew to Rob Ferreira Hospital in Nelspruit and landed on the helipad where a gurney was waiting.

With his adrenalin at last slowing, Michael sat on the tarmac and let out a huge sigh. Kobus joined him and both beckoned for Blessing to join them.

'Michael, I've always been impressed with the flying skills of Captain, but what you did today was impressive. And while I may have originally questioned the value of a medical doctor of your calibre becoming a pilot, if that woman is to live, she owes her life to you.'

'You saved my life too,' beamed Blessing, quite fluent in English after working with Michael.

'That's right!' exclaimed Kobus. 'What I don't understand is why you left Groote Schuur if you are so good a doctor?'

'What's changed is that I now see myself as a helicopter pilot first with medical skills as a bonus. Remember, not all my flying duties are about saving lives.' With a grin on his face, Michael said with slight sarcasm when he alluded to elephant culling, 'Sometimes I fly so that game rangers can take lives!'

'Point taken,' said Kobus. 'But seriously, why are you no longer a trauma surgeon? I'm sure you could have found work here if you didn't want to return to Groote Schuur.'

'I'll answer that in a moment. I was concentrating so hard during that rescue operation I didn't notice if you had eaten all the sosaties?'

'No!' exclaimed Kobus. 'I was so enthralled by what you were doing I completely forgot about them.'

'I'm famished. I'll answer your question while we eat.'

Kobus shared the sosaties and the three of them tucked into lamb cubes and many vegetables skewered on a stick.

'Truthfully, Kobus, as a trauma surgeon you are constantly working on cases where a person's life hangs in the balance. That part I don't mind. It's challenging work but I knew about that when I first decided to specialise in trauma surgery. But when you lose a patient, it's dealing with the loved ones that I could no longer take. The families think you are God, that you can perform miracles, and when you fail you know that when you exit the theatre to tell them the bad news, you are going to see that look of hope in their eyes turn to desperation and grief.'

'But no one can expect you to save them all!'

'No, and there's never been anger or blame directed towards me. But they will always want their loved one to be the one who is saved. And I understand. I know the sorrow and sadness of losing Anna.' Michael took a bite of his sosatie and continued, 'I'm not sure whether that woman we brought in earlier is going to live or not. But right now there may be a trauma surgeon working on her, and if she does die I am glad it will be him and not me who has to face her family.' Kobus nodded his head, understanding what Michael had said. Another bite and Michael continued, 'I'm very happy that I've found my calling. I love flying a helicopter, I am glad I can make good use of my medical expertise, and I am over the moon that I live in Kruger Park. Four years ago you and Sandra said that it would heal my sorrow and it did, mostly. All I need now is a woman in my life and I would be in heaven. And talking of women, your wife makes a darn good sosatie, just a pity we didn't bring a few bottles of your famous marula beer.'

'How little faith you have in me!'

'Really?' Michael queried as he saw Kobus climb the Flying Zebra to retrieve a cooler bag of bottles of marula beer.

Dishing out the bottles, the game ranger said to Blessing, whose eyes grew as wide as his grin of immaculate white teeth, 'Don't tell your father I gave you jabula or I will have to fire him.'

§

Two days later, Michael visited Rob Ferreira Hospital to check up on the woman he had rescued, first visiting the neurologist, Dr Ben Stevenson, a doctor that Michael had come to know over the past four years.

'How's my patient doing?' Michael asked.

'She incurred severe concussion in the accident,' Dr Stevenson said. 'She's come through that but I want to keep her in hospital for another two or three days to monitor her and also to see if there are any latent internal injuries.'

'I'll go and pay her a visit.'

Michael entered Scarlett's ward. At the foot of her bed was a file with the name Dr Rhodes written in bold. Michael had a quick scan through its contents.

Given that a man dressed in khaki shirt and shorts had walked up to her bed and started reading the contents of her medical file, a sceptical Scarlett asked, 'Are you sure you're a doctor?'

'I am,' replied Michael, looking up at Scarlett who was sitting up in bed. 'A sort of bush doctor. I fly rescue missions and—'

'Are you the helicopter pilot that rescued me?' asked Scarlett, her tear-stained face brightening.

'That I am, Dr Rhodes,' the pilot replied before introducing himself. 'My name is Michael, flying bush doctor at your service!'

'Then I must give you my heartfelt thanks for saving my life,' said Scarlett, her face showing genuine gratefulness.

'Oh, I wouldn't go that far. Dr Stevenson said you had severe concussion but nothing too serious.'

'Nevertheless, he said the rescue mission was extremely dangerous. Having to use a winch to bring the car from its side and back onto its four wheels, all on a small precarious mountain ledge. I'm eternally grateful to you.'

'All in a day's work,' said Michael, making light of what he had done.

Her face clouded with sorrow. 'My husband, did he—'

'You were wearing a seatbelt, but he wasn't. Why was that?'

'I don't know,' answered Scarlett, puzzled. 'Since I have regained consciousness, I have asked myself that a thousand times because by nature my husband was more cautious than me and always wore a seatbelt. We were in Kruger Park earlier that morning where one drives around so slowly that one doesn't really need to wear a seatbelt and I can only conclude that when we left, he forgot to put it on.'

'It was the seatbelt that saved your life. Not me.'

'My husband, did he suffer?'

Always the difficult question, even from a doctor. Michael looked into Scarlett's beautiful blue eyes and hesitated enough for her to know, her eyes tearing up. She turned to look outside and, unknowingly, Michael once again saw Scarlett's face peering through a window into the distance with a look of sadness etched on her face.

Michael gently held her hand and said, 'I'll leave you now, but I will be back in a day or two.

§

Two days later, Michael returned, having discovered from Dr Stevenson that Scarlett was to be discharged later that day. Michael sat on the edge of her bed and gave her the news.

'About time,' Scarlett answered forlornly. 'I have a husband to bury.'

'Dr Stevenson tells me that you are a medical practitioner. Where do you practise?'

'My husband, Paul, who was also a medical doctor, and I have been working for just on two years at a clinic about 20 minutes outside White River. A clinic set up by Swedish missionaries and associated with Themba Hospital.'

'Oh, I know that clinic. Flown over it a few times in my helicopter.'

'The one with black and white stripes?'

'Yes.'

Scarlett smiled. 'Of all the animals that my mother wanted to see, when she visited last year, it was a zebra. Unfortunately we didn't spot one when Paul and I took her and my brother to Kruger, but when we were having lunch one day at Skukuza, my brother Danny pointed to what I am sure must have been your helicopter and said to Mama that she had gone one better because she had seen a flying zebra!'

'He was spot on because I call my chopper the Flying Zebra!' After having a good laugh, Michael asked, 'You said just on two years, where were you before that?'

'In Cape Town. Paul had a private practice and I worked at the Red Cross War Memorial Children's Hospital.'

'In Cape Town?'

'Yes. Why do you ask?'

Michael's brow furrowed as he pondered the possibility, saying aloud, 'Dr Rhodes.'

'Yes?'

'No, I'm just thinking things through. I worked at Groote Schuur until 1977, and I'm pretty sure that you sent me many patients over the years.'

'I only know you as Michael. What—'

'My name is Michael Gibson.'

'Oh, my word! *The* Dr Michael Gibson?'

'What do you mean by that?'

'Well, I am sure you must know that in the medical fraternity around Cape Town you were regarded as a legendary surgeon.'

'I guess I had my moments. Some bad ones too. I wouldn't say legendary. But, I am dying to know, are you the Dr Rhodes that sent me all those patients several years ago?'

'It would most likely have been Paul as I worked at the children's hospital. I only did one year at his private practice.'

'In 1972?'

'Yes, but how would you know that?'

'You're not going to believe this, but you sent me my wife!'

'What?' cried a puzzled Scarlett.

'You sent me a patient in 1972 and I married her!'

'It could have been Paul.'

'No. It is true that her personal doctor was a Dr Rhodes, a man, but I clearly remember her telling me that she was referred by a woman doctor, and she was the doctor's first ever patient.'

'I do recall my first patient being a Swedish woman, but I can't remember her name.'

'Anna. Anna Lagerström.'

'Really? My boss is a Lagerström.'

'Stefan Lagerström?'

'Yes, how did you know that?'

'This is bizarre,' remarked Michael. 'Stefan and Ingrid Lagerström are my wife's parents! They are the Swedish missionaries you mentioned earlier.'

'Oh, my word!'

'You thanked me the other day for saving your life,' Michael said excitedly. 'But I owe you a huge debt of gratitude for giving me a life.'

A somewhat confused Scarlett asked, 'What do you mean?'

'Well, until I met Anna I was pretty much married to my work. For as long as I can remember I wanted to be a doctor. Actually, not a general practitioner but a surgeon. And especially a surgeon in trauma where every day would bring in a new challenge. The problem was that I wanted to get better at my craft and quickly, and so my job consumed me.'

'But it paid off because I'm not letting you off the hook, you became a legend.'

Michael ignored Scarlett's compliment and continued, 'Anna brought a whole new perspective into my life. A balance. She introduced me to tennis. We went hiking together. We took in the beauty of Cape Town, its restaurants, the winelands, the mountains. We went on overseas trips to the UK, Sweden, Germany and Austria. And we played music together, she on the piano and me on the guitar. She gave me life, which means you gave me life.'

'Why do you say gave me life as if it were in the past?'

Michael's excited relating of his time with Anna came to an abrupt end and with sadness in his voice said, 'She passed away four years ago. Breast cancer.'

'Oh, I am so sorry to hear that.'

'Thanks,' Michael said wistfully, nodding his head, but he soon perked up as he thought more about Anna. 'You know, in a strange way, her life was cut short, but she lived life more in that time than most others do in a full lifetime. She was the most cheerful person I have ever known. You know how devastating chemotherapy is—'

'I do', Scarlett said with emphasis.

'Well, it's hard to believe, but she dealt with her cancer treatment without ever losing her smile. Even three stillborn children could not dent her natural ability to be a light creator.'

'Three?' Scarlett cried out.

'Sadly, yes. We were never able to have children. We applied for adoption, and a newborn baby was to be ours just months before Anna passed away.'

'That is so sad. But I'm puzzled. What made one of Cape Town's leading surgeons become a flying bush doctor, to use your words.'

'Death. As I became more experienced as a trauma surgeon, I was given the difficult cases. Naturally, the number of lives lost increased. A great surgeon has to detach themselves from losing patients, but I never could. All those years dreaming of being a surgeon, and despite my parents being doctors, it never occurred to me that the death of patients would eventually wear me down. Then when Anna passed away I truly lost it. I felt that after my dedication to trying to save lives, medicine had robbed me of my most precious gift, Anna, my gift from you.'

'And you just gave up on medicine?' asked Scarlett.

'For a long while, yes. I needed to get away and work out what I wanted to do. At first, I had no idea, so I decided to tour South Africa and it seemed so weird that I had lived in the country for going on 14 years and I had never seen any of its magnificent wildlife, so my first port of call was Kruger Park and I have never left.

'From your accent, I take it that you are from England?'

'Yes.'

'When you say never left Kruger Park, what do you mean, since you are doing medical evacuation?'

'In a strange sequence of events, I befriended a game ranger in Kruger Park, came to love African wildlife, got introduced to flying a helicopter which is an absolute thrill for me and eventually found my calling. So now I work for Kruger Park where I help with game capture, census counting, fighting poaching and then also combine my medical trauma skills to do medical evacuations in Kruger Park and, when there is a need, in the greater area outside Kruger Park. After Anna's death, this new life became a great healer.'

'You mentioned that dealing with people dying drove you away from medicine, but you haven't escaped it completely. Surely you must experience losses. After all, you attended to Paul.'

'Occasionally. Mostly I pass them on to trauma at Rob Ferreira Hospital and give to them what they were giving to me at Groote Schuur. But I guess the doctor in me will always be a part of my life.'

Scarlett's voice became sombre. 'I asked you the other day if Paul suffered. Your silence suggested yes.'

'His injuries were severe. Severed arteries in the neck. But he was going in and out of consciousness so it's quite possible that he was in shock and mostly out of it.'

'Did he say anything?'

'No. He was too far gone to be able to speak. And then he went quickly,' Michael explained. To console Scarlett, he said, 'We doctors may think we know it all, but who are we to dispute that he hung on just long enough to know that help had arrived for you. It could be true and is something to comfort you in the difficult days ahead.'

Scarlett slowly nodded her head, not totally convinced.

'I'm sorry,' Michael said. 'We make a fine pair. Two doctors losing their spouses at such a young age. And, in my case, three unborn children, too.'

Tears welled up in Scarlett's eyes.

'Oh, no. Please don't tell me—'

Michael's plea was broken by the grief on Scarlett's face.

'You lost, what, a child?' asked Michael.

Scarlett closed her eyes, leaking tears down her face, whispering, 'A daughter.'

'Don't feel you need to talk about it,' Michael advised.

After a few moments, Scarlett found her voice again, saying, 'Actually, it may be cathartic.' Using a tissue, she wiped away her tears and said, 'I don't want you to get the wrong impression, because I loved Paul dearly. But for 13 years the centre of my life was my precious Robin. You need to understand that, unlike you, I never wanted to become a doctor. My life's dream was to become an Olympic swimmer. But that was thwarted by the whole South Africa situation.'

'Were you that good?'

'Well, I don't want to sound boastful, but I was in the team to participate in Tokyo. Did I have a shot at a medal? Perhaps. I'd like to think so. Then two months before the Olympics, while we were on a training camp in England, we were told that we were banned from participating. I was devastated. It would have been like you dedicating your whole life to becoming a surgeon and two months before graduation you are told that you may not practise as a surgeon. Not in England, not in South Africa, not anywhere.'

'Wow, at first I wondered if it mattered that much, but when you put it in those terms I feel your pain.'

'Paul was also on the team. Probably did not eat, sleep and breathe swimming like I did, so it wasn't as shattering an experience for him. I went into a black hole and I give him a lot of credit for pulling me out of it. In the end he convinced me to study medicine at the University of Cape Town.'

'What years were those?'

'I graduated in 1971.'

'That's interesting, because that means we were both at UCT at the same time. Our past is more intertwined than we may have thought,' pondered Michael. 'So did you and Paul get married early on?'

'No. I made a big mistake by getting pregnant with someone else. It was a one night stand, and had a lot of fallout but also gave me the greatest gift I could ever have imagined, my daughter Robin. All my life I desperately wanted to become an Olympian and win a gold medal, dreamed of it every day. But you could hang a hundred gold medals around my neck and it would not come anywhere close to what Robin gave me.'

'Even though she wasn't your daughter by Paul?'

'Yes. To use Paul's words, it's not about biology, it's about love.'

'And Paul was accepting of this?'

'More than accepting. He couldn't have been more supportive. He treated Robin as if she was his own flesh and blood and for that I will forever be grateful to him.'

'When in all this did you get married?'

'Just before becoming an intern.'

'Any other children?'

'No, though I am pregnant now,' replied Scarlett, which caused her to tear up.

'Hush,' said Michael. 'Don't feel that you need to talk about this.'

'No, I'm fine,' replied Scarlett, wiping away her tears. 'I am delighted I am going to have another baby, especially Paul's, this time. I just wish he were around, so we could be a family again.'

'If you so wanted a child with Paul, why didn't you have one earlier?'

'Robin was four when we got married and I think Paul wisely realized that she had become the centre of my world and that it would be unfair to have another child.'

'He sounds like a very astute man, your husband. And very unselfish.'

'He was indeed. I may not have realized that at first but I grew to love him more and more as time went on,' said Scarlett, swallowing a lump in her throat, the realization dawning that he was gone and would never know his child. 'He would always say that I was the brightest person he knew, but I can safely say that he was the wisest person I have ever known. And his wisdom came to the rescue many times during Robin's upbringing. You see, she was another me. Determined, strong-willed, and I am proud to say, a better swimmer.'

'Aah! I think I can see where this is going.'

'Yes, I started living vicariously through my daughter, hoping, no, desperately hoping that she would one day become an Olympic swimmer.'

'But wouldn't she have encountered the same problem as you? South Africa is still banned from the Olympics.'

'Yes, though I was prepared to emigrate to another country to get her to the Olympics, but—'

'And Paul?'

'He was an amazing man. He would have supported me, but in the end by some strange quirk of fate we managed to get Robin an Irish passport.'

'You are a very determined person.'

'I am. But all the determination in the world was not enough to fight Robin's ultimate adversary, leukemia.'

'Oh, gosh!' exclaimed Michael, because he knew the outcome.

'After she passed away, I took stock of my life and recalled a conversation that I had with Chris Barnard who said—'

'Chris Barnard? Dr Chris Barnard the heart surgeon?' asked a wide-eyed Michael.

'Yes.'

'When did you ever get to speak with him?'

'I would see him occasionally at the Red Cross War Memorial Children's Hospital.'

'He is my hero. He is the very reason I came to South Africa, studied at UCT and became a trauma surgeon at Groote Schuur,' said Michael. 'Sorry to butt in. What did he say to you?'

'That we are the privileged ones. That I should use my position to pay back to society. To those who are most in need. And that's when I decided to come to White River to work at the bush clinic.'

'And Paul agreed to give up his practice just like that?'

'He did. I think he knew that I was in a deep dark place with Robin having passed away. So, yes, he was very supportive.'

'He sounds like he was an amazing man,' said Michael. 'Now that he's gone what are you going to do? You can't live out there in the bush all by yourself.'

'I'll have to give it a lot of thought because in the absence of swimming, it has actually become a great calling for me,' said Scarlett. 'Though I'll have to find another doctor to help me.'

'And where do you propose finding a doctor willing to give up his practice to work in the bush?'

'Well,' said Scarlett, raising her eyebrows at the man in front of her, 'there is a bush doctor in my presence!'

Michael laughed out aloud at the same time that a nurse placed a tea tray on the table next to Scarlett's bed.

'We'll discuss that preposterous idea over a cup of tea,' said Michael. 'I'll do the pouring. Milk? Sugar?'

'Normally just milk, but I feel like something hot and sweet.'

Between sips of tea Michael said, 'You know, there's always a need for a partner on the Flying Zebra. My helper, Blessing—'

'Oh, goodness, no! Is his name really Blessing?'

'It is and you are blessed that Blessing is my helper or you may not be here. I've taken him under my wing, teaching him medical procedures, but I shudder to think what he might be doing with the patient while I am navigating the Flying Zebra back to a hospital,' laughed Michael. As he reached forward to relieve Scarlett of her empty teacup he suggested, 'Maybe we can come to some sort of compromise.'

Scarlett sat up a little straighter in bed, touched Michael's right eyebrow and asked, 'Where did you get that scar from?'

'I'm a bit embarrassed to say, but why not? It's a bit of a botched job I did when I was a medical student at Cambridge University.'

'But what caused the cut?'

'Well that's embarrassing, too! But, in for a penny in for a pound. It was drizzling, and I was riding my bicycle a bit too close to a bus, so I hopped onto the pavement and only at the last moment did I realize that I was heading straight for a lamp post. I squeezed the brakes tightly but the rain caused the tyres to skid and I crashed into the lamp post cutting open my eyebrow. It must have been quite a sight because—'

'In Cambridge?' asked Scarlett, a bewildered look on her face.

'Yes,' answered Michael, somewhat bemused at the question.

'In 1964?'

'Yes,' replied a puzzled Michael. 'How did you know that?'

'And while you were riding your bicycle you kept on looking at someone on the bus?'

Michael's eyes widened as he exclaimed with an enquiring tone, 'Scarlett?'

'No,' said Scarlett, looking slightly confused. 'My name is Missy. Actually it's Melissa.'

'No, don't worry about that,' dismissed Michael. 'But, was that you on the bus?'

'Yes.'

'And you remember?'

'There's not a day that has gone by that I haven't thought about you.'

Michael tenderly embraced Scarlett, then slowly drew back, looked into her mesmerizing sapphire blue eyes and said, 'Melissa, I have a collection of letters that I want you to read.'

THE END